THIRD FRONT

A DALÍ TAMAREIA MISSION
BOOK 3

E. M. HAMILL

STAR BARD BOOKS

For my mother
Sandy Warner
1944-2022
who encouraged my love of reading from an early age,
and supported my dreams until the end.
Love you forever.

ACKNOWLEDGMENTS

Coming to the end of this story arc is a bittersweet thing. Dalí will have more stories to tell, probably in novella form.

So many people supported me through all this. Thank you to my writing family, especially Jem Zero, cheerleader and critique partner through the entire process of this third book. Thank you to my alpha readers from the beginning, Mark Millham and Ashley Miller, and the mutual support community of Writers Refuge headed by the disgustingly talented Sarah Chorn. My beta reader Janean Dobos was here for the whole series, and Jessica Smith took on the challenge with *Third Front*. Thank you, a million times.

I want to extend my gratitude to Keshav Kant, my sensitivity consultant, for her insight into the Hijra community and spirituality and encouraging me to bring more of this rich culture into the story.

A standing ovation to Justin R. Gibson, who finally gave Dalí a voice via audiobook after all this time.

Kudos and huge hugs to Jami Nord and Evan MacGregor at Chimera Editing. Jami, my developmental editor and friend, thank you for your support, professional advice, and guidance through the series.

Thank you to artist JCaleb Designs for three brand new, gorgeous, exciting covers.

It was important to me to have Dalí come from a loving, supportive family. I was lucky to grow up in one. Not all of us in the LGBTQ+ community are. Paul Tamareia and Marina Urquhart are much like my parents were: loving, irreverent, and entirely supportive of their children. I want to express my thankfulness here, both for them and for my in-laws, who raised an exceptional human.

I am in awe of my children, Kylan, Gabriel, and Jayden, and Mark, my life partner of nearly thirty years, for making dinner and doing laundry for me while I worked full time as a nurse, finished my BSN, survived quarantine without maiming each other, AND put up with me writing this series for the last six years.

And last, but most ardently, I am thankful for all of you, who read *Dalí* and asked for more.

CHAPTER
ONE

I HAVE DONE a lot of stupid things. When I chose to man the turret of a stolen militia sandrail and chase Sol Fed drug dealers across the Martian desert, it was not one of my wisest moments.

The pulse rifle's sights bounced off the faceplate of my environmental suit as the MDEA officer behind the wheel swerved to avoid an outcrop of rocks. The buggy bottomed out in a divot pocking the sandy crust. "Don't you have a clear shot yet?" my driver demanded.

"I might if you stop hitting every crater on the goddamn planet, Cortez!" I braced my feet wider and re-sighted the weapon on the plume of dust kicked up by our target.

"Oh, so sorry, Tamareia. Didn't know galactic cops are such pussies," she retorted. "Can't handle a little off-roading?"

Another bump, and my teeth solidly clamped on my bottom lip. I tasted blood. "Fuck! When we stole this thing, I thought you knew how to drive it."

She snorted. "Hah! Who said I could drive? Where the hell is our backup?"

Good question. They should have been there by now. "Sumner, where are you?"

"Airborne." The clipped reply came over the private com implanted in my mastoid bone. "Sorry we're late. Williams wouldn't let the tower clear us for takeoff until they headed out."

"They're coming. Your boss is being a prick again," I told Cortez.

"Can't blame him, eh? We did just fine until you guys decided to stick your noses in our operation," she yelled back.

My team was dispatched to Mars to work with drug enforcement officers as part of a galactic response to curtail a sinister new drug's arrival in Sol Fed. Local authorities were still getting used to the idea of Remoliad agencies meddling in their business.

Drug cartels found a foothold in the crowded tenements of Mars, offering chemical bliss to exhausted shift workers from the food processing plants. The formula locally referred to as "vape" had made its way to our solar system five years before. It targeted humanoid physiology, manufactured elsewhere in the galaxy by insectoid Pilean chemists.

I first encountered the drug in the seedy illegal market of Rosetta Station's underbelly. Thanks to a Kadrelian doctor, I had recently subdued my addiction to vape for the second time in three years. It was still a struggle to stay clean. But things could be so much worse for humanity: the drug's most recent compound was far more threatening than its predecessor, rewriting human cells to pass the dependence on to future generations. We needed to cut off the supply line.

The whine of a projectile pinged off the bulletproof glass of the turret behind me. "Shit!" I twisted in the cylinder to locate the pursuing vehicle. "I think their backup got here first."

A bigger, flashier version of the sandrail we "borrowed" was rapidly gaining on us, glimpsed through the cloud of tawny sand thrown by our tires.

"The one up front is three kilometers from the canyon.

We'll lose them," Cortez said over the speaker in my helmet. "Can your team intercept?"

"Copy," Sumner said before I had a chance to relay. "ETA sixty seconds."

"They've got it!" I informed Cortez.

"We need at least one of them alive. Hold on to your ass!"

Cortez braked and yanked the wheel of the sandrail hard to the left in a low gravity spin out which carried us away from the path of the approaching buggy. They sped past and I glimpsed mirrored faceplates turning toward us. I got off a few shots from the mounted rifle as Cortez completed the arc. She floored the accelerator, coming in behind the buggy. Bullets careened off our vehicle's armored skin and I ducked out of instinct, cursing.

"Ignore them," she ordered. "We have military tech, they don't. Lock on their back tire and shred it. Let the gun do the work!"

I focused the sights on the left rear tire and squeezed the tracking trigger. Red crosshairs formed over the tire, and the gun took on a life of its own, following the target. All I had to do was hold down the firing mechanism. A volley of shots rattled out and huge chunks separated from the tread, but they still moved forward. Someone in an environment suit leaned out of the vehicle with a long, black tube that belched fire.

A magnesium-white explosion blossomed in our path. Cortez jerked the steering wheel to the side and avoided the worst of the violent eruption of rocks and dirt.

"What did you say about military tech?" I accused. "That was a fucking Pilean grenade launcher!"

"Okay, that's new."

My weapon locked back on its target, and I fired. More chunks of tire peeled off the rim until it disintegrated into elastomer snakes and the buggy unevenly bounced over the terrain. A badly aimed explosion went up on our right. When the dust cleared, I sighted on the remaining rear tire. With their speed already compromised, the gun chewed it up.

The heavy buggy wobbled on the uneven landscape and spun out in front of us, rolling over twice before Cortez swerved out of its way. We tilted at a heart-stopping angle in the low gravity before our sandrail tumbled back to four-wheeled contact. Three enviro-suited figures staggered out of the overturned buggy when we completed our wide circle. The laser tracking of my gun danced red dots over their chests as Cortez broadcast over the external loudspeaker,

"MDEA! Hands up if you don't want your suits ventilated, dickheads."

A soft *whump* from the rim of the canyon and a spray of ochre sand preceded the whine of *Thunder Child*'s atmospheric engines as she streaked overhead and away. "They're not going anywhere," Sumner advised over my implant. "Incoming MDEA vehicles. I think we should let them do the pickup. Peace offering. We'll meet you back at the base."

"Copy."

The battered cartel runners raised their hands as Cortez grabbed the rifle mounted in the sandrail's cockpit and spilled out the door. "On the ground. Now!"

They complied. I squirmed out of the turret and joined her, training my sidearm on their prone bodies. "The other vehicle's disabled. Tell your guys they can pick them up."

In the distance, the thick dust cloud created by the approach of MDEA's all-terrain transports veiled the sparkling trail of climate domes in a burnt-amber drift of Martian soil. Cortez muttered into her com and some of the group peeled off, headed for the lip of the gorge. The rest continued their arrow-straight path for us. As they got closer, I could see military vehicles in the fleet. Fantastic.

"Exactly how much trouble are we going to be in for liberating a militia sandrail?" I inquired. Cortez favored me with a wolfish grin.

"Williams will square it with them. I'll tell him this was your idea."

———

Back at headquarters, Captain Williams was having none of Cortez's bullshit. Or mine.

"Stop smirking, Lieutenant Cortez!" he barked. She straightened her expression, but my empathic nets still picked up the sparkle of self-satisfaction in her emotional broadcast. "I know it was your idea. You get to apologize to Colonel Tun. I'm done listening to her ride my ass, so you lick her boots. Make it good and maybe I won't chain you to a desk for the next quarter."

He spun, his dark eyes squinting at me. "And you? As soon as you and Cortez are done with reports and your people finish questioning the suspects, you can get the fuck out of my division, Tamareia. Don't let the door hit you in the ass on your way out. Understood?"

"Yes, sir." I couldn't resist a dig. "You're welcome."

Williams shook his head, sneering. "We were on top of this long before you got involved."

"Without our intel, you wouldn't have known where the drop was happening," I said evenly. "We identified six cases of the new drug in this shipment, Captain, but there's still more out there. Until we figure out how the cartel is getting it into Sol Fed, not to mention how the hell they got Pilean grenade launchers, we need to work together whether or not you like it."

"I won't have a division left if you and Cortez keep this up. But this isn't your job anymore, is it? Riga*nat is now the permanent liaison on this venture." His tongue clicked awkwardly on the glottal stop, but Williams was making an admirable effort to pronounce the Burkani officer's name.

Riga*nat was not my favorite being in the galaxy, but as

far as drug enforcement agents went, he was among the best. By Burkani standards, he was one of the more diplomatic examples of his blunt, outspoken species. Even though we weren't welcomed to Mars with open arms, he and Williams had surprisingly hit it off, in part due to their mutual dislike of me. As far as the MDEA was aware, the team and I represented their galactic counterparts in drug enforcement. Our status as a Remoliad intelligence unit was not something we shared with Williams.

"Get out of my office. Finish those reports." He sat down at his desk and glared at a screen, ignoring us. Cortez jerked her head toward the door, her lips twisted in a smug grin.

"Kind of refreshing to see someone other than me dressed down for making a dumb ass decision," I muttered when the port hissed shut behind us.

"Oh yeah? You think that was bad?" She laughed. "He's been worse. You? Sumner seems like a tight ass."

"Nothing I didn't deserve, but yeah. He doesn't hold back." Actually, Sumner held back a lot, but that was a whole different scenario. I changed the subject. "Do you want to grab a drink after we get the reports done?"

She paused. "Is this goodbye?"

"Yeah, I think so."

"Then you're buying. We'll bring the booze to my place."

"You're on." Cortez and I had worked together for three months on this assignment. We formed a bond based on competition and alcohol. In the last two weeks, we'd also branched out into casual, enthusiastic sex. She liked rough women. I had enough scars to pass her muster and the ability to sprout breasts with the right stimulation, so my lack of fixed gender did not constitute a deal breaker.

"Tamareia?" One of the other officers jerked his head at the enclosed local communications terminal. "You have a private call."

I frowned. "They asked for me by name?"

"Yeah." He shrugged and ignored me. I stood there, trying to figure out who the hell would call me at MDEA headquarters until Cortez elbowed me in the side.

"Did you forget to charge for a blow job or something?" She snickered.

I flipped her off as I slid into the booth and closed the door.

The second my fingerprint registered to accept the transmission, I regretted it. To get the word about the new drug's properties out to the public, I made a deal with the devil's asshole.

I promised sensational journalist Kiran Singh an exclusive story. Like a goddamned idiot, I didn't specify which one.

———

I was almost blinded by pearly teeth as he grinned at me. "You are a difficult person to reach, Dalí."

I groaned. "What do you want, and why are you on Mars?"

"I'm here covering the first joint operation between Sol Fed and Remoliad law enforcement." His smile slipped and his expression became more predatory. "And I have a message from Mother England and the Third Front."

"Whatever it is, I'm not interested."

"Oh, I think you might be." Singh paused and leaned forward into the lens. "Does the name Miriam Skadi mean anything to you?"

A haze of red threatened my vision, and I closed my eyes against it.

He was asking about my family's murderer, the terrorist who engineered the bombing of Luna Terminal.

"I take that as a yes." Singh's mellifluous voice darkened in the shadow of a frown I glimpsed as my gaze fixed again on the screen.

"What do you know about Skadi?" The weight of my need for retribution constricted my chest. I fought to breathe normally.

"Me? Nothing but what I can find in the records." He sat back. "Born on Europa to a militia officer. One of two Nos/human hybrids who were the products of a war crime."

That much was true. My commander, Rion Sumner, was the other hybrid— Miriam Skadi's half-brother. I doubted Singh knew that yet.

He continued, "She lit out for the galaxy when she was about eighteen. After a decade's absence, she returned to Sol Fed every six months or so to visit her dear old mater in a convalescent facility on Europa, right around the time things heated up with the Nos Conglomerate. But the last three years? No visits. No record of her coming in or out of Sol Fed. Her mother is still alive, but Skadi appears to have evaporated. Who is she?"

"No idea."

I was evading an answer, and his kohl-lined eyes narrowed in suspicion. At heart, Kiran Singh was a malicious, gossip-collecting bitch, and it drove him completely over the edge to not know everything.

"If you'd like to learn more, you're invited to a very exclusive party tomorrow night in the Hijra Quarter," Singh said. "Mother will talk to you there."

For a minute, I wasn't sure I heard him correctly. "She wants me to come to Luna?"

"Yes. And I want the story you owe me."

"I can probably get you a voice-only interview with one of the MDEA agents who made the arrest today," I offered weakly, still processing.

"No. I want *this* story." Singh's eyes gleamed. "I want to know what this is about."

"Ask Mother. You two are inseparable, right?"

"She doesn't really talk to me anymore," he said moodily. "We're estranged, at the moment."

That was interesting. "It's an ongoing investigation. I can't tell you anything."

"You trusted me with the information that took down President Batterson."

Oh, the irony. "I gave you the information because I knew you couldn't keep your fucking mouth shut. I counted on it."

"I recognize the look on your face, Dalí. The pain. This has something to do with the bombing."

A bleak laugh escaped me. "If you want something from me, you should stop talking now." But damn it, I was interested.

Despite the almost three years our team had been chasing Skadi and the malevolent entity for whom she worked, we had little solid information to go on. We finally gave a title to the organization: Residuum, a name coined out of frustration. Given that we could never find them, only the traces of where they'd been, the name stuck.

Skadi's "employer" remained faceless and nameless. The group's activities had always been targeted to cause strategic unrest in places that were not the most stable to begin with, like Sol Fed. The bombing of Luna Terminal nearly derailed the talks for membership in the Alliance. The colonies gained steady improvement with galactic relief efforts, but it wouldn't take much to tip the balance. News the Remoliad Security Council had been infiltrated by Alecto Sim, another of Residuum's "employees", left many worlds in near panic, wondering what defense information had been compromised.

This could be the break we needed.

"I have to talk to my team first. I'll let you know." I disconnected the call before he could say anything else and sat hunched over in the booth with my hands over my face, counting heartbeats and breaths until they were closer to normal.

Mars held no ghosts for me. It made it easier to pretend this was just another mission, until now.

I rarely visited Mars when I repatriated to Sol Fed sixteen years before, after my mother resigned her ambassadorial assignment on Zereid. I lived on Luna, and my parents near Jupiter on Rosetta Station, where my father had been in command.

I spent six months in Jupiter's blood-tinged shadow, chasing oblivion to relieve the pain and guilt of surviving the bombs which shattered Luna Terminal when my husband, wife, and the child she carried did not. My own ghost lurked in Rosetta's promenade bars and the station's underbelly, a twisting maze of pipes called the Labyrinth.

I hadn't planned on going back to Luna. Not this trip, anyway; maybe never again. The moon was too closely linked to my memories of Gresh and Rasida, our life together, and their deaths. Too many things to haunt me there, to threaten the fitful slumber of my grief.

I tapped my implant.

"Hey, it's me. Anybody listening?"

"I'm here, Dalí," Tommi acknowledged me. Even though it was only in my head, her translated voice held the same soft, breathy cadence the Cthash language patterns carried. My shoulders relaxed. Her voice always calmed me, maybe a relic of all our hypnotic debriefings, or just the fact I had grown to care deeply for her. She was my confidant and friend, and we had a platonic relationship important to both of us. "Is something happening?"

"Maybe. We need a conference call. I've been summoned."

CHAPTER
TWO

"DO YOU TRUST KIRAN SINGH?" Sumner asked after I filled them in.

"That he might have information, yes. Do I trust him? Not one bit." I shifted, rubbing my forehead. Singh would do and say anything to achieve what he wanted and had no respect for boundaries. He'd used our long acquaintance to gain access to me at the memorial for the bombing victims, then asked me on camera if Gresh and Rasida died because the explosion was meant for me.

I punched him in the face on a live broadcast in front of the entire solar system.

"What is the Third Front?" Tommi asked.

"On the outside, a political lobbying group. Third-gender reproductive rights to unedited genetic procreation are still a point of contention here in Sol Fed despite the Remoliad's stance against eugenics. The Third Front uses financial and political influence to defeat laws which encroach upon those rights. The head of the group is a third-gender named Justina England." I flicked a picture of her up on the screen. "Everyone in the Hijra Quarter refers to her as Mother, but like me, she's fluid in her presentation. She inherited an import company that's been in business with galactic partners since the early days of Remoliad contact. Her family has always been something of an underworld dynasty, the people who can get whatever you want if you have the credits. Gresh figured out she uses the group to launder money from their smuggling activity."

I took a steadying breath. "When Rasida and I decided to have a child with Gresh, we kept very quiet the fact we used unedited gene sequences from my DNA. Everyone assumed our child was Gresh's, but genetically it was more mine than his." The memory was still a serrated blade, twisting in what might have been. "What Sida didn't know—why Gresh and I parted ways with the Third Front on the rights movement before we got married—was that Mother England considered her genetics lab a viable target. The same facility housing Sida's research was also the front line for development of genetic sequencing which edited out the third-gender muta- tion as well as harmful anomalies caused by long-term expo- sure to cosmic radiation. Technicians were assaulted on one occasion. Plans for sabotage existed. We refused to legitimize that kind of action. I don't know what the group was mixed up in after the bombing because I stopped paying attention to . . . everything."

"We have been able to glean some information about Mother England from local law enforcement sources. I'm sending it to your device." Ra'sho's webbed hands danced over her heads-up display. "If we go to Luna, we will have access to her private data when we hack into her systems." Her translated voice oozed with confidence, no hesitation they would have any difficulty doing that. I had to grin in the privacy of the booth. Ka'pth and Ra'sho were brilliant at their job, and I had no doubt they were already halfway in.

My PDD ticked out a list of law enforcement investiga- tions against Mother England. Most of them didn't stick long enough to go to trial, and those that did were quickly dismissed in court. No surprise there. The team of lawyers to which she'd hoped to recruit Gresh worked very hard. One investigation stuck out, though, and made me whistle a Zereid expletive. "Smuggling tech-grade Ursetu rubies before the new trade laws took effect? That's interesting."

"It might be where her path crosses with Skadi," Sumner muttered.

"Agreed." Ka'pth scrolled through the list on her screen. "We must learn more about her enterprises."

A hesitation, a silence. For some reason, I knew it was Sumner who wavered but when he spoke it was decisive. "All right. Dalí and I will go to Luna."

"So, we're doing this," I whispered, mostly to myself, and dragged my hands over my face.

"You okay with it?" Sumner's quiet concern offered me a way out.

"Got to be. We need to know what this is about."

"What time will you be back on board?" Ozzie inquired.

I mentally calculated the flight time from Mars to Luna. *Thunder Child* was a hell of a lot faster than an intersystem shuttle. It would take less than twelve hours to make the trip. "Late-ish. Cortez and I have reports to finish and we're going to her place for a drink to celebrate the arrest."

"Be back by 0100 hours." Sumner's voice developed a chill, and I fought back the prickle of annoyance. He knew Cortez and I were sleeping together. If it bothered him, it was his problem, not mine.

"Yes, Commander." I paused a little longer than necessary between the words just to be a dick but kept my tone light. "Tamareia out." I tapped off my device and punched the button onscreen to call Singh back. He answered immediately.

"Where and when?" I said before he could gloat.

"Tripathi Hotel, 1900 hours. Dress accordingly." A smug grin tugged at his mouth. "Does this mean I get my story?"

"No promises," I snapped. "You have no idea what you'd be getting into."

"Try me," he offered.

It'd be tempting to let Singh get his throat cut. "We'll talk." I stabbed my finger against the screen and ended the call. Gray and white starbursts formed behind my closed lids as I pressed my palms against my eyes.

I was going back to Luna.

The crash of a fist against the booth startled me back into my surroundings. "Hey, are we going to finish reports and get to drinking, or are you going to sit in there all goddamned day?" Cortez called as she passed.

The drift of her pheromones lay heavy in the air when I exited the cubicle. She grinned at me from her workstation, and the warm flush of her sexual anticipation brushed suggestively against my empathic nets. The tissues in my chest and groin flooded with heat in response; my changeling hormones enabled the swell of my small breasts against the front of my shirt. Yeah, I was definitely going to be on the receiving end of her favorite strap-on tonight.

Bring it, Cortez. I returned her grin with a smirk and a raised eyebrow. As long as I could look forward to her assertion of MDEA dominance over me, the galactic interloper, I could put off the reality of going back to Luna for as long as possible.

————

With my face buried between Maritza Cortez's lush thighs, it was easy to forget everything in the scent of human skin and the sweet-and-salt taste of my partner as I reciprocated her earlier conquest of me.

My lips planted gentle kisses over the sensitive mound between her legs, tongue dipping into the slippery hollows in quick darts. I let my breath ghost over the skin beneath her dense curls. A shudder of desire wracked her body, sending a zing of pleasure through my heightened senses, and she protested, "Quit teasing, damn you."

"So impatient," I murmured against her, and flicked my tongue over the swollen head of her clitoris. She gasped and gripped my hair to pull me in tighter. I slipped my arms beneath her hips, belly down on the mattress to give her the attention she demanded until I sensed her orgasm building, and pulled back to prolong the session.

I lightly raked my teeth across the satin skin of her inner thigh, drawing a frustrated but appreciative purr from Cortez. My fingers stroked upwards across her soft, round abdomen to her breasts, teasing a tight brown nipple beneath the pad of my middle finger. She squirmed and arched her back against the mattress with a throaty sigh.

"You just like to draw things out," she whimpered breathlessly.

"It's worth it." The longer her arousal built, the more stimulating it was for me, too, capturing droplets of distilled mutual pleasure in my empathic webs. I turned my attention back to the glistening, rosy peak pushing through her damp curls.

She slowly rocked into my mouth, movements gaining rhythm and purpose as her breathing grew faster. "Ah, god, right there," she gasped as I sucked her clit between my lips. "Fuck me. Make me come."

Her moans tightened the flesh between my own legs as I slid my lubricated fingers into the silky depths of her body and worked in counterpoint to the gentle suction and stroke against the nub of engorged, heated skin. Her hands fisted in my hair, her legs trembling as her orgasm approached.

"Harder," she demanded.

I increased the tempo of my thrusts. Her cries built to crescendo and spilled over in a stifled shriek as she came. "Oh, god, yes!" The crest sent a rush through my empathic nets, my skin tingling with our shared release as I ground my engorged mons into the mattress and reached my own climax, groaning into her. She jerked against my mouth as the waves rolled through us.

I didn't relent until she fell slack and spent against the rumpled sheets. I bestowed another kiss upon the swollen pearl of flesh and each taut, erect nipple before I slid up to collapse, panting, beside her. She turned over and kissed me deeply, sharing the essence of her own sex. Her fingers found the small mound of my still-sensitive breast and I shivered as she rolled the nipple between her thumb and forefinger in a gentle tug.

"Another round?" she offered.

I lifted my head to read the chronometer beside her door. Already half past midnight. I was going to be inexcusably late if I didn't leave soon. "Damn, I wish I could. You'll have to settle for two."

"I guess I'll live with the disappointment." She handed me my almost-finished beer from the bedside table. I drained it in a long pull and stifled a hoppy belch, another reason I preferred whiskey. Cortez's wrecked bed, damp with sweat and lube and other secretions, reluctantly allowed me an exit from its tangled sheets. After a quick turn in the sonic cleanser, I fumbled for my discarded clothing.

"So do you and Sumner fuck?" Cortez asked from the nest of rumpled pillows where she nursed her own beer.

Open mouthed, I stared at her. While Alecto Sim was busy making plans to stab us both in the back, he pointed out that Rion Sumner cared for me—and I for him, something I'd known in the back of my head but wasn't ready to do anything about. And damn it, not long afterward, Sumner suddenly took a starring role in the feverish sex dreams which harried my sleep as often as my nightmares. It was one of the reasons I accepted Cortez's rather aggressive advances—I hoped it would soothe the sexual frustration and evict my commanding officer from my subconscious.

"Why does everybody assume we sleep together?" I mumbled, buckling my black kilt.

"He's the only other human on your ship," Cortez pointed out around another swig. "Unless you do it with the lizard people."

"Incompatible body parts, unfortunately. They're great cuddlers, though."

Her laughter pealed against the walls of the narrow room. "Are you serious?"

"Lizard-pile movie night is pretty damn awesome." I tugged on my shirt. "They let me hang out because I'm warm."

"I think I would go nuts without another human around. You never know, Sumner might be a great bedwarmer too." Cortez raised her arms over her head and arched in a satisfied stretch, the bedside lamp highlighting her brown skin in honey-colored shades. I took a moment to appreciate the sight. Something is hardwired into my pleasure centers about my own species, no matter how thrilling the sex was with certain other humanoids I'd encountered. The soft swell of breasts, the arc of a hip, the triangle where groin and thigh meet: the symmetrical geometry of a human body, regardless of gender, holds my worshipful admiration. Maritza Cortez's physiology was like a work of art.

"You are a goddess," I told her reverently. One knee on the bed, I braced myself on my hands and descended to kiss her for the last time, her tongue bitter with traces of beer. Cortez's hands stroked up the back of my bare thighs under the kilt and tightened on my equally naked ass. It sent a clenching spasm of warmth through my mons, stirring the chemical factories of my change hormones. I sighed against her mouth in regret as she pulled me down on top of her.

"I can't stay. I really do have to be back at the ship. We

have a deadline." I stroked a spiral of her hair away from her eye and pressed my lips to her closed lid.

"Ah, fine, you loser." Cortez groped my ass one last time and delivered a hard, stinging slap to the right cheek. She sat up as she released me and pulled a shirt over her head while I perched on the side of the bed and tugged on one of my boots. When I came up, she was watching me with a pensive expression, her faint sadness brushing my empathic webs. I cocked my head.

"You getting sentimental on me? I thought we said this was casual," I chided gently. She snorted in genuine amusement.

"You wish, Tamareia. We had fun, but I'm not going to pine for your scrawny ass." She skimmed underwear up her legs and stood. "I was wondering. You must get lonely out there for other humans. Our own kind."

"For certain individuals." I shoved my unshod foot into the other boot. "But our own species historically hasn't been kind to people who are different. Out there, when they hate me, it's usually because I'm an asshole, not because I'm a genetic aberration among my species."

"There's a faction out there, a fucking Pilean cartel who wants to enslave the human race to a drug." Her indignation flared, a lance of heat against my senses. "Eventually it will make it into circulation, and then what? We're still at war, but a sneaky one fought in a lab instead of an all-out, guns-blazing battle. You still want to tell me nobody hates us just because we're human?"

"My experience has been humans hate each other a lot more than the rest of the galaxy does." I strapped on the wrist sheath of my Ursetu dagger, securing the blade against my left forearm. "Anti-human sentiment does exist, but for the drug cartel, the real angle is what brings them the biggest payday."

"Or control of a specific sector." Cortez frowned as I got up and retrieved my coat. "It feels like somebody's setting themselves up to play out a long-term game."

Her words sparked something in me, and I froze with one arm halfway into the sleeve, my brain firing in a new direction. "You may be on to something."

"Anything you want to share with a fellow human?" she asked dryly, watching me. I shook myself.

"Not yet. Just an idea. If it pans out, I'll let you know."

I settled the coat around my shoulders, making certain the knife was covered. I had a permit for it courtesy of the Remoliad, but unlike other parts of the galaxy, carrying a blade was frowned upon in Sol Fed. Interesting, considering projectile weapons were far more dangerous to dome integrity, yet I carried a permit for one of those, too.

Cortez walked the six steps with me from her bed to the door of the pod. "Good luck out there, Tamareia. Watch your back."

"Thanks, Cortez. You too. Be careful."

"Ever ready." We said goodbye with a quick hug. She broke away first and closed the door behind me.

I made my way to the cage lift clinging to the outside of the high-rise and rode it down. Her pod occupied an outer row with a view of the desert landscape, almost skimming the top of the dome where the radiation shielding was thickest. The trail of humanity's footprints in Martian soil, a line of glowing domes and rectangular hydroponics fields, faded into the horizon. The blue-black night teemed with stars and the bright, moving dots of intersystem shuttles arriving at the terminal two kilometers over. That was my destination.

On the ride down, I thought about Cortez's impression of a long-term enterprise. The average lifespan in our galaxy for bipedal, oxygen-breathing types was around a century, give or take a couple of decades. Our concerns revolved around what could play out in the span of our lifetime.

Other species, like the Pileans, lived only the equivalent of half a humanoid lifespan and were more concerned with what came after them. The Pileans called it the debt to the next brood: each family group spent their adult life cycle amassing security in food, wealth, and shelter for the following generation.

Species which lived far longer did exist. I knew of only one allied system with beings whose slow metabolisms guaranteed them a lifespan of several hundred years. They weren't in a rush to accomplish anything, even eschewing FTL space travel for interplanetary hops if some other species didn't impose a specific deadline. But there were rumors of more out there, on worlds in other galaxies we'd just begun to contact.

Alecto Sim had infiltrated the Remoliad in a slow, methodical game, the moves of which we still hadn't been able to completely unpick, pieces set in place by an unknown player. I wondered if Skadi and Alecto's mysterious "employer" might be a member of one of those long-lived species.

The two opposing lanes of automated walkway belts at the center of the dome were packed with tired, dirty food processing workers getting home from the second shift. Some passively rode the conveyor's left inside lane, slumped in weary rest on benches, while those in a hurry paced the right side of the east-bound belt next to the handrail.

Crowds are rough on an empath in Sol Fed. It isn't a common psi attribute for humans and the lack of it undoubtedly contributed to our near extinction; consequently, no one ever learned to control their emotional broadcasts. Growing up on Zereid in a society of highly telepathic and empathic beings mindful of others' privacy had been a peaceful haven for me. When I came back to my native system, everyone's output bludgeoned my senses and overwhelmed me if I didn't shut it down. It had taken me time to learn how, and I still wasn't comfortable in a crowd.

Something nagged at the boundaries of my mind and

made me reluctant to draw in my empathic senses as I ducked with muttered apologies through clustered workers in the eastbound lane. Most moved aside without comment, but the hair on the back of my neck crawled as I glanced over my shoulder. I'd garnered someone's attention, and it wasn't friendly. Difficult to trace in the chaos of human emotions, it took a minute to pick out two individuals behind me, twenty meters down the belt. I did a double take.

Camouflaged in dark coveralls like the processing plant workers wore, their heads were covered in hoods and goggles. When they realized I was looking at them, they stopped and hung back for a moment, then surged forward with renewed purpose. The way one of them moved was odd; sleeves and legs flapped around limbs too thin to fill out the coveralls. The skull's shape beneath the headgear was not quite human. In the shadows of the deep hood, I glimpsed the curve of a sharp mandible.

Oh, seven fucking hells.

CHAPTER
THREE

I PICKED UP THE PACE, less polite in my passage, and tapped the implant behind my ear. "Anybody there? I have a situation."

Ziggy answered immediately. "What's happening, Dalí?"

"I'm on the eastbound belt outside the tunnel to the terminal. There are two subjects dressed in coveralls and goggles following me. I think one is a Pilean." I swallowed against the knot of dread in my throat for what that meant. "Warn MDEA there are strangers in the neighborhood. Cortez might need backup at her place."

"Copy that. Be careful. Sumner and Riga*nat are headed your way. I'm tracking you."

The crowd exited the moving walkway in front of a cluster of tenements and shuttered, ground-level storefronts. A hundred meters later, the benches sank flush with the surface, and the belt disappeared beneath the floor of the climate dome. I stepped onto the concrete slab and headed for the flight of stairs descending into the underground tunnel which led to the terminal.

The staircase leading up to the concourse was still half a kilometer away, and I took quick measure of my surroundings. At almost one in the morning, few people traveled, which was good if a fight broke out. But there was no cover, only an open metal handrail separating the opposing lanes of foot traffic and five hundred meters of echoing, deserted concrete tunnel. Not an ideal situation.

I reached into my coat sleeve to touch the hilt of the knife for reassurance and hoped the pair following me didn't have guns. The local cartel had a history of kidnapping people who crossed them and dumping them in the Martian desert to suffocate without an environment suit. Pileans just went for messy wet work using their mandibles.

I didn't particularly want to experience those unpleasant options. I didn't really want to get in a fight while I wasn't wearing underwear, either, but I'd be damned if it ever stopped me before.

Midway through the tunnel there was a clatter on the stairs behind me. My pulse sped up with adrenaline. Change hormones caused muscle and bone to slide beneath my skin in preparation for an oncoming fight. I turned to face them.

They no longer pretended they were not following me. Emboldened by the vacant tunnel, the Pilean gave up all pretense of being human and launched zerself toward me, knees bending backward under the coveralls, the hard exoskeleton on zer feet making sharp, skittering clicks as ze slid against the concrete.

I decided to run like hell for the opposite stairs. But I forgot Pileans could use those powerful backward-facing legs to jump.

I was halfway up the steps when the Pilean flew past my shoulder. Ze skidded to a stop on the landing two meters ahead of me and spoke. My implant translated the papery flutter of syllables as, "Going somewhere?"

The heavy footsteps of zer human counterpart came from behind. I ripped my knife from its sheath and tried to keep them both in view. The man raised his arm, the rectangular black barrel of a weapon pointed directly at me.

He pulled the trigger.

Two wire-tethered darts pierced the skin below my ribcage. Lightning crackled in the black tube. My body seized up; every muscle knotted and cramped until I thought they would rip themselves apart. I fell and could do nothing to stop it. My blade clanged down the steps. Pain drew a gray veil across my vision as I convulsed on the cold concrete. The agony stopped, and my breath shrieked in around a ragged gasp. Okay, that was just dirty. A fucking taser? Really?

The Pilean held my shoulders down with zer spindly hands, mandibles clacking an inch from my nose. Zer loathing was an oppressive pressure against my empathic nets. "Penumbra," ze breathed at me, the translator pendant beneath zer clothing doing the speaking this time. "I should tear your heart out."

"Too late," I rasped. "That happened a long time ago."

Ze cocked zer head at me, momentarily confused. The Pilean's human backup gave a shout, and I looked up to see a blond comet streaking down the stairs. Sumner vaulted over the handrail. His feet connected with the carapace beneath my assailant's coveralls and knocked zem away from me.

"Do not move!" Riga*nat's voice boomed and echoed through the tunnel in Sol Standard. The human took one look at the enormous Burkani thundering down on him and panicked, turned tail, and ran back west. I yelped in pain as the barbed darts got ripped out of my skin by his retreat. The sizzling purple flash of a stunner streaked overhead and the satisfying thud of a body hitting the floor echoed through the tunnel.

Sumner drew down on the Pilean and glared at the insectoid over the barrel of another energy weapon. "Are you okay, Dalí?" His vivid, blue-green eyes flickered over me in concern, and back to his prisoner.

My breath hitched out around my muscles' protest over their recent electrocution as I sat up. "Yeah," I managed, rubbing the blood-rimmed holes the barbs left in the shirt and my skin. "I'm fine."

"You are under arrest for the assault of a law enforcement officer," Sumner coolly informed the Pilean in Remoliad Standard. "Refusal to cooperate will be met with equal or greater force. Do you understand?"

"I deny the allegation." Zer mandibles sullenly clicked together over the projected voice of the translator pendant.

"Of course you do." Riga*nat snorted through his upturned nasal cavities as he thudded past us. With his thick, armored gray-green hide, wide shoulders, and a spiked horn jutting from his forehead, he reminded me of a now-extinct animal which once roamed the African plains on Earth. "Is Tamareia all right?"

My bare butt was chilled against the concrete, but I couldn't stand up yet. My entire body was one giant muscle cramp. "I'll live."

"How disappointing," he said.

Riga*nat and I had gotten off on the wrong foot as soon as he joined our team for this mission. He questioned Sumner's leadership decisions, something about employing unstable agents from underdeveloped species. I stuck up for Sumner and told Riga*nat he could kiss my unstable ass.

Funny how I never doubted he was talking about me.

The Burkani stepped over the rail and bent to fasten cuffs on the unconscious man's forearms. He grabbed the guy by one leg and dragged him over to lay next to the Pilean. Sumner moved aside, still holding the insectoid at gunpoint while Riga*nat removed the goggles and hood from zer triangular head to reveal the Pilean's crest.

The wavelike family pattern of the drug cartel rippled across the keratinous shield on its forehead. The Burkani grunted in recognition and placed restraints on the Pilean's slender wrists and around zer knee joints, which allowed zem to walk but effectively hobbled the ability to jump. The human prisoner began to stir and mumble.

"MDEA is on its way to take them into custody, but I will be responsible for the Pilean," Riga*nat said.

"I committed no crimes here," the insectoid being rustled in zer dry voice.

"I suspect you did not legally enter this system." Riga*nat's close-set eyes did not blink as he stared at the Pilean. "Sol Fed has unusually strict laws regarding immigration. At the very least, you will be deported."

"Sumner." I gestured for him to come closer. He holstered his weapon and extended a hand. I gripped it and rose, groaning, but leaned in close to speak quietly in his ear. "The Pilean ID'd me as Penumbra."

He pulled back to study me, a dismayed expression hardening his eyes into glacial ice. "We've been compromised."

"Sounds that way."

He swore under his breath.

"Ziggy, is there any news on Cortez?" I asked, suddenly afraid.

"Local law enforcement is on scene, medical on its way," Ziggy said.

My chest tightened. "Is she all right?"

"Oh, yes. Cortez has minor injuries, but she kicked her assailant off the walkway of her building."

"Outstanding." I imagined that scene with vicious satisfaction.

"Did you say you were ID'd?" Ozzie's sober inquiry came over the com.

"Yeah. I'm afraid so." From the terminal side of the tunnel, Martian drug enforcement agents spilled down the staircase with Captain Williams, his expression grim, in the lead. "MDEA's here. We'll get back to you as soon as possible."

Several sprinted for the beltway toward Cortez's high rise,

but Williams lingered with the officers swarming the two suspects, eyeing the Pilean with visible disgust. "So that's what the bastards look like, eh?"

"Become familiar with their appearance, Captain, especially the forehead crest," Riga*nat advised him. "I fear you will see others in the future."

Williams narrowed his eyes at me. "Were you and Cortez too focused on getting into each other's pants to notice they tailed you to her place?"

"With all due respect, sir, I'm not wearing any pants, and that's none of your fucking business." But the implications were unsettling. "I'm certain we weren't followed. They dressed in coveralls to blend in with the working crowd. They planned to be there during the second-shift commute. They already knew where she lives, or someone inside told them we were the ones who tracked the shipment and made the bust. They waited for me. The Pilean called me out when ze attacked."

Williams stared me down a minute before he averted his eyes. "Damn it. I didn't want to hear that." He exchanged a glance with Riga*nat, who gave a bob of his curved horn.

"I concur. They planned this attack."

"Son of a bitch." Williams's anger rose in surges; his fear of betrayal dashed against my empathic nets. "You think it's one of my own?"

"We have no way of knowing." Riga*nat began to lumber back up the stairs. "We must question the suspects. I assume the third is in no condition to talk?"

"Hard to say anything with your brains splattered on the floor of the dome." Williams pursed his lips. "I'm going to check on Cortez. We'll meet back at the division for interrogation. Tamareia, you'll need to come in and give a statement."

I exchanged a questioning glance with Sumner, who stepped forward. "I'm afraid they'll have to transmit it, Captain. Our team is leaving for Luna."

"Related to this case?" Riga*nat shuffled his massive feet, his head tilted in suspicion.

"No. Something's come up."

I managed to cover my surprise. If Sumner refused to tell the Burkani why we were going, he had a reason.

"I need your team's assistance in this matter. The prisoner must be transferred to a Remoliad vessel as soon as possible in compliance with galactic statutes." Riga*nat's indignant protest stomped my empathic nets like an inconvenienced rhinoceros in tantrum. "I realize the attack was unexpected, but this is ill-timed, Commander."

Sumner grimaced. Riga*nat was right; the joint operation was the whole reason we were in Sol Fed, but we both were reluctant to miss this opportunity. It was Sumner's call, though. It took all my self-control to keep my mouth shut. Maybe I was improving.

"You'll need at least twenty-four hours before transfer, more if interrogation stalls," Sumner said at last. "It gives plenty of time for *Thunder Child* to travel to Luna and return. Captain Ossixiani will take command in my absence. There is very little the team can't do enroute to assist your investigation if need arises. You have the frequency."

Riga*nat snorted through his bulbous nose. "Not ideal, but acceptable. However, transfer could take a matter of weeks depending upon the location of the nearest ship."

"We will initiate contact with the closest Remoliad vessel and speed things along," Sumner replied. "Dalí and I can book a commercial flight back if we have to."

"I'll meet you at the division for interrogation," Williams said politely to Riga*nat before he turned his scowl on me and barked, "I expect that report to be in the system by 0600. Far be it from me to delay getting you out of my hair."

"You don't have hair, sir." I guess I wasn't improving.

"Fuck you, Tamareia." He glared at Sumner. "I'm glad they're your problem and not mine."

To his credit, my commander didn't sigh in agreement as Williams stalked off toward the westbound belt; he only regarded me pointedly until I raised my hands in submission and accepted the silent reprimand. MDEA officers dragged the Pilean and the groggy, stumbling human suspect upstairs to the terminal. As soon as they moved out of range, Sumner turned to Riga*nat.

"We may have a bigger problem." He nodded to me. "Tell him."

"The Pilean specifically identified me as a Penumbra agent." I waited for Riga*nat to process the information, and a wet exhalation of shock erupted from the Burkani's cavernous nostrils.

"This is detrimental," he said. "Tamareia must be removed from all future operations. Their further involvement could endanger all we have accomplished."

My face grew hot. Before I could open my mouth and say anything caustic, Sumner's hand closed over my wrist in a warning squeeze, and he spoke. "Dalí's part in this case is over for now. We will re-evaluate our role in the operation since you are taking the position of primary liaison. You and Ozzie can discuss a diminished presence, but you will need human undercover agents."

"That makes your absence all the more difficult," Riga*nat complained. "I will be contacting my superiors to express my concerns."

"I respectfully request you do not contact anyone at the Remoliad about this team's status or activities." Sumner's voice was edged with steel. I did stare at him this time.

"Why?" The Burkani blinked in confusion, his close-set eyes fixed on Sumner's face.

"It's need to know. Not your mission." His voice softened. "We've worked together before, Riga*nat. I'm asking you to trust me."

The Burkani stared him down and finally spouted a cloud

of wet breath in reluctant agreement. "Very well." He mounted the stairs to follow the MDEA officers, each step sending a miniature earthquake through the concrete and rebar. "I will expect contact from you regarding the arrival of the Remoliad transport. But you must consider that keeping Tamareia on will compromise your entire team, Commander."

A cold sliver of ice slid down my spine as Riga*nat departed. His words resonated inside me like a tremor. I gripped the rail, both hands white knuckled, my blood boiling. *Fuck.*

We were compromised on our previous mission; there was no denying it.

The lab we discovered was destroyed in a bloody uprising of its captive test subjects: bioengineered warriors who possessed physiology tweaked with a direct addition of human DNA to support the Pilean cartel's research. These beings were unlike the Shontavians I had met before, both in their philosophy and ability to resist the base instincts ingrained by torture.

We thought we'd rescued them from their brutal fate, only to lose them again to Alecto Sim, a story everyone in the galaxy knew by now. Rion and I had placed our trust in him, and he'd cut us to the marrow with a blade we never saw coming.

But it was my face that was beamed out to galactic networks by goddamned media bots during the emergency session at the Remoliad.

I never stopped to consider how it might put our team in danger.

"I'm a liability," I said hoarsely. "I never thought—"

"Let's not talk about it here." He cut me off with quiet finality. "Ozzie, start preflight checks and contact the tower. We're on our way."

"Acknowledged." Ozzie said over the com. Sumner reached up and turned his off, so I did the same.

I followed him up the stairs, leaning heavily on the rail as I grimaced against the complaint of my still-knotted muscles. A bit of prescient dread sent dark, fluttering thoughts through my head as I watched Sumner climb ahead of me. Even though his Nos heritage bestowed a psychic null which prevented even the strongest telepaths from reading his emotions, I was intimately familiar with his body language.

Not that I studied him often . . . well, yes, I did. More so now since the last mission, and the moment of bleak despair when I thought he was going to die. I knew his relaxed posture and genuine grin when he was among our team, a close-knit family as well as colleagues. Straight-backed, rigid frustration set his features into hard, sculpted lines when I was being a dick. I had also come to recognize his gentleness and vulnerability, displayed in the too-rare moments when he revealed to me the man beneath a reserved veneer of cool, professional efficiency.

But this? The angle of his shoulders drooped with a burden he stubbornly carried alone. As he reached the top of the stairs, he looked back, noted my expression, and straightened. His customary demeanor snapped back into place so quickly I frowned at him in question as he slid a hand under my elbow to aid me up the last few steps.

"Later." He deflected the interrogation forming on my lips. "When the whole team can listen."

CHAPTER
FOUR

MY INFLEXIBLE MUSCLES finally decided walking was a good idea, but I still had a hitch in my step by the time we reached *Thunder Child*. Once we were on board, Sumner slid into the cockpit to take his place in the pilot's seat and I descended the narrow stairwell to the berth deck. I moved stiffly down the central corridor, headed for my quarters to strap myself in. Tommi's door was open as I passed.

"Dalí." She hailed me and patted the empty spot to her left. I joined her. "You have blood on your shirt, and you're limping. Did you and Cortez have rough sex?"

"No, all the screaming on the com was me getting tasered, remember?" I eased into the jump seat with a groan and buckled up.

"You were lucky he didn't shoot you. I can give you a muscle relaxant once we're out of orbit. It will help with the soreness."

"I'll take it. Thanks."

"Why didn't they use lethal weapons?" Tommi's chameleon-like eyes swiveled in their veridian sheaths, both bright irises trained on my face. "Did they plan on taking you alive?"

"Possibly." I thought about it. The Pilean said I *should* tear your heart out, not I *will* tear your heart out: a small distinction, but maybe an important one. Whether they planned to take me to a more gruesome death or somewhere for torture and interrogation, I hoped I would never find out.

The ship vibrated as the airlock arm detached and retracted from the hull. Vertical thrust jets fired, lifting us from the surface of Mars and away from the terminal before atmospheric engines cut in to begin our ascent. Beside me, Tommi's concern and dismay still tumbled against my empathic nets. I turned to her.

"What's wrong, Tommi?"

My translator whispered her words under the breathy hiss of the Cthash language. "Are you all right? You could have been killed."

"I'm kind of getting used to that." I closed my eyes for a minute, trying to articulate what I felt. "I guess it was stupid to think what happened on our last mission wouldn't come back to bite us in the ass."

The main engines fired, propelling the ship into the upper atmosphere. Our bodies tried to meld with the padded jump seats and speaking became more difficult. My thoughts spun like one of the red planet's sand devils, diaphanous and unpredictable, taking them in a direction I did not want to go.

Outside the narrow viewport, the Martian night yielded from the darkest blue to an impenetrable black freckled with hard white stars. After a few minutes, the pleats of my kilt lifted in the sudden loss of gravity. I smoothed them down to avoid flashing Tommi.

She noticed. "I've seen everything before."

"Maybe I'm getting modest."

"I doubt it."

We sat in silence a moment before I voiced the nagging fear at the back of my mind.

"If there's a price on my head, more assassins could be

coming. I should resign before the rest of you are endangered."

"There may be a bounty on all of us," she pointed out. "We'll be safer together. You could stay on board and just not do field work." Tommi stopped and hissed dismissively, her eyestalks rolling. "Never mind."

I laughed. She was right, but I couldn't resist teasing her. "What, you don't think I could do a desk job?"

"Could you?" Her eyes focused on me, telescoping in a quizzical gaze.

"No," I admitted. I liked the adrenaline. The work filled my waking hours and made me feel . . . alive. Nights were still too quiet.

Someone was always awake on *Thunder Child* when I couldn't sleep. Whether it was watching questionable twenti-eth-century movies snuggled up with one or more Clan Sustrix siblings, helping Ka'pth glean data from one of the Andari's many information dumps, or sparring with Sumner or Ziggy in the cargo hold, I had friends who helped me feel normal.

And I needed them. I needed them so much the thought of losing them tightened a garrote of panic around my neck. My composure threatened to unravel, and I shut my emotions down, unable to deal with it now.

Tommi leaned her smooth-scaled head against my shoulder in comfort, but I sensed her distress as well. "Don't leave. I would miss you terribly, even if you are a sore on my butt."

"A pain in the ass," I corrected around the lump in my throat, and rested my cheek against the coolness of her leathery skin. We stayed that way, each lost to our own unhappy thoughts until artificial gravity kicked in twenty minutes later. The summons came for the crew to assemble.

Sumner had something to tell us.

———

The command center was usually a noisy place. A hush loomed over it now, save for the low rumble of the ship's engines. Even gregarious Ozzie silently leaned in the cockpit doorway with the ship on autopilot. My crewmates' uneasiness tugged at my empathic senses, all of us sharing an undercurrent of dread.

Sumner supported himself on clenched fists at the central table, his gaze downcast. "I think we all knew this day was coming after what happened. We've just learned for certain Dalf's identity was compromised." He glanced up at us, drawing a deep breath. "And this morning, the Remoliad informed me I am relieved of command, effective immediately."

Not what I expected to hear.

"What?" I blurted. The rest of the team's shock and dismay coalesced against my empathic webs like burning sparks struck from metal.

"Alecto's infiltration of the security council embarrassed several high-ranking individuals. They needed someone to blame for the fiasco on Zereid, so they put pressure on the Penumbra." He ran a hand through his pale hair. "My genetic ties to Skadi and failure to disclose my previous relationship with Alecto was brought under scrutiny." He glanced at each of us in turn, meeting our disbelief with a resigned gaze. "As I told Riga*nat, Ozzie will see the Mars operation through to its conclusion."

"Once we finish here, we are to report for reassignment within the intelligence community," Ozzie said from the other side of the command center. "The Penumbra was terminally exposed when Sim was in charge and can no longer function in secrecy. We've been ordered to archive all our open cases until the Remoliad decides what to do with us. If we choose not to be reassigned, we are free to retire from service." His irony dripped from my empathic nets.

"But we're their most effective field team," Tommi hissed in disbelief.

"All cases? Including the investigation of Skadi and her employer?" Ka'pth's throat gills fluttered with indignance.

Sumner's gaze locked on mine, and I understood.

"We're getting too close," I said. "They're doing everything they can to protect themselves."

"There is more than one enemy operative in the Remoliad." Ziggy crossed his arms over his chest.

Pride glimmered in Sumner's wry smile. "And this is why you are the best team in the galaxy."

"You agreed to go to Luna even though you already knew," I realized. "That's why you asked Riga*nat not to say anything."

"I did. And he won't. He's a good being, even if tact is not a strong point." Sumner rubbed his forehead. "The rest of what I need to tell you is so far off the record it might as well not exist. While I am complying with the Director's official orders, he made a personal request. He wants us to continue the investigation on our own. If we agree, we will no longer be protected, nor can we seek assistance from the Remoliad fleet."

He held eye contact with each of us in turn. "I want everyone to understand you're free to be reassigned or to transmit your resignation once the Mars mission is completed. This isn't what any of you signed up for. I'm no one's commander now. The choice is yours."

A quick flurry of wordless communication went through the room. Ozzie straightened and said, "I speak for Clan Sustrix. We're in, Sumner."

"As are we." Ra'sho stepped forward, her mate moving a beat behind in that eerie Andari synchrony, like a waterless school of fish.

"To whatever end," Ka'pth added solemnly.

That left me. I kept my gaze on my hands, clasped between my knees. I swallowed hard. "I won't insist on remaining part of the team with a target on my back. I can go to Luna."

"You're not going anywhere alone, especially now," Sumner said. "I'm going with you."

I lifted my head and stared at him in defiance. The memory of him beaten, bloody, and ready to die for Alecto and me was sharp and terrible. "I have no idea what I'm walking into. I won't lose anyone else I love in the crossfire."

A microsecond later, I realized the implications of what I'd just said. Heat flooded my face. Sumner's expression flickered, his eyes going wide and soft as a flush crept over his features. He hadn't missed it. Judging from the triumphant surge of satisfaction against my empathic nets from a couple of unnamed lizard-like crewmates, nobody else had either.

I looked away hurriedly and stammered, "The team should make the call. I won't put any of you in danger. You're my family."

"As if there is a question," Tommi said softly.

"You're one of us." Ziggy touched my shoulder and gently squeezed it with their taloned fingers. I reached up and clasped their hand where it lay, moved by the warmth of affection and trust from my friends. It glowed in my empathic nets, and my eyes threatened to leak.

"Besides, we know you'd go after Skadi on your own like an idiot," Ozzie deadpanned. I chuckled as I spread my hands in sheepish agreement, grateful for the laughter of my friends even if it was at my expense.

"What about Melos?" Ka'pth inquired.

"I think we all know what his answer will be." Ozzie turned his bright gaze on Sumner. "The crew accepts the mission. It is time to meet the bastards head on. Commissioned or not, we follow you."

Sumner's eyes glimmered, and he ducked his head. His face bloomed with scarlet as he composed himself. When he looked up, determination hardened the angle of his jaw, and he nodded sharply.

"We have work to do. We will be in Lunar space approximately ten hours from now. Dalí and I will take *Three* down to the surface. We'll need the proper travel permissions and permits. It needs to look like a personal trip, not a meeting with a potential source."

"Already done," Ra'sho stated. "I reserved lodgings for you inside the Hijra Quarter using a Sol Fed credit account still active in Dalí's name. I had some difficulty locating vacancies for your arrival, but this proprietor was willing to open a room. There is some sort of festival happening. All the hotels were full."

Checking the date, it made sense. "Koovagam," I realized aloud. "The place is going to be packed." The colorful celebration lasted a week, but tomorrow evening had particularly profound meaning for the third-gender community on Luna. I was glad to focus on something else. "The Tripathi Hotel caters to a high-class crowd. I'm certain this party is no exception. There used to be a place where we could rent formal-wear in the Quarter." I rattled off the name of a shop, and Ka'pth nodded, his busy hands a blur over the screens.

"I see it here. I will transmit your sizes and reserve something suitable. Our mining programs will run against Mother England's databases as soon as we are close enough to receive confirmation of local network integrity."

"Excellent." Sumner straightened. "Tommi, let's shift Riga*nat off our backs. Find out where the closest Remoliad vessel is and schedule his prisoner transfer." He glanced at me, and his expression suggested nothing but the business at hand. "Transmit your report to Williams, then I want you to get at least six hours of rack time. Tommi can knock you out if she has to."

I watched him disappear into his ready room and fought the strange mix of dismay and irritation bubbling inside me. Great. I displayed my confused feelings for him in front of the whole crew. That was all I needed.

And why was I so pissed off Sumner barely acknowledged it?

I avoided looking at any of my shipmates and stalked off to my quarters to write Williams's stupid report, but all I did for the first five minutes was sit at the pull-down desk and scowl at the display with my head propped in my hand.

There was a tap at the door. Ozzie peered in, wiggling a bottle of water and a couple of small packets with tablets visible through the wrapping. "I brought you the muscle relaxant Tommi promised, and a sleep aid. She says don't take them until you're ready to crash."

"Thanks," I muttered, quickly pretending to be busy. "Just put them on my bunk."

Ozzie did so but, rather than leaving, he sat in one of the jump seats and closed the door. "Anything you want to talk about?"

I groaned, planting my forehead on the desktop. "What did I just do, Oz?"

The hiss of his laughter reached my ears even though I refused to look at him. "You're acting like no one else knows you have been dancing around each other ever since you joined us."

"I didn't even realize it until Alecto said so," I mumbled at the floor. "But in my defense, he was a goddamned liar."

For too long, I didn't see what was right in front of me, still navigating the devastated landscape of my heart after the loss of my spouses. I told myself Alecto's declaration was just another manipulation of my emotions. But there had been signs all along—some of them in bright fucking neon—over the last six months. The embrace Ozzie witnessed in Sumner's ready room had been the latest manifestation, but since that time, nothing. Until today, when I blurted out something I really wasn't prepared to confess.

"Humans are so bizarre," my friend mused. "There is no shame in love. It's a gift. You lot are too caught up in why it isn't practical instead of seeing the joy in it." Ozzie's tone softened. "I'm not dismissing your pain. Learning to care again isn't betraying Gresh and Rasida. But isn't refusing to acknowledge it another kind of loss?"

"I don't need a matchmaker, thank you." Raising my head, I glared at him. "Between you and Gor, you practically have a wedding planned." Even my Zereid crechemate had been sending me regular correspondence, asking *how is Sumner* and *how are things going*? "Besides, he's never said anything to me himself. Not one damned word."

"Fine. I'm pushing too hard." With a big, open-mouthed grin, Ozzie raised his hands in surrender. "Just consider it. You'll have time to talk on Luna if neither of you think too much and screw it up." He was still hiss-chuckling to himself when he went out the door.

I sighed and squeezed my eyes shut in frustration. Fatigue set in as the adrenaline of the arrest, my vigorous assignation with Cortez, and the taser experience began to take their toll. Dashing off a curt, concise report for Williams about the attack in the tunnel, I sent the encrypted message before I slammed the pills back with water. Face down in my bunk, I welcomed the drug-enforced coma and hoped it might somehow sedate the idea of loving Sumner.

CHAPTER
FIVE

ALMOST SEVEN HOURS later I awakened. My first coherent thought sent the muscles in my back stiffening by pairs up my spine. It was not a relic of my close encounter with the taser this time, but of a growing anxiety that haunted my sleep despite the meds Tommi gave me. My mind immediately began to race. I gave up any hope of sinking back into the darkness behind my eyelids.

The chronometer in my quarters said there were still hours left in our flight to Luna, but I wasn't ready to interact with anyone yet. I sat at my data station and started to comb through the most recent information dump Ka'pth prepared for me.

I got one every few days: unusual media reports, port authority alerts from the galactic hub, any odd activity which might signal a lead on the Shontavians. There was even a file on massive orders of raw meat. There was no possible way to hide six enormous, bioengineered mercenaries who enjoyed the taste of their enemies for very long. I refused to give up hope we might find Naru and the others. They had no other advocates, and I was responsible for them. Any potential clues I forwarded to Melos for him to check out.

My Nos teammate did not come with us. He was chasing leads on Residuum and Alecto Sim, but the primary reason he stayed away was the recent near war between the Nos Conglomerate and Sol Fed. It still festered in local memory. Sumner could pass as human, but Melos, with his ice-pale looks and moonlight hair, would be a beacon for any xenophobe in the system.

I delayed as long as I could, fighting the grumpy aftermath of my tranquilized sleep in the cleanser. The stimulating warmth and vibration afforded some relief from the tension but did little for my mood. My progression of thought shifted rapidly from the Shontavians, to Luna, back to the knowledge I had been targeted for assassination or kidnapping. Not knowing which didn't make it any less unnerving. Nor did the prospect of Sumner being in the way if they came for me again. It had not mattered to the explosive-laden media bot that killed Gresh and Rasida.

Stop it, Dalí, I admonished myself. I was getting better at cutting off the descent into despair, but it didn't make the fear go away. I was starting to wonder if it would always be a permanent, unwelcome passenger in my head.

I drew my hair back into a tight ponytail and stared at my reflection for a moment before acting on impulse. I didn't know what version of me the cartel was looking for, but I could make myself more difficult to recognize.

I grabbed my knife and sawed off the queue close to my head. Brown waves unraveled around my face. Clippers shortened the rest until I managed a passable look that was longer on top and short at the back and sides. I swept up the hair and consigned it to the garbage system to be broken down.

The chronometer in my cabin still showed an hour left in our flight to Luna. I dragged on a pair of black duty pants and a long-sleeved shirt before wandering down to the mess to make myself some volatile Ursetu tea. I managed to smuggle some off the planet after our previous mission; it afforded a powerful kick, and I hoarded it for emergencies. One cup later, my brain buzzed with synaptic activity, and I was ready to hit the ground running.

More or less. The twisted coil of anxiety had taken root inside me and quivered with potential energy. The tea did not help that. Nor did replaying last night's confession in my head as I passed Sumner's still-closed cabin door on the way back to my quarters. I resolved to stay cool and professional and pretend it didn't happen if he came out.

The door stayed shut, but I couldn't even fool myself.

I put on my jacket. Shoving toiletries and a few changes of clothes into a bag, I dropped them down the ladder tube where *Three* waited in her snug little berth before I joined the rest of the crew on the command deck.

Tommi gave me an approving nod from the com station as she took in my short hair. I responded with a crooked smile and a thumbs up. Ka'pth and Ra'sho were in high gear in front of the bank of computers, webbed hands flying over tablets and heads up displays as the hacking programs began to collect information about Mother England.

Ziggy held out an inner pants holster and a small-caliber sidearm. "With your current credentials, you should be able to get this through security without any questions."

After last night, I was more appreciative of the gun no matter how far against the tenets of *zezjna* it went. The Zereid path of the peacekeeper was a variable one; maiming was allowed if I didn't kill anyone. I should use all the tools at hand to protect myself and my teammates. I nestled the weapon in the small of my back. Ziggy tapped the blade buckled over my forearm with their first talon.

"That might draw attention. Should you leave it here?"

"My local permits allow it." I hesitated and shrugged. "I feel better having it than not."

Sumner walked in, as bleary eyed and sleep hungover as I

was before my near terminal caffeination. His gaze rested on me, studying the abrupt change in my appearance with an enigmatic expression before he inquired, "Status report?"

"*Nova Twelve* will rendezvous with us at Neptune Station in six days to transfer the Pilean into their custody. The prisoner will be remanded to a Remoliad holding facility pending trial," Tommi said. "I notified Riga*nat we must leave Mars within twenty-four hours to meet their timetable."

"We will stay in orbit for at least three hours to ensure we receive the best quality data before we return to Mars." Ka'pth handed both of us pocket-sized versions of our normal PDDs. "Dalí is familiar with the location, but up-to-date maps of the Lunar domes, caverns, and utility tunnels are loaded. Access to Mother England's personal databases should be achieved within the hour. If there is something important, we will advise before you make contact. Otherwise, we will transmit a synopsis to your devices."

"Pre-flight checks on *Three* are done. She's ready to take you down." Ziggy gave Sumner his own rig, the commander's favorite sidearm in the holster. "Ozzie's going to put us in an apogee orbit. We shouldn't attract as much attention for not broadcasting an identification signal that way, but we know how to handle it if it happens."

"Great work. Thank you all." Sumner nodded and checked the chronometer. "It's 1600 local time. We'll have enough time to check in to our lodgings."

"The rental shop you recommended delivered several sets of clothing to the hostel where you are staying tonight," Ra'sho informed me.

That pricked up my ears. "A hostel? Which one?"

"The owner's name is Devan Patil."

It now made sense why the proprietor had made room for us, but it was another tweak on my already questionable nerves. "Well, then," I said, and hated the way my voice went ragged.

"You know him?" The Andari cocked their heads in synchrony.

"Yes."

"Is that a problem?" Sumner asked.

"No. The Patils were good friends of Gresh's. And mine." Clearly, Dev wanted to see me. I wasn't sure how I felt about renewing contact, other than ashamed I hadn't done so earlier and terrified of what demons might be resurrected when I did. It had been almost three years since I saw Dev and Michael; not since the memorial for the bombing victims.

Before I could overthink it, I straightened and got back to business. "If we want this to look like a personal trip, that's excellent cover."

"Good. Ready to go?" His expression told me he knew I was struggling.

"Yeah. Let's do this."

"Have fun storming the castle." There was a playful note in Ziggy's voice, but their next words were more serious. "Be careful down there. Don't take any chances without backup."

"Thanks, Zig." I gripped their forearm in appreciation and gave Tommi a farewell squeeze as I made my way to the narrow stairwell with Sumner close behind.

He grabbed his own bag from his quarters as we passed. I kept walking, descended the tube to the bay and moved my duffel away from the bottom of the ladder.

"Catch?" Sumner dropped his luggage to me before he stepped down a few rungs and sealed the hatch behind him.

The narrow port in *Three's* side was open. Glowing instrument lights created a soft aurora of color against the bulkhead. Her engines emitted a low hum, ready to carry us away. Another restless shift from the anxiety coiled in my chest made my breath catch. I shoved it back in denial and stowed our bags in the tiny, enclosed space behind the two-seated cockpit while Sumner did a final walk-around.

The emergency storage locker where I secured our

luggage, already full of environment suits and rations, took up most of the space. The ship swayed in its magnetic cradle as I moved. The cabin had just enough headroom for me to stand in, but Sumner had to crouch to enter. I slid into the co-pilot's spot, checking the pre-set instrumentation for launch.

"All systems go?" Sumner asked as he folded his tall frame into the pilot's seat.

"Go." The port sealed with a thump and a hiss. Our little craft's manifold system began to pump air through the cabin. I put on my headset and strapped in. "All right, Oz. We're ready to start the depressurization sequence."

"Copy. Beginning depressurization of ventral bay."

My ears popped when the cabin pressure compensated for the bay's atmosphere as it bled out at a controlled rate. I watched the barometric readings advance and retreat on the display. "External pressure seventy-five percent."

"Seventy-five percent," Sumner responded.

"Fifty percent. Thirty percent." I swallowed to relieve the fullness in my head. "Cabin pressure at maximum."

"Prepare to open bay doors," Sumner advised the crew.

"Depressurization complete."

"Copy that. Opening ventral bay," Ozzie confirmed. *Three* shimmied in the magnetic boom as the doors receded. The arm lowered us to dangle in space below *Thunder Child*'s hull.

The flint-blue curve of Earth filled the transparent alloy windshield. Even gravely wounded, humanity's ancestral home was breathtaking. Phantoms of arid golden continents haunted breaks in the heavy cloud-cover; oceans glinted like winks of mercury in Sol's light. The atmosphere was beginning to clear, but it would take the surface longer to purge the toxic aftermath of war and pollution from soil and sea.

How in the seven hells did we manage to fuck up a whole planet?

"Prepare for drop," Sumner murmured into his headset. I braced myself.

"In five. Four. Three. Two . . . "

The magnet released us. Sumner fired top thrusters to quickly maneuver the ship away from the hull and we floated free. "We're clear."

"See you soon," Ozzie said. *Thunder Child* left us in her wake, heading off to complete the surveillance mission. Sumner throttled the little craft into motion and carved an arc in space, putting the planet behind us.

And there it was.

The moon's disc swelled before us, painted in silver and ash. In the nightfall of Earth's passing shadow, the lunar plains of Mare Nubium sparkled with lights, and at the southern horn of the penumbra's crescent, where light and darkness embraced, lay the place I once called home.

"Have you ever been to Luna?" My uneven voice betrayed the winding tension inside me.

"No." Sumner glanced at me, but I kept my gaze on the moon, unable to meet his eyes. "I've only been to the major space stations before Mars. Where did you live?"

"Kepler. You can just make out a hexagon of complexes north of the crater."

"I see it."

"The apex dome, Galileo, is where the Capitol is. The university is under Kepler, at the middle left. That's where . . . where we . . ."

Memories lay bitter and sweet on my tongue, the ache in my throat a hot coal. Oh, coming back was such a bad idea.

"The—" I coughed to clear the suffocating thickness from my voice. "The old city is in the industrial complex at the bottom of Bullialdus Crater, that cluster of rectangular structures near the shuttle port."

A sparkle of transparent alloy and steel caught my eye as we got closer. My palms grew damp.

Luna Terminal gleamed against the void of space. Intact, as if the explosion that shattered the Earthward docking arm and killed so many innocent people had never happened. As if my heart was still whole and strong, not the bruised piece of meat thudding too fast in my chest.

The restored line of windows where Gresh and 'Sida once stood to bid me goodbye were blank and flawless. Empty.

The spring-coil of anxiety suddenly exploded into shards and hollowed out my insides. I forgot to breathe, my white-knuckled fingers clenching the edge of the jump seat.

Fuck Kiran Singh. No matter what Mother England wanted to tell me, I should never have agreed to come back.

My breath ran shallow in the heavy gravity of blind panic. I fumbled with the stiff buckle of the five-point harness.

"Dalí? You okay?" Sumner's quiet voice cut through the noise in my head.

"I can't . . ." The clasp wouldn't give, my sweat-slick fingers numb and buzzing. "Goddamn it! I need to get out of the cockpit."

"Hey, hey." He extended his right hand and gently laid it over mine where I scrabbled at the release. "We're in *Three*. Where are you going to go?"

I gave up trying and gripped his hand, pressing it against my chest.

"I'm here," he said, his voice low and soothing. "Breathe. A deep breath. Come on, you can do it."

I drew in a shuddering gasp, filled my lungs with air, and just as unevenly let it out.

"Again."

The second one was less painful. "I'm sorry," I managed to wheeze. "I didn't think it would hit me this hard."

"You thought you were prepared. You weren't. Not yet."

His hand was warm, and I hugged it like an anchor against the freefall of chaos. I didn't let go until my breathing was closer to normal and I knew I wouldn't fall apart. His touch calmed me, and at the same time it created a ripple of longing I wasn't ready to deal with. That was finally what made me let go.

"Thank you," I mumbled, releasing his hand with a sheepish press of gratitude, and scrubbed my wet eyes with my palms. It was the first episode in months since I'd started the meds. I was fiercely glad *Thunder Child* was out of our implanted coms' range and my teammates had not been remote witnesses to this meltdown. "I feel ridiculous."

"Never feel that way." The gentle admonition made me glance up and meet his eyes. Aquamarine sparks snapped in the depths of his irises as he held my gaze. "What you witnessed can't be processed all at once. It comes out in pieces because it's too much."

"That felt like a huge chunk." But the empty space had begun to collapse on itself. The void softly filled with a new substrate and covered the scree of old trauma as we stared at each other. Once again, Rion Sumner showed me the side I wanted to know better, and I desperately wanted to know it when I wasn't a fucking mess he had to prop up.

"Port Armstrong to approaching vessel." *Three's* com blared as Luna Station's control center registered our presence. The emotionless mechanical voice in our headsets startled both of us. "Verify identity and destination."

Sumner toggled his mic with what I swore was irritation. "Port Armstrong, Midak 3 requesting approach."

"Midak 3, transmitting approach vectors," the artificial controller's voice replied.

The instrument panel came alive with lights and coordinates. Auto-piloting sequences blinked suggestively on the data screen. Of course, Sumner chose to pilot *Three* manually, our moment of connection sublimated into preparation to enter lunar airspace.

I silently cursed the cock-blocking AI running the tower and sat back to watch him guide our little craft into the deep well of Bullialdus Crater, a bright path of syncopated flashes leading us into the underground terminal. The small, rocking thump of landing sent a shiver through me.

Luna. The people who had made it my home no longer existed, yet here I was.

CHAPTER
SIX

WE MADE it through inter-system customs without a hitch. Our law enforcement IDs subjected us to the bare minimum of immunization verification and exempted us from DNA scanning. Sumner's Nos heritage would have taken some explanation.

The Hijra Quarter glittered with riotous color as we threaded our way through jubilant crowds. Excitement and anticipation thrummed against my empathic nets in a constant buzz, and I employed what mental remedies I could to dampen the psychic noise. Despite my conflicted emotions about being there, the festival atmosphere was almost irresistibly contagious.

The old city had been built at a time when its grid architecture mimicked the layout of a surface town on Earth. Actual buildings were erected within the two-kilometers-square climate structure, the tallest—the Tripathi Hotel—soaring to nine stories under the roof's steel girders. The street was already packed with revelers. Music and laughter echoed throughout the district.

We passed a crowded pub on the first level of an apartment complex. A bear of a man in suspenders and very little else spun on impressively tall heels to watch Sumner walk by. He offered him a drink, and Sumner grinned at him, shaking his head.

"This is quite a party," he acknowledged as we side-stepped a woman and her third-gender partner embracing passionately in the middle of the walkway.

"This is nothing," I assured him. "Wait until tonight when it really kicks off." I preferred to be out of the thick of the main district by the time it got wild—my empathic nets and sensitivity to human pheromones made the enthusiastic crowds expected at First Night an uncomfortable experience.

The colorful event had its roots firmly planted in Earth. The religious festival of Koovagam celebrated the role of transgender individuals in the Mahabharata, but it was trans-formed by the settlement of Hijra who emigrated to Luna before the wars decimated humanity. The story of the god Krishna taking the female form of Mohini, her wedding to Aravan, and his subsequent sacrifice was played out in lavish theatrical productions during the week leading up to the final, sorrowful day, when the Hijra faithful still mourned Aravan's death in the white sari of widowhood.

That part resonated differently with me now. It was some-thing I understood.

But the cultural cocktail shaken together by the evacuation of Earth had taken on a new flavor, peppered with the defi-ance of the Stonewall Riots in the face of third-gender oppres-sion. Mourning ended at dawn, and celebration began anew.

Tomorrow, the government would observe a decorous and patriotic observation of the Moon's part in preserving mankind, but this colorful incarnation of Lunar Pride, called First Night, focused on the Hijra community's role caring for refugees evacuated from our dying planet.

Unable to escape on the limited number of corporate space shuttles headed for Mars and Europa, those who survived the nuclear wars found themselves trapped planetside. The bloom of toxic biological weapons hijacked jet streams and turned the atmosphere into virulent soup. By the time the other colonies could respond, it would all be over. Luna answered the fading cries for help, sending ships to rescue as many people as it could.

The pleas inevitably ceased.

A district built for the recreation of those employed by the vast technological industries on the moon, the Quarter was home to dancers, entertainers, and professional companions from the South Asian subcontinent. Many members of the group were among the first in Earth's history to be recognized as a legal third-gender.

Theaters and businesses flung open their doors to the refugees when they were released from quarantine. People housed them for nearly thirty years before construction was completed on the dome habitats. They shared their homes, their food, and genetic material—both naturally and via test tubes. Geneticists like my wife suspected this was where a bottleneck of the human genome occurred, allowing intersex and third-gender mutations like changelings to proliferate.

The Hijra Quarter was, in many ways, the cradle of modern Sol Fed humanity.

I glanced up through garlands, a dense forest canopy in rainbow hues draped between the narrow thoroughfares of the old city. The emergency shielding was rolled back from steel and transparent alloy skylights for this celebratory event. One hundred feet above my head, stars glinted, and the slate-gray face of Bullialdus Crater's rough-terraced cliffs loomed between the flags and bunting.

The upper rim of the crater bristled with anti-meteorite missile batteries and the ever-vigilant sweep of radar. I had served required rotations on meteor watch in the Lunar militia, long periods of boredom followed by piss-yourself flurries of action when the sirens went off. The batteries were all that stood between Luna's one million citizens and certain death by atmospheric breach. Man-made cave systems served as emergency shelters, but meteorite warnings and drills were a common enough occurrence that people often ignored them. The truth was it would only take one small space rock to decimate Luna's population.

Or one intentional act of terrorism.

In front of the Tripathi Hotel, my gaze was drawn to a media bot as it maneuvered around a performing Kinnar dance troupe. Even though I knew for a fact every one of the intrusive little robotic bastards had been detained and thoroughly inspected for explosives after the Batterson scandal, my fight or flight responses still surged when I saw one.

Thankfully, the hotel was not yet our destination, though my impulse to flee grew as I led Sumner down a less-crowded thoroughfare toward the hostel owned by Devan and Michael Patil. We turned a corner into the familiar street, and I stumbled against the uneven footing of my own emotions.

Damn the memories. Gresh and I—and later, Rasida too—walked down this lane to visit the Patils more times than I could count. I stopped in front of their establishment, a three-story building owned by Dev's family since its construction. I hesitated as I remembered nights filled with Michael's home-made sorghum rum and warm laughter, seated around a table crowded with family not related by blood, but by choice. Scenes flooded through me with a pleasant, aching sweetness. Sumner noted the change in my demeanor but said nothing, waiting for me.

"The Patils are good people." I gripped the strap of the bag hanging over my shoulder. "Michael's a human rights solicitor who worked with Gresh, and Dev and I went to university together. I should warn you Dev has never known a stranger. You'll be instant family and inundated with questions you might not want to answer. Kind of like my mother, but with more testosterone."

He laughed. "Thanks for the warning. I'll follow your lead."

I didn't move, my hands still wrapped in a death grip around the strap of my bag.

"Are you going to be all right?" His expression stayed neutral, ocean eyes warm with concern. Rion Sumner still had the most beautiful eyes I'd ever seen, even if I could never say it sober.

"Yeah. I think I will." I took a breath and pressed the entry buzzer.

"Patil's. We're full tonight, sorry." I thought the voice was Michael's.

"I have reservations," I responded. "Dalí Tamareia."

Before I got out the last syllable of my name, the door slid open.

"Dalí, where the fuck have you been?" Michael demanded as I was engulfed in his strangling hug.

Devan rushed out the door, his dark eyes swimming with tears, and I lost it.

It was a kind of homecoming, after all.

———

Devan squirreled under his husband's arm to wrap himself around me. The three of us cried together, keenly aware of who was missing from this reunion. My empathic nets were awash in their affection and welcome, but hurt throbbed like an old bruise below their fondness. Not only had they lost Gresh, but in a very real way, they'd lost me too.

Even so, there was a lightness growing inside me, the weight of bearing my grief alone suddenly relieved as I allowed my friends to take some of the burden from my shoulders. It was—healing. There was no other way to describe it.

Michael finally stepped away from where Dev and I

hugged it out. I heard him introduce himself to Sumner, and the murmured reply.

"We've been worried about you," Devan said softly against my ear. "Not a word in almost three years, and the only person who says they've seen you is Kiran."

"I'm so sorry. I wasn't ready to come back. For a long time, I couldn't even think about it."

"Well, you're back. That's what matters." Dev pulled back and for a moment held my wet face in both his hands, beaming at me through his own tears. He hooked his arm around my waist, and as he turned us toward Michael and Sumner, he whispered, "So, Kiran says you're a spy now. Is that why you're wearing weapons?" He patted the bulge at my back.

With a beleaguered sigh, I gave him my mostly true cover story. "I work in Remoliad law enforcement and special negotiations. Nothing so glamorous."

"Mm-hmm." Devan raised an eyebrow, unconvinced. "Well, introduce me to your boyfriend."

I didn't bother to correct him. It wouldn't have mattered. "Dev, this is Rion Sumner."

"It's lovely to meet you, Rion." Rather than shaking hands, Devan hugged him, and Sumner, red-faced but smiling, returned the embrace without demur.

"What are we doing out here?" Michael swept us through the door. "Come in! You're staying upstairs with us, not in the hostel. I know you have somewhere to go. There are fancy clothes waiting and you must want to get cleaned up. Are you here for a party?"

"On business, but yes," I admitted cautiously, glancing at Sumner.

"Well, we have to prepare dinner for our guests, but we'd love to catch up." Devan's wistful expression sent a pang through me. "Most of them will be out clubbing until the wee hours. I know that isn't your thing, so maybe you could come back here after? We just decanted a batch of rum."

"That would be fantastic." I hoped we would be able to take him up on it. A little normality in the bedlam that had become my life was a seductive thought.

The jaded part of me wondered when the shit would start.

———

The room in the Patils' upstairs apartment was only big enough to hold two shikibuton side by side with a little room to walk around the bedding. The mattresses were folded and tucked neatly into the same narrow closet where we found the clothes and shoes the rental shop delivered.

They weren't terrible considering the short notice. Because of Sumner's broad shoulders and height, his choices were limited to an austere black tuxedo-style suit and a lapis-blue sherwani with gold embroidery at the cuffs and collar.

I chose a wine-colored men's kurta and churidar. None of the clothes in my size accommodated ease for a waistband holster, but the tunic had sleeves wide enough to conceal my knife and its forearm sheath. I slid my credentials into one of the pocket slits in case anyone questioned my carry permits.

While Sumner changed into his formal wear I sat at Michael and Dev's dining table to wait for him. Ka'pth's initial download arrived with a shrill beep on my device, and I browsed the file. The mugshots were several years old, back when Mother presented as male, but the more recent holos the Andari hacked from her personal system showed her leaning heavily toward femme.

Mother had branched out in her questionable enterprises. The contraband business was unsurprising, but this new information read like a minor Shontavian Market list: she was dabbling in small-scale arms dealing. She *did* have shady galactic contacts, and that was probably where Skadi came in.

Mother's exclusive corner on the Ursetu ruby trade in Sol Fed hadn't changed since Urset joined the Remoliad. She must have had industries on Luna eating out of her hand. It would have seriously pissed off any competing Sol Fed manufacturers who had to wait for the legal import of tech grade rubies until after galactic trade agreements got hashed out.

Companies like Batterson Robotics.

The corporate empire maintained a low profile after President Simon Batterson's downfall and exposure of the company's illegal weapons manufacturing, but they still conducted steady business. Unfortunately, so did Europa's New Puritan Movement, a socio-political niche with a private militia, some strong ideas about human purity and reproduction, and a particular hatred for genetic anomalies like Mother England, Kiran, and me.

During my first mission, one of the NPM's leaders was literally eaten alive by a Shontavian. The other decided blowing himself up was better than facing the consequences of dealing in human trafficking and treason. I thought the NPM was quietly licking its wounds under the ice-covered domes of Europa, but the more I read, the more dismayed I became.

The NPM and the Third Front were engaged in a war—or more specifically, Simon Batterson and Mother England were. Violence erupted more than once between the two factions during demonstrations at the capitol. Accusations of corporate sabotage flew back and forth between Batterson Robotics and England's company, Artemis Imports. No charges ever stuck, suggesting Mother had local judiciary on her payroll.

Federal law enforcement kept her firmly at the top of the list as a person of interest in the murder of a Lunar Homeland Security officer and two Europan citizens. I was willing to bet they had ties to the NPM. I wanted to know more about that. Ka'pth and Ra'sho hadn't been able to hack the federal database during their three-hour deadline, but it was just a matter of time.

"Did you see the download?" Sumner asked as he exited our room.

"Yes. This makes me think—" I glanced up at him briefly and did a double take.

Sumner had chosen the blue sherwani and trousers. I'd never seen him wear anything except some version of a neutral-colored uniform. The effect was, frankly, breathtaking. The rich lapis color accentuated his pale golden hair and made his strange eyes, the only visible tell of his Nos genetics, more startling in their intensity.

An appreciative "Wow" was all I managed.

"Too much?"

"No, just right. You look fantastic." I turned my attention back to the data in front of me, struggling to regain a line of thought that didn't involve me taking his clothes back off. "Ah . . . anyway. It looks like Mother's little feud with the NPM is getting nasty. I can't say for certain anymore there aren't human casualties."

"It's certainly the kind of thing Residuum takes advantage of." He stood behind me and peered over my shoulder, which didn't make it any easier to concentrate. "Turf wars, ideological tension. Anything to destabilize the Remoliad or its member systems from the inside."

"Chaos for the sake of chaos," I mused aloud, and shook my head. "But what's the end game?" I glared fiercely at my screen as if I could make the puzzle pieces fit together by sheer force of will. "Residuum's MO feels like distraction. Something bigger is happening while we're focused elsewhere."

"That's an interesting theory."

"Yeah, well, it's just a theory. Same as everything else on this goddamned case." I slid the device into my pocket. "Shall we see what England wants to talk about?"

CHAPTER
SEVEN

WE MANAGED to evade the media bot's lens as we ducked through the growing number of celebrants in the street and slid unmolested into the hotel's foyer. A concierge stood behind a podium outside the crowded hall and waved us inside when I gave my name.

Sumner scanned the roomful of glittering elite, cataloging potential threats and noting the exits. "Are we supposed to find her?"

"No need." I nodded to a table in the corner where Mother stood out in a luxurious fuchsia and silver sari, holding court with some of Luna's celebrities and corporate giants. She'd seen us come in and rose from her seat in a shiver of silk, her hands extended in front of her as she got closer.

I allowed the embrace and endured her overpowering cologne as we planted ceremonious kisses on both cheeks. Her relief to see me was genuine, but there was a hint of fear beneath. I wondered what that was about.

Her husky voice warmly greeted me. "Dalí. It has been far too long."

"I was surprised to receive the invitation," I admitted.

"I'm glad you came. I wasn't sure you would, given that

Kiran insisted on delivering the message himself." She cocked her head at Sumner and extended a hand. "Justina England. Everyone calls me Mother. I suspect it's really short for *Motherfucker*, but nevertheless, it has a nice maternal ring to it."

"Rion Sumner." He accepted the handshake.

I listened underneath with my other senses as they sized each other up, but mostly I watched her face, my empathic nets billowing in the gale of the partygoers' emotional output. There was no recognition on Mother's part, only a hint of caution. It was difficult to mistake Sumner for anything but a soldier, even in a formal sherwani, but at least she did not expect Skadi's brother.

"Welcome. We'll talk privately later. The bar is open, so find yourselves a drink and I'll be with you soon." England gave us a bright, false smile and turned away. She went back to her table. I noticed a woman who'd been standing nearby drift away in Mother's wake, her eyes scanning the room—a bodyguard, and a discreet one. Something was up.

"How many guns?" I asked Sumner as we walked to the bar.

"I counted three bodyguards."

"Seven hells," I muttered. "I saw the woman, but who are the others?"

"Big guy behind her table, brown kurta. He's the showy one. The other ghost is the short one in black."

I glanced back and found the individual in question watching us, a third-gender with dark, kohl-lined eyes. They averted their gaze as our eyes met.

"England's scared," I told Sumner quietly. "Something could go down at this party. I can't pick a lot out above everybody else's noise." I rubbed my forehead, where a tightness was beginning to grow in response to the constant empathic stimulation. "Is this a good time to mention I hate being in crowds when I'm sober? Let's take her up on the drinks."

A surly bartender handed out the spirits dispensed by his

robotic coworker. I added him to the list of those carrying, based on the bulge in his jacket. There was something to be said for Luna's elite parties, though. The whiskey was real, not a synthetic distillation, and heavy, lunar crystal tumblers were a welcome change from recyclable cups.

The atmosphere in the room roiled against my empathic senses in frothy waves—I tasted overpowering excitement and the usual sparks of pleasure people gave off in this environment. No one else seemed to anticipate anything but a celebration. As I completed the futile scan of the room, a snap of recognition and flood of joy to my right assaulted my senses a millisecond before a shrill, excited voice squealed, "*Gresh!*"

Startled, I turned. Someone flung herself into my arms, and I lost grip on my whiskey. Sumner's quick reflexes saved the crystal from certain doom as I realized who was strangling the hell out of me.

"Holy shit. Dru?" It was one of the third-gender changelings we rescued during my first mission. She clung to me as I hugged her back, bewildered to find her here.

"Oh my god, it is you!" Dru babbled. "I thought I was seeing things!"

Blinding LEDs bathed us in a harsh spotlight. I flinched away from the media bot zooming in to catch the reunion and instinctively whirled her behind me to take a defensive stance. Kiran Singh's smug, dazzling smile appeared beside the floating paparazzi drone. Anger burned through me as I heard him announce in his sonorous, media-rich voice,

"The mysterious identity of the changeling who rescued Dru Goldstein and Kai Anderson from the Shontavian Market, known only as 'Gresh', is finally confirmed as none other than former Ambassador Dalí Tamareia." The son of a bitch grinned at me in triumph.

My fists clenched. "Get that thing away from me, or this will be the second time I punch you in the face on camera."

He blanched at my emotionless tone and barked an order at the hovering globe. "Party shots, Joan." The abrupt cessation of harsh light left blobs in my vision, and the media bot obediently purred away.

"I'll deal with him," Sumner said grimly, and I gripped his arm in thanks. His fingers trailed against mine, tightened, and withdrew. I turned my back on Singh and gave my attention to Dru.

"Still shielding me after all this time." She laughed, carefully wiping tears of happiness away from her flawless makeup. "I'm sorry, I forgot your real name is Dalí." She knew me best by the alias I used on the mission—my husband's nickname. "I was just so excited you were here."

"Don't worry about it." I was genuinely pleased to see her. "You look happy, and absolutely stunning." Dressed in a russet and gold gown, her auburn hair caught up in a complicated twist, the wary Dru I knew during her captivity had been replaced by an individual with confident poise. "Did Kiran bring you to the party?"

"No, but he introduced me to Justina. I work for her now. I'm studying political science at the university," she said with pride. "No more protein processing plants for me, ever again. She hired me to do public relations for the Third Front. I'm going to make sure what happened to us never happens to anyone, ever again."

"Congratulations, Dru. That's wonderful." It didn't escape me that England employed her to do what was once Kiran's job. That intrigued me. But I marveled at the change in her. The ordeal she went through brought her strength to the surface. It was a radiant thing.

She tilted her head closer and said in a hushed tone, "I'm so sorry. I had no idea Kiran was going to ambush you like that. He didn't mess anything up, did he—if you know what I mean?"

I'm not sure my life could be messier at this point. I kept that pungent thought on the inside, unwilling to tempt Fate, and pressed Dru's hand between mine. "No, don't worry. I'm actually here on a personal visit."

"Good." She glanced over my shoulder. "The tall blond number seems very protective of you. Kiran's about to shit himself."

I stole a glance at Sumner, who conducted a seemingly innocent conversation with the tight-lipped, uncomfortable Singh. "I need to chat with our friend Kiran, too."

"I wish I could tell the whole galaxy how you rescued us, but I understand." She sniffled and shook her head. "Damn it, I'm going to ruin my makeup, and we're going live in a minute for Justina's speech. Kai's going to be so jealous when I tell him I saw you."

"Tell him I said hello."

"I will. Can I give you my contact number? If you have time, I would love to get together."

"I would like to, but I don't know how long I'll be on Luna." We exchanged information. After another tight hug, we parted so she could go to work. I joined Sumner and Singh.

"Was it a live feed?" I asked tersely.

"Yes," Sumner confirmed, and handed me the drink he'd saved.

"Just fucking great." I downed it in one swallow and glared at Singh. "Well, I guess you made it back from Mars in time for me to kick your ass for setting me up."

"I didn't set you up," he said, sulking. "The opportunity presented itself."

"So naturally you took advantage." I breathed in, counted to ten, and was still furious enough to bounce him off a table. "You want a story? Here's one for you. Tell me why Mother needs bodyguards at a First Night party."

Singh's shrewd glance darted around the room. "That's a new

development." His emotional broadcast painted a picture of someone who had screwed up one too many times and lost privileges: irritation shimmered in an oily aurora, threaded with a dark ribbon of guilt. "Like I said, she doesn't talk to me anymore."

"And she hired somebody else to do your job. You overstepped your bounds with Mother, too?" I gave him an exaggerated stare of wide-eyed innocence. "Shocking."

"I'm a journalist, damn it. My ratings are falling. The Batterson scandal broke almost two years ago, and I refuse to go back to small-time gossip." His eyes gleamed. "This is something important. I have to know what's happening. If we work together—"

"Back off and don't get in my way."

His sigh of surrender was too quick, his slumped shoulders a parody of dejection beneath embroidered purple silk, but his mind was alive with excitement. He was not giving up; this was falling back. He gripped my arm in apology, squeezing it a little too long. "I'm sorry, Dalí. I realize I abused your trust in the past."

I shrugged off his hand. "Who said I ever trusted you?"

"You're right. You probably shouldn't." His dazzling smile was back. He was already up to something. "If you decide I can help, I might be persuaded to part with some interesting information about one of Europa's favorite sons. I have a new source on the inside at Batterson Robotics who is eager to set the record straight."

"Batterson?" I scowled at him. "Are you holding out on something?"

"You know how to find me."

"I'll just look under the nearest rock."

Singh's expression faltered, and anger marred his handsome features before he stalked away to catch up with his media bot.

"He's going to get himself killed," Sumner muttered.

"Like I have that kind of luck." I inspected my empty tumbler with disappointment. "I need a refill."

"Your attention, please," Dru's voice announced as we reached the bar. The crowd parted around Dru, who held the slender wand of a microphone. Her smile glowed in the spotlight of Kiran's media bot as it zoomed in and illuminated her.

"Thank you for coming to celebrate with us. We hope you are enjoying yourselves. Your generous contributions tonight will fund our lobbying efforts for another quarter as we work to defeat Senate legislation discriminating against third-gender citizens."

The room erupted in applause. Dru made a sweeping gesture with her free hand. "Please welcome businessperson and founder of the Third Front, Justina England!"

Mother made her way to the center of the dance floor, shaking hands and giving air-kisses. She didn't spare a glance for Kiran Singh as she walked right past him, his media bot swiveling to capture her approach. The enthusiastic guests began to clap, and she beamed at everyone as Dru handed her the microphone. Two of her bodyguards took up a protective stance in the nearby fringe of the crowd.

"Good evening. Happy First Night!" England's jubilant greeting was amplified above the renewed ovation. "I'm delighted you could join me tonight to celebrate our pride in Luna's history and the heroic role of the third-gender community here in the Quarter."

More wild cheers. "When Earth's survivors begged for rescue, who answered those calls for help?" Mother demanded.

"Luna!" the crowd responded.

"That's right. Luna sent their ships, risking personal injury, disease, and high radiation levels to save more than three thousand people from certain death. The Hijra community opened their homes and their hearts, providing food, shelter, and safety through the long quarantine period. Service industry employees. Professional sex workers. Entertainers. The third-gender citizens of Luna were the champions Earth needed, and they changed the face of the moon forever."

The room was wild with excitement. England was on fire, and she was only getting started. "Lunar industries keep Sol Fed safe with the manufacturing of radiation shielding and technology. Our tradition of keeping the arts alive entertains all the Colonies and makes this solar system a better place for its citizens.

"Luna has never forgotten the third-gender's contribution to the early days of Sol Fed, but some representatives of our federal government have deliberately played down this history to further their barbaric legislation. Genetic editing and the restriction of our reproductive rights is nothing short of genocide."

The crowd's combined response exploded against my empathic nets, a multi-textured barrage of indignation, anger, even fear.

"The Third Front continues our work to defend Sol Fed's third-gender citizens. We appreciate the financial contributions you made to support the cause. Others here tonight are unsung heroes who protected members of the third-gender community, risking your lives when they were threatened." For a moment I held my breath and hoped to hell she wouldn't say my name as her gaze sought me out. England merely raised her drink to salute the room. "To you, we give our most ardent thanks."

Sumner glanced at me and tapped the rim of his glass against mine. I grinned at him and lifted my empty tumbler, but in the moment of silence after England's toast, a high, hysterical voice rang out, "Human purity!"

I quickly turned my head in the direction of the sound. The huge bodyguard grappled with a woman in the doorway.

"Sterility is death to humanity! Eradicate changeling muta-tions now!" she screamed.

But as everyone focused on the scuffle in the back, I glimpsed a sudden movement in my peripheral vision. I whipped my head to the left and saw the bartender bring the gun out of his jacket. He pointed it toward the center of the room where England stood in the glare of Singh's media bot spotlight.

He was no bodyguard.

I hurled the tumbler. It shattered against the wall behind him in a crash of breaking crystal. He flinched in defense and searched for the source of the attack, but I was already halfway across the bar. My foot caught him beneath the chin and knocked him backward into the robotic dispenser. He fell to the floor. Straddling him, I ripped my blade out of the wrist sheath and pressed it to his throat, hard enough to draw blood as he scrabbled for the dropped gun.

"Don't. I promise I'll cut you," I warned. He sneered at me but lay still as we gained an increasing number of witnesses staring down at us, Sumner among them.

"Everything under control?" he inquired casually.

"Yeah." I shrugged, glad to be under the counter and out of Singh's robotic camera eyes. Hotel security appeared on the scene. I slipped the knife back into its sheath before they could ask any questions and drifted away into the crowd with Sumner as they took control of the man and his weapon.

Kiran got a decent story after all. The media bot illumi-nated him and a pale but composed Dru, rehashing the details of what just happened. Party guests wandered about in shock, spilling out into the lobby. England was nowhere in sight, hustled off during the incident to somewhere more secure.

"Damn it. I think we lost our chance to meet with Mother," I griped.

"Maybe not." Sumner nodded behind me.

The third-gender bodyguard in black approached. "Will you come with me? Mx. England wants to see you now."

We followed them to a closed lounge adjoining the hall. The guard stopped Sumner outside the door. "Not you."

He started to protest, but I shook my head. "I'll be fine." I camouflaged the tap activating my implant com as a nervous adjustment of my collar. Sumner gave me a stiff nod, taking a vigilant stance next to the door. He would listen in.

The bodyguard opened the door. Mother England was waiting with her hair disheveled, the silken folds of her sari rumpled. Her emotional broadcast was more irritated than terrified; a strange reaction, since a few minutes before a gun had been pointed in her direction.

"Thank you, Loki," she said to her employee. The door shut out the party, and she smiled halfheartedly at me. "Well, that was exciting."

"The NPM must really be pissed at you if they sent hitmen."

"They should stop sending amateurs." She motioned to a decanter and glasses on the side table. "Would you like a drink?"

"Let's just get straight to it, shall we?"

"Your negotiation tactics have deteriorated." England gave me a lopsided smirk and waved for me to sit, taking the opposite chair. "So it's true. You're some kind of Remoliad secret agent?"

I ignored the inquiry. "Kiran said you have information for me."

She poured herself a double. "You recognized the name I gave him."

"Yes."

"She's extorting me."

I fought my sarcasm and lost. "What kind of dirt could she possibly have on you?"

The thick, sticky deluge of her guilt enveloped my

empathic nets and stunned me with its heaviness. Dread punched my gut with an ice-cold fist.

Staring at England, I was suddenly reluctant to hear what she had to say. "What is this about?"

"I'd hoped to ease into this, but we'll do it your way." She shifted. "You're here, so I think you know what she did. And I'm afraid I bear some responsibility for the bombing of Luna Terminal."

CHAPTER
EIGHT

THERE WERE times I strangely missed the thick, insulated detachment of depression. And oh, this was one of those moments. Pain sizzled its way through my nervous system like molten lead and left seared, black-edged fury in its wake.

"In what way?" The question dropped from my lips in syllables so jagged they cut me on their way out.

England's skillful makeup floated over a suddenly pallid complexion, her eyes wide and dark. Her perfume soured with the scent of fear, and I was sure she regretted leaving her bodyguard outside. She remained motionless—a wise decision. As far as I was concerned, she was in more danger than she'd been ten minutes earlier.

"Several years ago, a non-human entity who wanted to expand their business into Sol Fed contacted me," she finally answered. "Our interests overlapped. They said they didn't want to compete. Honor among thieves, I suppose. They became my supplier of certain out-system goods in a way which avoided customs scrutiny. It seemed like a lucrative opportunity. The benefits outweighed the risk."

"Too good to be true." The roar of vengeful fire filled my

ears, but I reminded myself I had to think, to ask the right questions. "What is this entity called?"

"I've never had a knack for speaking alien languages. It's something like Orlogon," she said, her stumbling pronunciation so humanized I couldn't be sure of the word's planetary origins.

"Is that an individual, or a group?"

"I'm under the impression it is several beings who act as one."

This was new information. A spark of interest crackled through me.

England went on. "I should have known a deal like that came with conditions. Everything went as promised, but in return for their continued patronage, twice a solar year I was required to legally purchase other products from specific vendors which could be shipped into the Fed without undue questions. A few cases found their way into each of my containers. An associate would retrieve them from my warehouse—a Sol Fed citizen by birth, but an alien hybrid."

"Skadi."

"Yes." Mother pursed her lips.

"What did they ship in?"

"Off-world technology and parts. Nothing that looked out of place in my business, so customs wasn't unduly suspicious. Individually, the shipments were meaningless, but I realized when the elements were combined, they could be used to make weapons."

"Where did they go when they left here?"

Mother raised an eyebrow. "Europa."

Well, well. For people who hated galactic interference, the NPM and Batterson Robotics certainly did a lot of illegal out-system business. "You were helping Batterson build his weapons trade under the radar."

"Orlogon was, at any rate. Not long into our association with them, that son of a bitch got elected President. People weren't just talking about editing genomes anymore. Third-gender genocide was becoming a matter of government policy and I began to wonder if the weapons were meant for us." She paused and clasped her hands in front of her. "I was willing to do anything that might bring them down. I thought it would be wonderfully ironic if Batterson's own illegal tech was used against him. Skadi made a purchase for me at the Shontavian Market."

"You bought the media bots." My voice almost strangled in coils of disbelief.

We'd never been able to track the sale of the bombs through the flawed data I managed to steal from the Market. I merely operated under an assumption Skadi made the deal.

I never suspected the transaction was made on behalf of someone I knew.

"I came to my senses before they arrived. My legal team is good, but not good enough to get me acquitted of presidential assassination. It would delegitimize everything I worked for with the Third Front. Skadi called me a coward but said she had use for them. I never thought . . ." England closed her eyes. "So many people were killed. Even if I wasn't the one who detonated the bombs, I brought them here. I can't tell the authorities without indicting myself. She knows it."

Her grief, though heavily laced with self-interest, was genuine. If it hadn't been, the urge to beat her senseless might have won. "Why are you telling me this? Give me one reason I shouldn't turn you in."

"Because I think you want the person who pressed the button more than you want me." She leaned toward me and carefully enunciated her words. "I can give you Miriam Skadi."

I snorted. "Right. She hasn't come back to Sol Fed since the bombing."

"Until now." Her gaze locked on mine. "A shipment arrives

two days from now. She's going to personally retrieve something in one of the crates as soon as it gets to my warehouse."

Skadi was coming here.

My emotions careened wildly between excitement, anger, and suspicion. This was the reason I joined the Penumbra: to bring my family's murderer to justice.

If Skadi's employer was unmasked in the process, we could go after the head of the beast itself. But she was too smart to walk into a trap. Nothing I sensed empathically from England suggested a setup, but something seemed off. I couldn't see the pattern. What I needed was to talk it out with Sumner.

But I could not lose this chance.

"You have proof tying her to the bombing: shipping records, credit transfers? Anything that will hold up in a court of law."

"I do, and more. The cost of her silence is I have no choice but to work with her when I'm told. I'm more complicit in her activities than I ever wanted to be."

"She'll spill your involvement if she's arrested," I said at last.

"She can't talk if she's dead." England raised one lofty eyebrow.

"Are you insinuating you want me to take care of that problem for you?" I frowned at her. "I personally don't give a shit if we take her back in morgue stasis or as a prisoner, but the truth is, we need her alive. What's your price?"

She lifted her chin. "Immunity from federal and galactic courts in return for my testimony."

"I don't carry the authority to promise that." Especially not with our impending rogue status.

"I'm sure you can negotiate something. You have contacts in high places."

I didn't know Sol Fed's political cast the way I once did. We couldn't say anything to Remoliad officials without the chance it might be heard by the wrong ears; however, England did not need to know that.

"I give you my word I'll try to negotiate immunity, but I want proof you have the data we need." I leaned forward. "Every being responsible for killing Gresh and Rasida is going to burn. You owe me and each person who lost someone they loved in that explosion the means to drive them into the ground."

I held her gaze, and the side of her mouth twitched. "I don't remember you being so fucking scary," England said.

"You have no idea."

She blinked first.

"I'll show you the data." She produced a holo card from the folds of her sari. I couldn't help myself and reached for it with greedy fingers. She snatched it back. "No downloads." There at last was a flicker of rebellion. "When you secure my immunity, you'll get everything you need to prosecute her."

"Then I have a deadline, and a lot of work to do." I stared at her until she relented and handed it to me. I fished my device out of my pocket and inserted the holo card to scan quickly through the data.

It was all there. Dates. Communications. Transactions. Account numbers. Shipping origins. Everything England promised.

We had Skadi in our sights, and perhaps the first real information on her mysterious employer.

I hated giving the card back. "I need the warehouse location so we can check it out before she gets there."

"Does that mean we have a deal?" She stood and extended her hand. I didn't take it.

"Yes. But for the record? Fuck you, Justina. There is nothing I would like more than to shove you out an airlock."

"I deserve that from you." She gave a tight nod of her head. The black, encroaching cloud of her shame made me draw back my empathic senses. I refused to feel sorry for her.

"Give Loki your contact information. They'll send you the details. The security guard at the warehouse and I enjoy a mutually beneficial arrangement. I'll tell him you're coming."

I let myself out while England collected herself. Sumner turned a grim expression to me as I emerged and exchanged frequency codes with Loki.

"Where are you staying?" they asked.

I wouldn't put Michael and Dev in harm's way by running a mission out of their hostel. We'd need to find other lodgings. "It will change after tonight. This contact is sufficient."

They gave me a curt nod. "You should leave now if you don't want to attract attention. The constabulary is taking statements in the lobby." Loki jerked their head to the left. "Follow that hallway and it will let you out the service door onto Johnson Street."

"Thanks."

Sumner and I walked away. "There's something wrong about this," he said when we traveled out of earshot.

"I think so too, but I can't put my finger on it. She didn't lie to me, though." A tentative spark of excitement grew in my chest. "We need to go to the capital tomorrow and see if I can beg the use of a secure subspace line. If we can contact Kap'th and Ra'sho before they leave for Neptune Station, they might be able to find out more about Orlogon—who they are, where they operate—while we bring in Skadi."

"Right," he said quietly. I glanced at him. The still-solemn set of his mouth made me remember that, despite everything, he and Miriam Skadi shared genetics and a history.

"I'm sorry we didn't get a chance to talk about it before I agreed. Are you all right with this?"

"Yes." The answer came on an exhalation, heavy and resigned. "Don't misunderstand me. She can't escape justice for what she's done. You know I'll do everything in my power to bring her in." He glanced at me. "But I won't be her executioner."

"I know. It sounds like England's all too eager to do it unless we can guarantee what she wants."

As Loki promised, the side door opened into a street full of revelers, where a DJ's sound system provided a brain-liquefying beat that had people dancing with abandon. We melted into the frenetic crowd, trying to make it back to a main thoroughfare to reach the Patils' hostel.

Sumner and I were spun and pushed by strangers' bodies. The psychic onslaught of so many people's emotional output left me reeling in confusion, even with my empathic nets furled as tightly as I could manage. I'd never tolerated large crowds well, and only made it through the public memorial service for Gresh, Rasida, and the bombing victims with chemical assistance.

The noise of hundreds of human minds in celebration bludgeoned my senses, too overstimulating for me to function. Separated from Sumner, his pale blond head several feet away in the crowd, I faltered, dazed by the pounding music and the excitement surrounding me. My hands rose to cover my temples in a useless, protective reflex.

I drowned in other people's happiness, the recirculated air laden with the musk of sweat, skin, and pheromones. A hormone cascade flooded my bloodstream, muscles beginning to slide and shift as if anticipating a fight—or looking for a violent fuck. If I stayed here any longer, it might not matter which one.

Sumner's hand reached through the crowd and gripped my arm. He pulled me forward and broke a path through the crowd until we emerged from the seething mass of dancers across the street from the Tripathi. Sumner drew me into a narrow alleyway between buildings, barely more than two feet wide, but dark and quiet. The aftermath of an unwanted change sent convulsive shivers through my body as things started to settle down.

"Sorry," I managed, my teeth chattering. "It's been a long

time since I've been in a crowd like that. This is why I never went clubbing."

"Take your time." His null was a soothing balm against my overtaxed senses. It made it easier for me to breathe out the tension, but his proximity in the small alley created another issue. The hormones still fizzed and played havoc in my body. My engorged mons ached in a way which made it difficult to think of anything but how close together we stood in the cramped passageway.

"I have to get out of here." Braving the masses was the last thing I wanted to do. "I think we can go all the way through the alley back to Dev and Michael's and miss the main strip. I'm going to need that rum."

CHAPTER
NINE

I HAD FORGOTTEN how it felt to sit at a table with friends and talk—not about data, shipboard duty rosters, or who might want to kill us. About events, careers, and people we had in common. Even though I knew those things existed somewhere in the debris of my old life, it seemed impossible I once attended dinner gatherings almost weekly here at Devan and Michael's.

The Patils had not changed. Dev brimmed with gossip and wicked nudges, while steady, grounded Michael made sure everyone's glass stayed full of his home-brewed sorghum rum and managed to coax more information out of Sumner with his friendly inquiries than I ever dared.

"So, Rion, did you go to university here or on Mars? What colony are you from?"

Sumner shook his head. "I'm not from Sol Fed. My mother was from Europa, but I didn't grow up here. She was a security officer assigned to the Sol Fed Embassy on Kadrel. I had private tutoring with the rest of the staff's children until I went into military service."

"Aww, you're an embassy kid like Dalí. That's sweet. Is that how you met?" Devan cocked his head.

"No. We met on a commercial flight to Zereid a few years ago."

"Wait. The one that was all over the news?" Michael's eyes widened and he turned to me. "I forgot. You and your blue friend beat up goddamned Nos pirates."

"They asked for it." I tipped the last of the rum into my mouth, and Michael poured another shot as soon as I put down the glass.

"Were you involved with the pirate thing?" Dev inquired of Sumner, wide eyed.

"I was there, but that was all Dalí. They piqued my interest." Sumner grinned at me. "When a job came up fitting their talents, I tracked them down on Zereid and asked if they wanted to work for me."

"Oh. You mean you're their boss, not their boyfriend?" Dev's voice dripped with disappointment.

I waited to see what he would say, waiting for the telltale flush indicating Sumner might be embarrassed by the question, but it never came.

"Partners," he answered carefully, a word laced with multiple possibilities. He looked at me in surprising challenge. To my chagrin, heat rose and blossomed in my cheeks.

"Uh-huh," Dev said with satisfaction.

The rum was more potent than I remembered. Michael's personal brand, distilled from hydroponics-grown sorghum, carried a hell of a lot more proof than any synthetic variant thanks to his husband's chemistry degree. The first small bottle disappeared without my notice, and only after the pop of the seal on the third did I briefly register we might be completely drunk.

By that time, Dev and I were well past the point where everything was funny and moving into the nostalgic level. Even Sumner picked his way through sentences, stumbling over syllables with uncharacteristic clumsiness.

"How long have you known Dalí?" he asked Devan.

"Since university." Dev screwed up his face, thinking. "I can't recall where we met first."

"Debate society," I reminded him. He made a noise of agreement.

"I remember that night." Michael brightened, but said quietly, "That was when Kiran introduced you to Gresh."

I nodded, a liquor-softened smile stretching my mouth. "Yeah. It was an epic night."

"Singh introduced you?" Sumner squinted at me.

"His only redeeming act, the little fucker." I shook my fist, and Dev giggled. "Kiran was trying to talk me into joining a debate club and invited me to a practice meeting where he affirmed third-gender reproduction rights. This tall, red-headed grad student on the opposing team argued like he believed the fate of all humanity rested on banning natural procreation for us thirds. I was totally confused because my empathic nets told me a different story. In the middle of refuting Kiran's most forceful point, the guy looks at me and winks."

"Gresh?" Sumner asked, grinning.

"Yeah." I let the smile spread across my face. "Afterward he and Kiran were laughing together. I figured out we were all on the same side. I walked right up to him and introduced myself."

"How long before you started dating?" Sumner inquired.

"Are you kidding? It's me. I asked him out that night."

"Meaning Dalí took him straight to bed," Devan tattled.

I made a conceding gesture. "We ended up in one. Eventually."

Laughter, then: "I miss that ginger bastard." Michael's sigh was uneven and threatened to undo me. The excess of alcohol afforded a bit of cushion against the sorrow.

I realized this was the first time I had talked about Gresh since his death with anyone who had called us both friends. The shared loss made it somehow easier to bear than when I was alone in my bunk at night. I'd cut myself off from others far too long, hoarding my grief as if it were the only thing left of Gresh and Rasida. The connections with those who loved them too, our communal memories, would keep them alive.

"What was he like?" Sumner asked softly.

"Smart as hell. Compassionate, but he took no prisoners in court. Gresh could argue diamonds out of moon dust." Michael smiled in remembrance.

"Sounds like someone else I know." Sumner gave me a sidelong glance.

"The Lunar government didn't stand a chance when he and Dalí teamed up to lobby a change in the laws to give third-gender citizens equal rights to triad marriages." Dev's voice broke with emotion. "They changed a lot of lives here in the Hijra Quarter."

"*Omnia vincit amor,*" I breathed, and remembered how proud we had been of our accomplishment, how Sida had cried from happiness when Gresh and I asked her to be part of our family before the law was one minute old.

Dev sniffled. His mood was rapidly turning melancholy, something Michael and I recognized at the same time.

"Bed," our host said firmly. "We have to cook for the lodgers in the morning. Breakfast is in the dining room from seven until ten, since everybody will be out late. Dalí, Rion, you're welcome to stay here as long as you want—as friends, not guests."

I shook my head in apology. "We have work to do in the capital tomorrow. We planned on taking rooms at one of the hotels there."

"So, you're just going to disappear again?" Dev wore an expression of hurt. "I don't think I like that. Stay here one more night."

I hesitated, reluctant to explain why that was not a good idea and too soused to guarantee I wouldn't say too much.

Sumner wisely stayed out of the conversation, grinning as Dev swept me a dismissive wave.

"Yeah. You're a big bad spy and you can't say anything. We'll argue about it tomorrow night when you're still staying here. I've spoken."

"Yeah, you've spoken, love, now let's get you to bed." Michael patted him and glanced at me. "You remember where everything is? Bathroom, all that."

I gave a thumbs up. "Thanks."

"Good night." They disappeared down the hallway as Michael shepherded a weaving Dev to their bedroom.

Sumner finished off his rum and rose with an uneven wobble. I wasn't much better. We stumbled to our room, and he waved at their closed door. "I like them."

"Told you they're good people."

The lights in the other room automatically shut off before we were ready. I tripped over the bedding and sprawled onto the mattress, snorting with laughter, and Sumner tumbled down next to me as the bedroom's dim illumination rose a moment too late.

"I guess you're better now after the crowd?"

"Yeah. Drunk helps."

"I don't know how you know what you're feeling with everybody's emotions in your head." He made a fluttering motion with his fingers beside his temple. "That must be confusing."

"Nah." I rolled my head to regard him. "I know how I feel most of the time. It's only confusing when I'm around you."

"Oh yeah?" He propped himself up on his elbow and leaned toward me. "What am I feeling?"

"I told you. I can't sense you at all, especially not as marinated as I are." I frowned. "As we are. I don't know how you feel."

"You could try asking for once." His expression grew

softer, voice thick with the effects of Michael's distillation. "Or I could show you."

"Are you flirting with me, Commander Sumner?" My question came out wrapped in a laugh of delicious uncertainty as he moved closer.

"Not your commander anymore. You really can't tell, can you?" His breath was warm with the sweetness of rum. "I'm not flirting. Confessing. It's been hard to be your commanding officer."

"Because I'm an asshole who doesn't follow orders," I agreed.

He bobbed his head. "Yes, you are. But it was hard not to show how I feel about you. Even if you are an asshole."

He touched my face, clumsy and gentle and so very inebriated.

Something bloomed in my chest: a sunburst of warmth saturated in rum-drenched delight, wrapped around an icy core of sheer terror. "We can't even talk about it unless we're drunk or sedated," I stated with the gravity only an excess of alcohol can muster. "We have issues, Rion."

"We'll probably never discuss it sober. Right now, I want to kiss you while there's nobody listening in, and I don't have to pretend. Can I kiss you, Dalí?"

"God, yes, please."

His lips brushed mine with such tenderness. Unexpected and sweet, as if he feared I might break. I opened my mouth to his and Rion deepened the kiss, the tip of his tongue a caress in exploration.

Warm excitement unfolded inside me; its edges fluttered in my mons and stirred changeling hormones, making my pulse speed up. I was too drunk for anything else, afraid this shining, fragile moment would crack and fall away to join the rest of the broken, temporary fragments of happiness in the last two years.

"You taste like rum," he murmured against my lips.

"So do you."

Rion closed his eyes with a sigh. "I've wanted to do that for a long time. I like Luna. I wish we could just stay here and drink rum."

"Trust me. We are so going to regret rum in the morning." But that didn't stop me from pulling him back down.

———

I woke up on the shikibuton still fully clothed in rented formal wear, with a pounding headache, the taste of stale alcohol in my mouth, and something stabbing my right bicep.

Groaning, I shifted and rubbed my arm. My fingers found a pin with a round head on it, stuck in the sleeve of my kurta. I pulled it out, squinting with blurry eyes at the tiny sharp thing, and suddenly realized I was alone.

Oh, shit.

Last night oozed back in fuzzy detail, but I was pretty sure I spent at least thirty minutes dry humping my ex-commander before we both passed out. I lay back with my arm crossed over my eyes as a pitiful whimper escaped my throat.

The humming sound of the cleanser told me where Sumner was. I stuck the pin into the strap of my discarded wrist sheath and slowly folded the bedding into neat thirds in time with the pounding in my skull. The mattresses went back in the closet before I stripped off my wrinkled kurta and hung it up beside Sumner's equally distressed sherwani. I wandered back to the scene of last night's rum carnage with my PDD in hand, bare chested and wearing only my pants.

I found two liter-sized containers of water on the table with a note in Dev's looping handwriting: DRINK ME. Next to the water was a small bottle of analgesic gels. Silently blessing him, I shook out two painkillers and took a long pull on the water to wash down the gel caps and swish away some of the foul taste in my mouth.

My PDD's display was too bright, but I connected to the local networks and started looking up old diplomatic contacts until Sumner entered the room with careful steps. He sat slow-motion in the chair opposite me, one hand rubbing his forehead. I slid the remaining water and the meds in front of him.

"Still like rum?" I asked and did my best to ignore the Burkani-sized question pirouetting in the back of the room.

"Ask me again later." He gulped the capsules and chased them down with water. "What are you looking at?"

"Seeing if I still know anybody who can help us. I don't have enough undamaged brain cells for anything else."

"How long does it take to get to the capital by tube?"

"About forty-five minutes." I checked the time. "It's still early enough for breakfast." The idea made me slightly queasy, but we both needed real food. We only grabbed a portable snack after we landed at Port Armstrong.

We sat in silence, slamming water. The Burkani—who looked suspiciously like Riga*nat in a tutu—did a thunderous *grand jeté,* and I decided to risk it. "So. Last night. Was it just the rum talking, or is something really happening between us?"

He sighed heavily. "I shouldn't have said anything."

"No, just keep filtering it through other people, I guess." I couldn't keep the frustration out of my voice. "Ozzie. Alecto. Gor. They say they see it, but I have no fucking clue. The only person who didn't say anything until last night was you." I stood. "I'm going to clean up."

"Wait." He grabbed my wrist as I rose and tugged me back. "Sit. Please."

I lowered myself into the chair, and he met my gaze, his expression soft. "I'm not sorry about anything I said, only the timing. I never intentionally filtered through anyone. I guess you weren't ready to see it, or you didn't want to." He pinched the skin between his eyes against what had to be a nasty hangover headache, if mine was any indication. "I don't want to be just another one of your sex partners. I want more, and I don't know what you're able to give."

It stung, but he was right. "What do we do about it?"

"Take it a step at a time. Most people talk when they need to know something." He gave me a half smile. "I'm sorry you can't cheat and see what I feel, but I guess that gives us even footing to start."

The sensation in my chest was close to terror, tangled in loneliness and want and all the messy, unsorted emotions still littering the floor of my psyche. "It might be tricky."

"Complicated," he admitted. "I don't want to jeopardize our working relationship or the team's dynamic."

"And there's a price on my head."

"Now you're just making excuses."

I laughed and instantly regretted it as pain lanced behind my eyes. "We have a lot to work out." I drew a breath and met his gaze. "I want this, Rion. I want you." I didn't say *I might love you*. I wasn't ready to feel it yet. Grief still echoed like a scream in the back of my head, and only one thing would silence it forever. "But I have to finish this before I can move forward. This is the first time we've been even half a step ahead of Skadi. I can't lose the chance to bring her in. I need . . ." I gestured helplessly. "To end this."

"I understand." His hand covered mine. "But I'm not willing to miss this opportunity either. I'm done with rum, though. We'll try it sober when you're ready."

"No promises about sobriety." I interlaced my fingers with his.

"You told me once there's always room for negotiation."

I smiled at him through the haze of headache. Whatever I was going to say promptly evaporated into hangover mist when the screen of my device flashed and emitted an eardrum-piercing beep. Wincing, I pulled it over to silence the alert and read the text from our teammates.

"Holy shit." My pulse rate shot up.

"What is it?"

"Some data Ka'pth and Ra'sho mined from Mother's systems yesterday turned up another hit on the database. Skadi may not be the only one running things through England's shipping." I slid the device to him. "That's a Martian drug cartel account. I think we just found out where they got the grenade launchers."

"Makes you wonder about her real motive for demanding immunity from prosecution." Sumner's eyes glinted as he looked up from the data. "What happens if you can't broker an agreement, and she decides we're too much of a risk to let go?"

"She can get in line behind the Pileans, I guess." I swallowed the last of my water, adrenaline and hydration beginning to clear away the fog. "I have an idea where to start asking for help, anyway. Give me ten minutes. We can get some food and head out."

I grabbed a clean set of clothes and my hygiene kit out of the room we shared, adding my knife sheath to the top of the pile. In doing so, I dislodged the pin I'd found and stabbed myself.

"Damn it!" I jerked out the barb. A scarlet globe welled up on the pad of my middle finger as I glared at the pin—and did a double take.

A tiny light inside the round head blinked in the dim room. Now that I was more awake, I made out microscopic perforations in the material.

"What fuckery is this?" I muttered to myself and padded back into the dining area. "Sumner. Look. Is this what I think it is?"

He examined it. "A microphone." His eyes narrowed as he grimly confirmed my suspicion.

"I found it stuck in my sleeve this morning." Anger surged through my veins and pounded against the aching insides of my skull. I crushed the head of the pin between the tabletop and my thumbnail. The bug died in a smear of micro tech. "I can guess who put it there."

"Singh." Sumner's mouth set in a hard line. "He listened to your meeting with England."

CHAPTER
TEN

WE STOPPED LONG ENOUGH to eat some of the high protein, anti-hangover breakfast Michael prepared on demand for the guests. Dev looked a little better than we did and cheerfully gave up Kiran Singh's contact number when I told him I needed to kill him.

I was only half joking. If he fucked up our operation, I'd be sorely tempted to commit murder. A quick scan of the latest headlines showed Singh hadn't yet broken the news about England's culpability in the terminal bombing. The feed of the NPM's assassination attempt was being replayed all over his network, but thankfully I didn't see Sumner or myself in the holos.

I was doubtful Singh would spill anything too soon; he was after a story that would grab coveted galactic bylines. If he turned Mother in, Skadi might abort her visit to the warehouse.

The prick didn't answer my call. I left a scathing message warning him to stay away and gave clear, violent details about what I would do to him if I found him lurking.

What to do about England? Giving her a heads-up about Singh's potential double-cross could have the same negative effect on her willingness to cooperate. I needed to transmit my inquiry on immunity from prosecution before the story broke and make a contingency plan. I had an idea, but no guarantees.

The chemical magic of painkillers and food soothed my head and made the walk to the underground tube station more tolerable. Wide tunnel platforms on the opposing transport lines, designed to double as a meteor-warning shelter, were practically deserted as the inner airlock port at the tunnel's mouth yawned open, the near-silent train gliding to a stop at our feet.

Luna still held to a traditional five-day work schedule in the private sector. The transport system was not as crowded as it might have been on a weekday. Only a few dozen zombie-eyed travelers returning to their homes after last night's revelry milled about the station, and I was thankful for the reprieve. My empathic nets remained tightly furled after the onslaught of First Night crowds and today's hangover. I really didn't want to test my ability to block at the moment.

We headed to the least populated car and strapped in. Once the train traveled beyond range of the city's artificially generated gravity fields, the human body was still susceptible to Newton's laws of motion in Luna's light Gs. When the ports closed, I transmitted a copy of the match report on Mother's files to Sumner's PDD. We continued to dissect the information during the trip, conversing in Remoliad standard for privacy since it was still less likely to be understood by most Sol Fed citizens.

"Where do you plan to beg to use a secure subspace array?" Sumner glanced up at me as he scanned through the data.

"Our credentials won't get us into the Sol Fed capital structure, but we should be admitted to the Zereid embassy easily enough. Ambassador Tem is an old friend of my mother's. We can trust her." I thought a moment, tapping my finger against the PDD's case. "It would be nice to have an ally if things go sideways. If Singh runs his damned mouth too soon, this is all for nothing. I want to talk to Tem about giving England asylum in the Zereid embassy until we have a solution for immunity from prosecution. Any thoughts?"

Sumner considered the matter, frowning. "Does the situation meet criteria for political asylum?"

"As a stopgap measure, maybe. It will take some legal sorting out, but we should have Skadi in custody by then."

"What if Skadi wants to make a deal?" he asked softly. "As a citizen, she has the right to be tried in a Sol Fed court of law rather than the Remoliad. She might refuse to be extradited."

"Do you think so? I assumed she would want to be prosecuted in a galactic arena. She can be assured of friends there. If Alecto and their employer try to break her out, it's easier to disappear."

"It's a huge risk coming back at all. She knows we're watching Sol Fed." Sumner glanced moodily at the passing walls of the tunnel. "I wonder if it was her choice."

"You tracked her before the bombing. When she came back every six months, was it just to receive the smuggled goods, or did she have personal reasons?"

"Her mother is still in a convalescent facility on Europa. Singh was right, she did visit. I think she used it as a cover for travel because they were never close." He met my gaze. "Anna Skadi suffered a severe brain injury about two years prior to the bombing. Official records called it a fall, but there were witnesses who reported a woman had pushed her off an elevated walkway after an argument."

"You think she tried to kill her?" I reflected on what little I knew. "You told me once her mother was psychologically abusive."

"She should never have been forced to raise her, but you know Europa and their laws. Anna never touched her—not to hit her, hug her, or kiss her. Just spewed hate when Miriam did something to make her angry, which was often from what little she shared with my mother and me. Because she looked more Nos than human, Miriam was a target for animosity from xenophobes who were familiar with the circumstances of her birth. I can't imagine what it must have been like."

I knew something about being different among one's own species, but I was fortunate to have parents who embraced my unique traits without hesitation. Without even the most basic support system, it was no wonder Skadi turned out warped. I didn't want to feel sorry for her, but Sumner was making it difficult. "I'm guessing one day, she had enough?"

"When you're repeatedly told you're a monster, it stays inside and eats you alive. You either prove them wrong, or you become what they say you are. You can't run away from it."

His gaze flickered away, and he stared out the port. Sumner knew that pain all too well. He'd spent the last fifteen years proving to himself he was not a monster.

I let my leg press against his in casual contact. After a moment, the rigid muscles in his thigh relaxed and sagged against mine.

"She found my mother and me on Kadrel," he said, staring straight ahead. "I was home on leave, recovering from being mostly dead on Lymo. She drifted around the galaxy for a few years, doing whatever it took to get from one place to the other before she looked us up. She was so broken. Angry at the universe. My mother took her in on sight because that's the kind of person she was."

He smiled, his eyes soft with affection as he spoke of his mother, but the glow quickly dimmed. "Miriam and I were genetic half-siblings, but complete strangers. Even so, I somehow felt responsible for her. When I went back to my unit three months later, she came with me as a recruit. She blossomed in the mercenary corps like a vicious flower. Warfare suited her. But I abandoned her, in her eyes. After years of fighting for causes that weren't always the right ones, I started to lose interest in whether I would survive the next battle. You know what it's like." He met my gaze again and I nodded in silent accord. "I had to get out. The day I resigned, she punched me in the face and walked away. We never spoke again."

"What did you do after the corps?" I realized I didn't know.

"I applied to the Remoliad's allied fleet. They had no idea what to do with me. I was officially a citizen of Sol Fed, but a Nos hybrid, and neither one was part of the Alliance yet. But I caught the attention of the Director. He had the foresight to recognize a human-appearing agent would be an asset. Galactic crime syndicates were already making their way into the Colonies, allied or not."

Sumner had spoken of his superior several times, always couched in anonymity. "Since we're not Penumbra anymore, what can you tell me about the Director?"

"I can tell you he is not a member of the voting body. He appears to be relatively low in status, but his job gives them an opportunity to be unobtrusive. He hears things representatives might not say out loud if anyone in authority was lurking around."

"Interesting. Nobody else gets to meet him but you?"

A faint grin claimed the right side of his mouth. "You met him at the Remoliad."

"I did?" Startled, I tried to remember anybody who could have been the Director. We'd only been there a few hours.

Fuck me.

"The Tolkish ancillary?" I gaped in surprise as I received a silent affirmation. Tikker, a secretary for the Remoliad security council, had showed me how to find Sim's office before he and Sumner disappeared under the guise of checking out our assigned ship. At the time, I assumed Sumner was avoiding contact with Alecto Sim.

"Does he know about Lymo?" I asked.

With a heavy exhale, Sumner gave a stiff nod. "I told him when he recruited me. But I didn't tell him I recognized Sim. I still don't know why. I wasn't thinking clearly. My mistakes gave him a lot to answer for."

A series of digital tones on the overhead com verified our train had entered the hexagonal circuit of domes under which most Lunar citizens lived and worked. At the first pair of airlocks beneath Hubble, the returning pressure of my own weight made me take a deep, instinctive breath. People drifted into and out of the cars before it eased back into motion on the electromagnetic track. The well-lit platform and benches rushed past the windows until white-tiled walls abruptly transmuted back to gray lunar stone beyond the second airlock.

The closer we got to Kepler, the more my shoulders tightened. Tones for the stop sounded over the intercom and my hand twitched toward the buckle of the harness in some vestigial muscle memory. I stilled it and laced my fingers in my lap.

One glance outside the port was enough to bring back a flood of memories. The tile and concrete walls were the same as any other station, an escalator leading up to the University and its surrounding dwellings. But I knew every inch of Kepler. Our apartment had been a ten-minute walk from the station, on the outer curve of the dome.

Memories dragged out, spilling like the links of a chain. *Waking in the morning in our tiny apartment, entwined with Gresh or Rasida. The three of us, laughing as we ate breakfast and prepared to separate for our respective workdays. Walking hand in hand to the tube station.*

I realized I was twisting one of my wedding rings around my finger, like a talisman to ward off the expected storm of pain. The clouds broke open, but it was soft and warm, like a summer rain on Zereid.

I closed my eyes. No blind, black maw of grief waited in the shadows to swallow me whole, just a familiar sadness. An emptiness, not so hollow as it had once been, where new friendships took root and thrived between the cracks and old ones returned to life after the long winter in my soul.

And a new, tentative bloom in a place I thought nothing could grow anymore.

"How are you doing?" Sumner's quiet voice cut through the rattle of my thoughts, and I opened my eyes. He was aware of my withdrawal, as attuned to my physical cues as I was to his. Even without an empathic connection, we weren't doing badly.

"Better than I thought." The train slowed as it entered Galileo station. "This is where we get off."

———

Galileo's geometric dome looked deceptively delicate, but the structure was engineered to withstand the pressure of an artificial atmosphere against the vacuum of space. Sol's harsh rays still bathed the western horizon and illuminated the landscape in a silvery half-light, but not for long. The strange beauty of Luna's night phase would soon be upon us. Sunrise wouldn't come again for two long weeks.

The metallic thrust of the Sol Fed Capitol Building, a windowless, tiered climate structure within Galileo's heart, dominated the center of the complex. Most citizens referred to it as the Fortress, but more sarcastic souls called it the Hive.

The Fortress had its own atmosphere and in emergent situations could be sealed to protect the government officials inside—a waste of oxygen in many cases, but arguably necessary to the solar system's function.

The Zereid embassy lay outside the Hive, a two-story building constructed of warm-colored concrete, with doors built especially tall to accommodate the average furry, blue humanoid height. We were immediately escorted to the ambassador's receiving room once we presented our Remoliad credentials to the azure-pelted security officer.

Ambassador Tem's lidless, silvery eyes grew angular with the Zereid equivalent of a curious smile when she entered the room. "Dalí Tamareia. I see you." She stooped to rest her forehead against mine, one six-fingered hand on my shoulder. I returned the greeting, sharing breath and mind in a gesture of trust.

"I see you, Ambassador Tem."

She brushed my empathic senses in a gentle acknowledgment, but with characteristic telepathic courtesy, she pushed no further than the surface and repeated the welcoming ritual when I introduced her to Sumner. Her puzzlement spiked when I assumed she encountered his psychic null.

"To what do I owe this unexpected visit?" Tem stood back and regarded us.

"I must ask for our presence to remain off the record, Ambassador. Is the room secure?"

"It is." Her interest flowed over me.

"Commander Sumner and I are on Luna as part of an open investigation. The case has widespread galactic involvement and I need to make a data transmission on an encrypted system. Will you permit us the use of your subspace communications array?"

"I see no reason to decline. It is a reasonable request. But there is something else you wish to discuss." She cocked her head. "How may I be of assistance?"

I glanced at Sumner. "A criminal informant gave us a confession on the promise I would try to strike a deal guaranteeing them immunity from prosecution. The information may come to light much sooner than we hoped," I told her. "If so, they will almost certainly be arrested by local authorities. I hoped you might be open to offering asylum until we can secure their terms."

"I see. Would there be danger to me or the embassy staff?"

"It is possible," Sumner admitted.

"Ah." The space between Tem's reflective eyes widened in interest. "It is not without precedent to offer asylum within a Zereid consulate. However, I fear I must know more about the circumstances before I can agree."

I summarized the criminal activity without giving any names, mentioned a connection to the attack on Luna Terminal and the intended arrest of a galactic terrorist. It was good enough for the ambassador. She agreed to shelter our informant for an unspecified period. While Sumner, Tem, and the embassy's head of security hashed out preparations, I used the subspace array in the ambassador's office to update our crew on the new information.

Afterward, I composed an encrypted message to my mother via her private com system, filling her in on the situation and England's request for galactic immunity.

My finger hesitated over the command to send.

We had no way of knowing how deeply the Remoliad was infiltrated, or by whom. What if they were monitoring her communications because of her relationship with me? If she innocently approached the wrong person with details of the inquiry, Mom's life could be endangered.

I deleted the message. I would probably regret it later.

We were on our own.

My PDD chimed for attention, and I glanced at the screen. It was England's right hand, Loki. I answered at once, and their image flashed up.

"Tell Mother we may have a temporary solution until the question of immunity is decided."

"She'll be pleased to hear that," they said.

"Maybe not. I found a bug on the kurta I was wearing last night. Someone at the party was listening in on our conversation, and my bets are on Singh. The details might become public sooner than she thought."

Loki muttered a string of gutter Hindi about Singh's sexual inadequacies, a little too detailed for casual acquaintance. "I was about to contact you anyway. The freight arrived early, but we've heard someone else is asking questions about the shipment. You might want to get there sooner rather than later."

"We're on our way."

"I'm sending you the dock number now." Loki ended the call. I tucked the PDD into the inner pocket of my coat and exited the ambassador's office. Tem, Sumner, and her security officer studied a holographic blueprint of the embassy which rotated slowly as they discussed preparations. Sumner glanced at me and raised an eyebrow in question.

"We need to get back to Port Armstrong. I'll fill you in on the way." I inclined my head to Ambassador Tem, allowing my gratitude to brush against her mind. "Thank you for your assistance. We will keep you informed."

Sumner and the Zereid officer traded codes and we left the embassy. "What's up?" he asked as we hurried back toward the train station.

I relayed the discussion I'd had with Loki. Immediate understanding flooded his expression. "If the freight's early, Skadi may be, too."

I quickened my pace. "That's what I'm afraid of."

CHAPTER
ELEVEN

THE USUAL CROWDS populated the train station at Port Armstrong. Rather than follow them upstairs into the terminal, Sumner and I boarded a tram for the short trip through the tunnel linking the adjacent caverns to the port.

Hewn into the side of Bullialdus's crater walls, the vast system of man-made caves housed the majority of Luna's industrial district. Manufacturing plants crowded the harshly lit caves on the southern side.

Freight from other colonies and incoming relief supplies from Remoliad-allied worlds was offloaded in orbit from leviathan transport barges and ferried down to Port Armstrong, riding into the caverns on mechanized beltways through another double-airlock system. Inside, the containers got scanned and directed to appropriate storage areas for customs and processing.

Metal containers soared noisily overhead, gripped in the giant clamps of robotic conveyance systems. Automated forklifts followed gleaming metal circuits set into the floor and sped about with smaller crates held carefully in front of their spinning wheels. We disembarked the transport in the warehouse district and kept to the green lit walkway, neither of us keen on getting crushed.

"It'll be in this row." Sumner indicated the gleaming numbers posted on a fenced block of warehouses, each delineated by three roofless cement walls dividing tracts of floor. The enclosed security booth at the gate was empty, though it appeared to have been recently occupied.

"Great. We arrived during somebody's break," I muttered. "How do we get in?"

"Climb?" Sumner suggested, surveying the fence.

"Yeah, that wouldn't look suspicious at all." There was another security post about a hundred meters down the center aisle, but that probably was not an option. Mother said she had an arrangement with one guard, not the whole port.

Suddenly, the gate began to roll aside.

"Watch it!" I grabbed Sumner's arm and pulled him aside as a robotic forklift pivoted into the opening and narrowly missed us.

"Guess they aren't programmed to slow down for pedestrians." He gave the equipment a dirty look as it buzzed past and down the row. We slipped through the closing gate and followed the forklift until we reached Mother's dock.

Stacks of crates lined the walls. A large transport container with Kadrelian script squatted in the middle of the floor, harsh lights from above throwing angled pools of shadow around the base. It stood a little taller than Sumner and twice as long. I checked the number against the information Loki sent me and came up with a match. "Whatever she came for will be in there."

"Did they give you the combination?" Sumner examined the container's control pad.

"No. Is it one you can work with?" He knew a few tricks to unlock transport containers, having run undercover on a cargo ship several years ago.

He frowned and stepped back. "No need. It's already open. The customs seal is broken."

"Not good," I muttered, my heart sinking. "Did she get here first?"

Sumner pulled his sidearm and stood to the side of the door. I reached beneath my jacket at the small of my back and drew my gun, the grip still an unfamiliar shape in my hand. At his signal, I swung the crate door wide. He rolled to peer into the opening, leading with his weapon.

The unmistakable scent of blood and death assailed us.

"Clear." He holstered the gun, his face wrinkled in disgust.

There was a touch pad on the inside wall. I activated the strip of cold lights running down the ceiling of the freight container.

Splayed over a long, low case like a sacrifice on some ancient altar, Kiran Singh lay in a pool of gore and the spill of his intestines. His eyes were open, a startled expression frozen forever on his handsome features.

"Fuck." I stepped away and holstered my own weapon. The reek of copper and shit choked me. "I don't think this was the headline he wanted."

———

We didn't have time to investigate. Half a dozen uniformed officers charged down the center aisle, guns drawn.

"On the ground, now! Hands on your heads!"

Sumner and I glanced at each other and complied.

"We are Remoliad law enforcement officers," Sumner said loudly above the shouting as he went to his knees. "Identification is in my left front pocket. We are both armed."

I didn't move fast enough for the officer behind me. He dragged me down by my coat collar. My cheek hit the concrete with a smack, and he slapped a cuff on my right wrist. His knee dropped into my back when he discovered the sheath on my left arm. "We have a knife here!"

"I have a permit," I protested, my voice muffled against the floor as my weapons were confiscated. "It's with my other credentials."

"Oh god." Somebody's weak voice cut off into retching noises.

"Hudson, get out of the crime scene before you contaminate it." A female voice, authoritative and in charge. "How long has he been dead?"

A pause. "Not long," another voice answered. "Still warm. Blood's just beginning to congeal."

"Who are these clowns?"

"They claim to be Remoliad law enforcement."

"Well, let's just see about that, shall we? Stand them up."

Someone's hand in my armpit yanked me to my feet. I struggled upright and attempted to shrug off the assist, but the officer didn't let go and warned me to stand still. The commanding voice belonged to a woman in black uniform coveralls with government insignia. She was tall and muscular with copper skin and close-cut raven hair.

Sumner, flushed with anger, repeated the location of his ID. One of the officers fished Sumner's credentials from his pocket and handed it to the woman as another scrabbled in my coat. Her gaze flicked from the holographic photo to Sumner's face. They handed her mine, and her dark-eyed stare did the same cold dance over my features. I had the odd sensation of being permanently cataloged and filed, and not in a friendly way.

"Uncuff them," she said. "Keep their weapons."

The reluctant officer freed my hands, and I resisted the urge to rub my wrists as the agent in charge handed our identification back with crisp movements. Her building anger grated against my empathic webs.

She glanced into the crate, took in Singh's desecrated

corpse, and turned back to us with her eyes narrowed in suspicion.

"Special Agent Preeda Saetang, Lunar Homeland Security. Nobody notified me of any joint operations here, so what in the seven fucking hells is the Remoliad doing in my jurisdiction? You thought you'd just walk in and start poking around?"

"The booth was empty, and the gate was open." I was stretching the facts, but it was all true. "The cargo container was unlocked when we found the body."

"Is this related to anything I should know about?" She crossed her arms over her chest, waiting.

"Nothing we are at liberty to discuss at the moment," Sumner admitted.

"That's a problem, Commander—Sumner, is it? I have the still-warm body of an informant disemboweled inside an uninspected container, and your partner has a knife. I can't let you go until I have proof you are who you say, and security recordings are reviewed."

Singh? A federal informant?

"We would like to see those recordings, too." Sumner glanced at me. "If you contact Captain Morgan Williams at the MDEA, he'll verify we were working with him on a joint operation on an unrelated case less than two days ago."

"That still doesn't tell me why you're here." Saetang scowled and motioned for two of her officers to take charge of us. "They can wait in the interrogation room until I get some answers. They don't leave, understood?"

Sumner and I got marched down to the gate. Every step I took shuddered through my body, an endless loop of *Fuck, fuck, fuck* reverberating through my head as we were bundled into a security shuttle. Singh was never a friend, but he was someone I had known a long time. He was a prick.

He still didn't deserve to die that way.

Federal law enforcement was now involved whether we

wanted it or not. And Skadi might be long gone by the time Saetang was through with us.

———

In the windowless interrogation room, I started to get pissed off. I amused myself for the first half hour by staring expectantly into the blank camera eye watching us. After that, I wore a path in the concrete between the table and the locked door. It shouldn't take this long to receive answers from Mars unless Williams was being difficult.

"Sit down," Sumner said quietly in Remoliad standard, though his red-flushed face told me he was more than annoyed at our predicament. "There's nothing we can do."

"What if we lose her again?" I paced restlessly for another turn before I sat in the chair beside him. Being detained like this when Skadi could be so close was maddening.

"We don't even know if she's here yet."

We never would if we didn't get out of here. I paced a while longer, seething until Agent Saetang finally came in, carrying a data device and a bin containing our IDs and confiscated weapons.

"So you're the ones who discovered the new formula of vape hitting the system." She didn't offer our property back yet and sat opposite Sumner. "Captain Williams had a lot of opinions about your involvement in his case—nothing particularly positive, but you helped him do the job."

"It took you more than an hour for that?" I bristled, but Sumner lifted his hand, first finger raised in caution. *Play nice with the local authorities.* I subsided, biting back my words. He was better at that game than I was despite my background, a subtly different strategy from interspecies negotiation.

"Why are you on Luna?" she asked. The words evaporated into frost clouds, her suspicion condensing against my empathic nets. "If you're working a case, it would have been polite to let Homeland Security know the Remoliad was here."

"It's a personal visit," he said.

"Bullshit." She sat back and glared at Sumner. "You don't turn up at a known smuggler's freight dock on vacation."

Sumner shrugged. "We were given a lead on an open case."

"So was I. You two showing up at the warehouse when you did was extremely convenient, especially after spending the evening at Justina England's party."

Saetang tapped out a code on the tabletop and a holographic image flashed into the air between us. The time stamp showed it was recorded less than fifteen minutes before Sumner and I arrived. The image showed Kiran Singh walking down the aisle to Mother's warehouse, accompanied by a uniformed guard.

"The guard for England's warehouse is employed by a private security firm, not Port Authority. That is not the regular guard. We're still looking for him." The individuals stood in front of the container with their back to the crate and looked around as if waiting for someone. The holo paused, recognition software zooming in on the face of the other man and bringing up data.

"Robert Conway," Saetang said as information ticked up the image. "The security company says they've never heard of him. He's Europan. He's listed as an employee of Batterson Robotics, but he's got a rap sheet for fighting all over the system." She raised an eyebrow. "Recognize him, Tamareia?"

"No." I frowned. "Should I?"

"You had a close encounter with the ex-President's sons and some buddies a couple of years ago that almost left you a corpse. Forensics picked up Conway's DNA all over you." Saetang's eyes gleamed. "You refused to press charges, but considering two of the four men who assaulted you are dead, I imagine you still might have bad blood there."

Sumner glanced at me as I processed this information. I helped bring down President Batterson when I sent Kiran Singh my evidence files against the President's oldest son and his human trafficking crimes. "Jon Batterson and his associates were kidnapping third-gender changelings with intent to sell them as sex slaves. I didn't know it when they attacked me. I'm not responsible for their deaths, but they got what they deserved."

"For what it's worth, I agree." She restarted the holo. "That doesn't explain why he was here, or what happened next."

Both men approached the crate. Singh consulted his PDD and entered a code on the pad, releasing the sealed door. He peered cautiously through the crack and swung it wider to stick his head inside.

Conway reached into his jacket and moved in behind Singh. A knife flashed in the harsh overhead lights as Conway pushed him into the container and out of the camera's view.

"I guess we know who the murderer is," I muttered.

"Here's where it gets weird," Saetang directed us back to the recording.

Conway backpedaled into view, the bloody knife still in his hand, his eyes wide and startled.

A nightmare skittered out of the freight container.

My first thought was *that is a fucking huge arachnid*. Eons of ancestral revulsion for eight-legged creepers sent a shudder down my spine.

But then it contorted into angles impossible for any organic life-form to achieve. I realized this was a mechanical construct. It rearranged in seconds, spiky parts forming into a skeletal, humanoid shape. Suspended in the center of the artificial skull was a fist-sized sphere of something so dark it burned a white-rimmed, amorphous ghost of its shape into the image.

Conway straightened and spoke intensely, the knife brandished before him, his other hand raised in a warding-off gesture.

It leaped on Conway, enveloping him in the spiky exoskeleton. He screamed as the dark blob flowed down his forehead into his open mouth. His face went blank; his body jerked, held upright in the grip of that ghastly, delicate framework. The blade dropped to the floor of the warehouse as the thing disappeared inside him.

"What the fuck is that?" I whispered, recoiling.

Saetang paused the holo and frowned. "I was hoping you could tell me."

"Replay the last fifteen seconds." Sumner leaned forward and watched the horrific recording again. "It's definitely a life-form."

"What kind?" Saetang asked.

"Unknown. The exoskeleton seems to be a vehicle of some kind."

"Conway spoke to it." I leaned forward to re-watch his attempt to keep the creature at bay. "Is there audio?"

"No, but lip-reading apps confirm he knew something." She touched her PDD, and Conway's words scrolled out.

STOP DON'T HURT ME LOOK I'M JUST THE PICKUP GUY NO DON'T

The holo continued to play out after the thing violated Conway's body. The man-shaped framework separated, found openings in his clothing, and crawled beneath his jacket. Conway straightened and experimentally flexed his limbs. He took a few stiff, cautious steps before looking directly at the lens of the security camera.

His eyes burned with the same obsidian flare that had inhabited the mechanical suit a moment before. Conway picked up the knife and walked out of lens range with rigid, unnatural movements.

"It's using him as a vehicle." I swallowed against a wave of revulsion.

"Not anymore. Cameras tracked him as far as the departure terminal. He disappeared into a public restroom and never came out. We found Conway unresponsive in a stall after we shut everything down. He's at the hospital."

"The entity may have changed bodies." Sumner's grim expression echoed my horror. "How many people went in and out before he was found?"

"Six, of varying genders."

"Trains and flights left before the terminal got locked down?"

"Two trains," she admitted.

"It could be anywhere," I muttered.

"This is where I could use some help." Saetang eyed us grudgingly. "Conway said he was just the pickup guy. The holo could prove Justina England's not only smuggling contraband for the NPM, but she's branched out to trafficking aliens into Sol Fed. I've been trying to bust her ass for years."

"I'm not sure that's what's happening here." I exchanged a worried glance with my partner. "If our suspect is involved, this could be bigger than smuggling."

"How big?"

"It could be terrorism," Sumner confirmed.

Saetang stared at us. "Please tell me you're joking."

"Afraid not," I said. "She's a galactic terrorist with ties to organized crime. Our informant said there was something in the crate she planned to retrieve in person."

"Well, she's not getting in now. It's a murder scene." Saetang shook her head. "And it looks like her package might have walked off by itself."

Sumner leaned back, his posture open and relaxed. "I take it you've isolated the trains." I admired his ability to sound so unassuming and calm. Saetang's defensive attitude dialed down a notch.

"One is in the maintenance dock between the old city and the terminal. The other is on a sidetrack between Port

Armstrong and Hubble. Teams are on the way to clear them."
Her lip curled. "We're under pressure from local government
to make it quick because of the celebration tonight."

Dread took my breath. The city wasn't quite as heavily
populated on the weekend when the industrial sector operated on skeleton crews, but tonight's continuing festivities
would draw crowds from all over Luna. Hubble, the moon's
largest residential structure, was thick with pod-style tenements and dome-scraping apartment buildings. Almost three
hundred thousand people lived there.

Families with children.

I stood. "What are we waiting for? If it escapes into a residential district, it will be damned near impossible to find
without a door-to-door search." I shoved my sidearm back
into its rig and asked Sumner, "Do we split up?" I didn't like
the idea, but it made sense.

Saetang jumped on it. "It would be faster to clear both at
the same time."

"Will you let us take the lead?" I asked soberly. "We don't
know if this being is here of its own volition, or if it really was
trafficked. Maybe we can convince it to cooperate and come
with us."

"I'll notify the tactical teams to stand by until we arrive.
Stay here." She picked up her data device and hurried out,
muttering into her wrist com. The door remained open this
time.

"I guess she decided we're on the same side." I strapped on
my knife. "Are you okay with splitting up? We'll be out of
implant range, but we should be able to communicate via
Saetang and her people with their hard line." The thick-
walled caverns made radio contact over any distance impossible. Old-fashioned cable still ran along the tunnels in metal
conduit.

"I'm not crazy about it, but we don't have much choice."

He retrieved his sidearm and holstered it. "What else do you think England didn't tell you last night?"

A flush of anger worked its way through me. "Residuum has her against the wall. She could be tangled in a lot of things she hasn't confessed yet." I would not appreciate being played for a fool. Again.

Our gazes brushed and held as Sumner spoke. "Be careful out there."

"Yeah. You, too." I hesitated. I didn't like knowing we wouldn't be able to watch each other's backs. Was it getting weird? Damn it.

"All right, let's go." Saetang came back, pulling a vest over her head. "I have tactical gear for both of you. This conversation is not over. When we get back, we're going to have a nice long talk about our mutual problems."

CHAPTER
TWELVE

SAETANG'S PARTNER was a lanky man with graying brown hair and laugh lines furrowed into the skin around his eyes and mouth. He introduced himself as Evan Rama before he took Sumner to the location between the terminal and Hubble.

Agent Saetang and I climbed into an electric cart and sped through claustrophobic tunnels running parallel to the high-speed tracks until we reached the service area outside Port Armstrong. We emerged into a cavern frosted by harsh LED work lights. Equipment used to repair and clean the cars crowded the cement floor, and an electromagnetic crane hovered above the group of eight armed officers in full tactical gear.

Everyone bristled with tension. Alarmed passengers peered at the waiting squad through the tempered glass of the train's windows.

If the entity was on board, it knew we were coming.

Saetang gestured to me and instructed the tactical officers. "This is Dalí Tamareia with Remoliad law enforcement. They are taking point in this operation. I want two of you in each car with the exits covered. Tamareia and I will enter the first car and work our way down. If we find the alien, the civilians need to be moved off the train and out of harm's way. Consider it armed and dangerous. This thing can jump into other bodies, so keep your distance. One man was critically injured. Tamareia will attempt to convince it to come quietly."

"What if it doesn't want to cooperate?" a gruff voice demanded beneath one of the tactical visors.

"There is a possibility it may simply be frightened," I answered. "If there's no response to negotiation, we seal off the cavern until we can contain the life-form. It can't be allowed to escape into the general population, or we may never find it." I glanced around the anonymous circle of visors. "My partner and I have never seen anything like this. It has a small mass"—I made a circle with my thumbs and forefingers in demonstration—"and it uses a mechanical construct as a means of conveyance and as a restraint. Do not shoot unless there is an immediate threat."

Saetang signaled the officers and they moved to breach the first car, identifying themselves as they went in. "Homeland Security! Remain seated. Do not remove your harness and keep your hands visible." The warning echoed in each car as teams proceeded down the aisle. Saetang and I followed them in, her weapon drawn and pointed at the floor, but I left my hands open and empty.

A bludgeoning onslaught of fear and indignance, all very human, slammed into my empathic nets. Moving slowly down the middle, I met the gaze of each passenger in turn, looking for telltale dark, burning eyes like we had glimpsed on the security footage.

The cars were jammed with travelers, cases and bags crowding the overhead storage. Saetang's boiling energy distracted me, and I wished for Sumner's cool, detached null at my back instead of her adrenaline riot.

Without exception, every passenger we encountered was

anxious, irritated at being delayed, and free of alien possession.

"What do you think?" Saetang asked me, her eyes on the increasingly restless passengers.

"It isn't here."

"And we haven't heard from Rama." A muttered curse escaped her. "Did we miss something? Is it just walking around the terminal biding its time?"

Neither scenario was attractive, but we didn't have long to consider the alternative. One of the men outside hailed her.

"Agent Saetang, you have an incoming message from Rama on the hard line. He says it's urgent."

"It was on the other train," I said. A cold frisson of dread went through me as we exited the rail car and hurried to the communications node where her gear's umbilical was patched into the data cable.

"What's your status?" she inquired.

"We made contact." Rama's voice was tight with stress.

"Is Sumner negotiating with the alien?"

"No, the thing fucking took him."

My pulse stuttered to a painful, jolting stop and lurched back into rhythm as I shoved past Saetang and demanded, "What happened?"

"The alien was hiding behind luggage in the overhead compartment and jumped on him," Rama reported. "The passengers went crazy. Everybody screamed and started running into the next car. We couldn't reach him in time, but I don't know what else we could have done. It's inside him."

———

Back at Homeland Security headquarters, I watched the feed of the interrogation room from Saetang's office, my fist pressed hard against my mouth. Rion Sumner stood eerily motionless under the watchful eyes of two armed officers.

The metal skeleton gleamed in geometric array over his torso, giving the tactical vest a sheen like medieval armor. The entity hadn't allowed anyone to approach but offered no resistance either. It silently complied with all orders and directions thereafter and willingly guided Sumner into the armored transport for the ride back.

But the threat was clear. One segmented tentacle lay curled around Sumner's throat and tightened when anyone came too close.

Fear wormed its way out of me in a groan, and I stifled the sound behind my fingers, reminding myself to breathe instead. Zereid mental disciplines helped focus my thoughts. I couldn't fall apart, not when Sumner's life might depend on me.

But my thoughts kept up a steady beat of accusation: *You should never have split up.*

A few minutes passed before I was able to drive back the fear until it crouched, snarling, in a dark corner of my psyche where I could deal with the mess later. Saetang stalked back into her office a moment afterward. The door closed before she started in on me, her displeasure blasting through my empathic webs.

"Rion Sumner. Son of a Europan expat, and half Nos. More goddamned aliens," Saetang grated, tossing her PDD on the desktop. "Any connections to the NPM?"

I snorted. "Are you serious? Definitely not."

She flung herself into her chair and glared at me. "Time for you to tell me what you're really doing here."

Pulling up the file on my device, I slid it across her desk, ready for all the help I could get. "Yesterday, we received a tip on the whereabouts of Miriam Skadi, another Europan expat and Nos hybrid. Before you ask, yes, she and Sumner share genetic history. Skadi is responsible for the attack on Luna Terminal."

Saetang jerked in shock, her face hardening as she scanned

the data. "You weren't going to notify Sol Fed authorities, just ride in and take credit? I've been investigating the bombing for almost three years without a solid lead and you assholes were hoarding this information!"

"It was a case in progress. We had nothing concrete to tie her to the bombing, and we didn't even know where she currently was until last night."

Licks of fire from her building rage crackled against my empathic nets. "How is England involved?"

"She's got a guilty conscience about a purchase she made, but not enough to take the fall." I explained England's role in the bombs' import, and Skadi's impulsive decision to use them against Sol Fed. "Mother says she will provide us with hard evidence against Skadi on the promise of immunity from prosecution. The preview she gave me last night will do the job. With England's testimony, we have everything we need to charge her with the crime."

"Do not tell me you gave her immunity." Her voice dropped to a threatening rumble.

"All I told her was I would make the appropriate inquiries."

"Did you?"

"Not yet. There are . . . complications."

"Tell me more about these complications," Saetang demanded. "I saw you lost your family in the bombing when I checked out your story, and I'm sorry. But why would you and Sumner choose not to alert the Remoliad? I'm beginning to think you're not supposed to be here."

Sighing, I confessed. "Technically, we aren't. Someone is working very hard to prevent us from investigating anything to do with the syndicate Miriam Skadi works for." I gave her a rundown of how Singh contacted me at England's request, and last night's meeting. "The organization usually covers their tracks so completely we haven't been able to trace them back to any one solar system. After talking to England, I believe what happened here with Luna Terminal was a crime of opportunity because she showed me a clear trail leading to Skadi. The whole thing was too sloppy to be sanctioned by her employer. We can't risk extradition. Skadi should be charged by Sol Fed authorities and tried here as opposed to a galactic court."

"Using England's get out of jail free card." She shook her head in disgust. "Fuck."

I listened to what she wasn't saying, a rumble of anger vibrating my empathic nets. "This isn't just about smuggling. This is personal for you, too."

The psychic flash of her pain blindsided me and disappeared almost as quickly as it had come. Saetang shifted irritably and slid my PDD back across the desktop. "England is playing you, no matter how much she pretends to be cooperating."

"Something doesn't feel right," I admitted. "After the attempted hit yesterday, more is going on."

"You aren't telling me everything, either." She tapped out something on the PDD she held, and an audio clip began to play. My own voice filled the room, and I winced at the venom of the message.

"Kiran, I found your little present this morning. Do not fuck with me. If you interfere, you won't have to worry about anybody else killing you. I'll do it myself. Keep your mouth shut and stay away from me."

"We got that from Singh's device." Saetang turned her piercing black gaze on me.

"He planted a bug on me last night and eavesdropped on my meeting with England. It pissed me off. He has a history of invading my life." I thought for a moment. "He and Mother were always in perfect sync with the Third Front before the bombing. Last night he told me they were 'estranged', a big enough rift she hired someone else to be her public face. What was his business with you?"

"He's been feeding me information about Mother England for a year. Singh found out she was smuggling for Simon Batterson. He called this morning and told me I should check out the dock but wouldn't tell me why. He said he'd meet me at the warehouse."

"Let me guess. He wanted an exclusive story." Her expression said I was right, but something else occurred to me. "How did he learn the container was already in port? England's people contacted us because it arrived early."

Saetang's eyebrows lifted. "Maybe it was supposed to arrive today all along, and she knew it?"

"You still have a missing guard, and a high-level Batterson flunky who conveniently happened to be in the right place at the right time." This was getting more fucked up by the second.

"I can probably guess why Conway was there. Singh claimed he was talking to someone inside Batterson's company, somebody high up, who said this shipment was important." Saetang growled in frustration. "Now he's dead, and we don't have the name of his contact so we can keep tabs on whatever they're up to. But we obtained a warrant for England's arrest. Officers are on the way."

"They'd better hurry. We made a contingency plan for her to request asylum at the Zereid embassy if he ran his mouth or local authorities got involved."

She gave a bark of bitter laughter. "That fucking figures."

"Any word how Conway is doing? Can he be questioned?" His recovery might also give me some idea how much physical danger Sumner was in.

I saw her face change. Her voice softened. "He's in critical condition. Brain bleed."

Hope drained out of me in a cold rush.

"How are you holding up?" Saetang asked.

"How do you think?" I stood. "I want to talk to it."

"You're too close."

"I'm an interspecies negotiator."

"It might want to manipulate you because it has your partner in thrall." Saetang shifted in her seat. "What if Sumner isn't in there anymore?"

I screwed my eyes shut in agony, torn between what I hoped and my fear she was right. "I know what I'm doing."

"I get it. I do." Saetang's pain was back, dark and biting at my empathic nets. "But you need to make sure you don't mistake that thing for your partner."

"That 'thing' is an intelligent being. We are obligated to give it the same treatment we would any other species, no matter how dangerous it seems. We still don't know why it's here."

Saetang shrugged in resignation. "Go find out."

———

Rama lingered outside the interrogation room, his expressive face grim and hard. Through the one-way glass window, I observed Sumner. He stood with his feet braced hips-width apart, hands relaxed and open at his sides. Beyond the slow, even rise and fall of his chest, he was utterly still. The two officers in the room were attentive but not on alert, still wearing full tactical gear and with rifles at the ready.

"Any changes?" I asked.

"No, he's just standing there," Rama said. "He hasn't said a word."

"I want to talk to him alone. Is that possible?"

"Sure. But is it smart?"

"I don't know if I'll get anywhere with weapons pointed at him."

"That thing *is* a weapon. You didn't see it in action." Rama shrugged. "It's your funeral. If anything goes wrong, I'll be watching out here."

"Thanks," I said dryly.

Rama opened the door and motioned the armed officers out. I went in.

Sumner turned his head when I entered the room. My insides churned as the inhuman, burning-black gaze rested on me, his expression blank, without acknowledgement or recognition. That hurt more than I anticipated. Drawing closer, I caught a glimpse of his familiar blue-green irises behind the veneer of darkness superimposed on his features.

I had to believe he was in there, somewhere, and I could still reach him.

A pins-and-needles sensation against my empathic nets disconcerted me, like nerve pain in a limb after being deprived of circulation. Cloaked in a veil of static electricity, the entity's broadcast had no comparison to any other being I'd previously encountered. I wasn't certain what I sensed, or if they were even emotions.

"Close enough," Rama warned me when I stood six feet from my partner's compromised body. "I'll be outside."

The door shut, and we were alone.

"Who are you?" It spoke Remoliad Standard. Sumner's throat flexed when air was forced through his vocal cords in a parody of his voice. His mouth barely moved.

"I'm Dalí Tamareia. I'm an interspecies negotiator." I focused on the requisites of first-contact protocol. "What is your name?"

"My designation is Kitryd."

"I haven't met anyone of your species before. What are your requirements for life support and sustenance?"

"I am an artificial intelligence suspended in an organic energy matrix. I have no physical needs but will comply with the essential functions of my host's body."

An AI? "Has Rion Sumner been harmed by your actions?" I asked, fighting to keep the sharpness out of my voice.

"I have temporarily reprogrammed his nervous system to obey my commands."

"You gravely injured another human being at the terminal when you attacked him."

In the curtain of white noise against my empathic web, a hesitant stutter interrupted the static fuzz.

"My knowledge of your species' physiology is limited. I made an error. I did not intend to harm him."

"Where are you from?"

"The Sovereign Collective."

"In what star system?"

"It varies."

Evasive bastard. I took a couple of deep inhalations and refocused on the alien presence in my partner's eyes. "The man you injured is in a medical facility in critical condition. I'm concerned for Sumner's well-being."

"I compensated for the initial miscalculation. My current host's biology is not entirely human."

Not comforting at all. "Why are you in Sol Fed?"

"I require assistance from local authorities. I have come to retrieve Miriam Skadi for crimes against the Sovereign Collective."

CHAPTER
THIRTEEN

LEFT MOMENTARILY speechless by the pronouncement, words stumbled out of my mouth." Are you a bounty hunter?"

"I am not." Kitryd managed to sound offended.

"What crime did she commit?"

"Skadi removed six immature consciousnesses from an incubation module. I will fully integrate with the criminal when she is found, and her memories will enable me to locate the undeveloped collective. She will be terminated after I rescue them."

The muffled sound of Sumner's usurped voice unnerved me. As much as I wanted to learn what the hell was happening here, I needed to negotiate my partner's release. "However urgent your business might be in Sol Fed, what you did is wrong. You violated Rion Sumner's free will when you took over his body. Let him go before you do irreparable damage and we will find another way to talk to each other."

"I cannot do that." The prickly buzz sharpened against my senses and made my ears itch. "I must locate Skadi immediately."

"Let me talk to him. I need to know if he is all right."

"Intercranial pressure in your species has already proven to be more delicate than anticipated. It is less dangerous to keep his consciousness submerged. If he fights against me, there may be physical and neurological consequences."

It sounded like a statement of fact in the flat, emotionless tones from Sumner's throat, but the coil of gleaming, articulated metal around his neck canted me toward menace. "You did not enter this system legally. Your actions thus far are not exactly benign, and I cannot prove you are not a threat. I do not believe I can negotiate your release under these circumstances."

"I have no agenda but to retrieve the criminal Skadi. When I locate the immature consciousnesses I will immediately return with them to the Sovereign Collective."

"How did you know she was coming here?"

"I tracked her from our home to the travel hub near Kadrel. I failed to capture her there but intercepted two incoming transmissions to her ship. The first contained a set of instructions. She was to divert a shipment to Sol Fed and remove something from the container before customs inspection. The second transmission originated from Sol Fed with an unidentified sender, an agreement to purchase what they referred to as six pieces of exclusive technology. I believe they were speaking of the immature consciousnesses. I integrated with the hub's computer system to discover what vessel the freight would travel on and entered the container she diverted. I expected those for whom I search to be to be inside."

Kitryd paused, an odd surge in the tingling static against my empathic nets before it continued. "They were not. Instead, I concealed myself in the container and waited. I believed she would be first to open it when it reached Sol Fed. This was an error."

Skadi brought the AIs to Sol Fed because she had a buyer.

Shit. The Batterson thug called himself the pickup guy.

Conway must have expected to meet her at the warehouse, but Singh showed up and threw him off.

Artificial intelligence technology was a field not even Remoliad Allied worlds dominated. It would give Batterson Robotics an advantage over the entire galaxy if they were able to reverse engineer these AIs—and if Kitryd represented a common example of their kind, they were highly sophisticated. The company financially suffered under relief agreements which allowed free tech to stream into the Colonies, not to mention the highly publicized fallout from Jon Batterson's extracurricular activities. They probably couldn't wait to get their hands on them.

Saetang opened the door before I could fully process this information. "Tamareia. I need you."

I pulled myself back into focus and addressed Kitryd. "I will return as soon as I can."

"The longer we delay, the more likely Skadi will evade me."

"If you attempt to leave, Sumner could be injured. I will not allow you to do that." I met Kitryd's black-hole stare. "If you want our help, stay here."

Armed officers moved back into the room when I exited and fell into step beside Saetang. "What happened?"

"I put out an APB on Miriam Skadi after our conversation." She handed me her data device. "Facial recognition software pegged her in the old city twenty minutes ago."

I stared at the image. Tall, like Sumner, her hair gleamed almost white rather than his more human light-blond coloring. She appeared to be wearing cosmetics, her stark, alabaster skin several shades darker than I remembered from the mocking holo she and Alecto sent us after they abducted the Shontavians. But her eyes were unaltered, an ice-pale gaze looking directly into the camera.

"She's not hiding, despite the makeup," I murmured. "She wanted to be seen. Where was this taken?"

"A block north of the main street in front of a hostel."

The world swung on a dizzy pendulum. My lips grew cold. "Patil's?"

"Yes." Saetang drew the word out until it curved upward like a question mark.

No random hit on surveillance: this was communication aimed at Sumner or me. I started to think we were the ones being set up. "That's where we're staying. They're friends of mine."

"How did she find out you were there?"

"Until yesterday morning, we didn't even know we'd be there." Sudden fear for Michael and Dev punched me in the chest. "Will you send someone to check on the Patils?"

"Absolutely." Saetang quickly entered something on her device and consulted another app. "No record of her arriving through immigration anywhere in the system. None of the exit points from the old city tagged her leaving on a train or a flight since that image was captured. She's still here."

"We need to find her." Still shaken, I relayed Kitryd's origins and my theory the stolen AIs were brought to Sol Fed for sale to Batterson Robotics. She snorted in disgust and dropped into the chair behind the desk when we reached her office, her fingers rubbing her forehead.

"Great. Damn. The last thing I need is a headache. This AI society wouldn't be a member of the Remoliad, would it?"

"No. The Remoliad has yet to recognize artificial intelligence as a species. None came forward and claimed a society unto themselves until now. As far as I am aware, this is a first contact situation."

"Fucking marvelous. Congratulations, you just became indispensable. Should I alert the diplomatic corps, too?"

"Not yet. Please." I had resigned my commission when I joined the Penumbra, and I doubted they would recognize my authority in this case without contacting the Remoliad. It would not go well.

"We had a whole train car of witnesses, and I'm informing my agency of the need to issue a heightened security alert. It's only a matter of time before bureaucrats show up on our doorstep, Tamareia."

She was right. Damn it; I couldn't wait around for that to happen. They would take Sumner out of my reach.

"I have to get him out of here. He's a hostage. If the government tries to contain Kitryd, Sumner's going to be caught in no man's land. Release them both into my custody and let us go look for her."

Saetang squinted at me. "The AI hijacking his body assaulted a Sol Fed citizen and wants to eat your suspect's brain when it finds her. Whatever she's done, she's a Sol Fed citizen too, and I have issues with just allowing it to do whatever it wants. Are you willing to risk Sumner ending up like Conway?"

Flint-edged fear struck a spark of anger and sent heat through me. "I have zero ideas how to get the AI out of him. Asking nicely was a bust. There's no guarantee he won't come out of this unscathed, no matter how we play this." I swallowed the rising burn of acid before my words turned into a shout. "If it will leave him voluntarily, I want to cooperate."

"Goddamn it," Saetang muttered, but she was considering my plea. "The officers couldn't take his gun away without endangering him. We don't need that thing running around with a projectile weapon."

"According to Rama, the AI won't need a gun if we find her." I straightened. "I will take full responsibility for its actions."

"You think I'm giving you free license? You don't have any jurisdiction here. I'm coming with you. We do this as a joint action, or not at all. I suspect you don't give a shit about accountability."

I had to give her points for figuring me out that fast. Saetang was not wrong. With Sumner compromised, I needed a cooler head to temper my actions. But I was beginning to wonder about her acquiescence. She'd accepted my request too quickly, without consulting her superiors.

She had her own agenda with Mother England. Kitryd constituted an unknown factor, but I was willing to lay odds the AI would do anything necessary to take down Skadi. Between the three of us existed staggering potential for collateral damage.

We needed a grown up. Fuck.

I guess it had to be me. "We'll lay out some ground rules for Kitryd and see how it reacts."

Saetang and I returned to the room where Sumner and Kitryd were held. She dismissed the guards and stood near the door.

"This is Agent Saetang. She's coming with us," I told Sumner's invader. "She represents federal law enforcement with access to surveillance that will help us find Skadi. Do you accept her authority in this operation?"

"I will cooperate," the AI responded in its flat, un-Sumner-like way. It didn't say yes, which gave Kitryd more leeway in its answer than I liked.

"There are conditions to which you must agree before she will let you out of this room," I informed it. "First: you will take no action which risks the lives of any Sol Fed citizens or deliberately endangers Rion Sumner, and you will tell us immediately if Sumner needs medical assistance."

A scratchy shift in the AI's static field brushed against my senses as it considered this. "I agree to those conditions. Proceed," Kitryd said.

"Second: any information you learn regarding the location of the stolen consciousnesses must be shared with us. It may be related to further criminal activity here in Sol Fed."

"That is acceptable." Kitryd shifted, its impatience showing.

"Last." Kitryd would not like this one. "You will give us

ample time to question Skadi once she is in custody. She committed crimes against Sol Fed and is an accomplice in the kidnapping of life-forms for whom *I* am responsible. I think you understand I must do everything I can to retrieve them."

"When I access Skadi's memories, I can provide answers to the questions you have," Kitryd said.

For a moment, I almost said yes. To have all the details of Skadi's network of illegal dealings, her employer's agenda, and the Shontavians' location, everything at once? My better self was horrified I even considered it. What was wrong with me? "No. It is not an allowable interrogation method in our society. Our species' most cherished condition is our autonomy. We cannot question her that way."

"If I must concur, I also have conditions." Kitryd stared at us. "You will not hinder what is required to rescue the immature line. I will give advance notice if your directives will be violated."

"That's some broad language." Saetang folded her arms over her chest.

"You will give us sufficient time to find alternative solutions," I countered.

Kitryd remained silent for several seconds as the waterfall of static ebbed and flowed.

"Agreed," it finally said. "Let us find Skadi. But now—" Kitryd squirmed again. "I believe my host's body needs to excrete waste. And I do not yet know how."

———

While Saetang filled in her officers and changed into street clothes, one of the guards and I escorted Kitryd to the lavatory. Anyone who never coached an alien AI through the act of releasing humanoid bladder and sphincter muscles for the first time should be considered fortunate. Afterward, Kitryd imitated me scrubbing my hands, though there was no way in hell I could ever scour that experience away. I only hoped Sumner's consciousness stayed submerged long enough to never know it happened.

In the mirror, I studied the metallic cage surrounding Sumner's torso, curious to understand how it moved and reformed. The construct gleamed in the overhead lights, conspicuous even if it wasn't arranged over a tactical vest with Homeland Security insignia. Kitryd turned Sumner's head and caught me in a frown.

"You are dissatisfied."

I wanted to see it in action, close enough to discover if it could somehow be disrupted. I hadn't stopped thinking of a way to free Sumner. "We won't blend into the crowd with him looking like that. Will you allow me to remove the vest? You can hide your construct from view under his coat, like you did with Conway."

Segments folded in on themselves. Each piece moved independently of the others, flat sides joining or rolling with a flurry of soft clicks: magnetic, possibly, the poles flipped at will to rearrange at Kitryd's command. The construct formed a thick belt around Sumner's hips below the bottom of the armor.

Kitryd lifted Sumner's arms, and when I unstrapped the Velcro on each flank, dipped his head to allowed me to lift off the vest. The AI watched me all the while with fathomless eyes, but I faltered when I thought I glimpsed Sumner's gaze beneath the inky veil. His expression minutely changed, and his lips twitched in the beginning of a word.

"Sumner?" I whispered.

"Do not attempt to communicate," Kitryd warned. "He must remain quiescent. If his neurological system is damaged by stress, the host will no longer be useful to me."

The AI's casual disregard of Sumner as something to be used and abandoned when defective ignited my fury. I threw the vest on the sink top and rounded on Kitryd.

"His name is Rion Sumner. He is a living being, not a host for your use. He did not agree to this." Leaning close, I glared into the dark void of Kitryd's eyes. "That makes you as much of a criminal as Skadi in my estimation. I will help you find her so you can get the fuck out of his head. But if anything happens to Sumner, I will destroy you. Understood?"

Silence hung between us for an endless, tense moment. "Affirmative," Kitryd said at last.

CHAPTER
FOURTEEN

WE LEFT headquarters and caught the automated beltway spanning the length of the old city. The moving sidewalk teemed with people heading to the ceremony. An underlying current buzzed through the crowd in anticipation of the evening's events, which promised to be no less jubilant than last night's proud, unabashed revelry, but with more historical focus.

Saetang and I flanked Sumner and his body thief. Under the AI's influence, he moved at first like Kitryd's mechanical construct: stiff, deliberate, with sudden stops and inhuman stillness. The longer it was in contact with Sumner, though, the more it gained some of his quick, easy grace as muscle memory took over. I didn't like it. A stranger inhabited my friend's body.

Eight other officers rode with us on the belt, most in plainclothes and interspersed through the groups of festivalgoers. We were all linked on a single com channel except for Kitryd, who had not been issued one. My fingers brushed the bump of my implant com as I adjusted my earpiece, and I had a thought.

"May I touch Sumner?" I asked Kitryd.

"Why?" Sunglasses borrowed from Rama concealed the alien gaze beneath tinted lenses as Kitryd regarded me.

"He has an implanted device which will allow us to stay in contact if we get separated."

Although its coils of metal were hidden beneath the jacket, a glinting curve like the torque of some ancient Earth king still lay visible around Sumner's throat. Kitryd finally spoke. "You may activate the device."

I tapped the small rise on Sumner's mastoid bone. Kitryd continued to study me. With its black gaze hidden by reflective lenses, I could see only the man I knew with his head tilted down to look at me. It was unnerving, and I quickly stepped back.

I will speak to you this way if it is less disturbing. The artificial voice of my translator sounded in my head, just as if I was receiving a transmission from one of *Thunder Child's* crew.

"You can interface with his communicator?"

Yes.

"It's better to keep talking out loud unless we're separated." When I was finally able to evict the AI and return Sumner's autonomy, I now knew it could use a communication device to speak. That Kitryd was concerned about my discomfort with it using Sumner's voice was something I couldn't afford to dissect right now.

The belt became more crowded as people merged in from the train station's plaza. Uneasiness clawed its way up from my stomach into my chest as I took note of the sheer number of families present. Children with shining eyes danced around their parents, their joy colliding with my tightly furled empathic nets in sparkling bursts. The lives of innocents meant nothing to Skadi. She'd proven that at Luna Terminal.

"She's going to use this crowd as a shield," I said, my voice cracking. "It's too risky."

"We'll find her." Saetang adjusted the tactical lens over her right eye and glanced at me. "I have people watching the rail station and departure gates at the terminal. She so much as passes in front of a camera and we've got her. There's a continuous alert running on facial recognition all over Luna."

So long as she wasn't inside the Patils' hostel. Saetang's officer had reported Dev and Michael appeared to be in no danger and now patrolled their street, watching the crowds. It was a small comfort, but in the larger scheme of things, it didn't make much difference. Back on Luna for one day, and already people I cared for were in peril. If I had told Singh and Mother England to fuck off, Sumner wouldn't have a murderbot riding him, and if they'd never known me, Gresh and Rasida—

Stop it, Dalí. I shoved my thoughts away from the gravity of that dark spiral before it could suck me in.

People filled the streets. Music and laughter fluttered through the air under the canopy of decorative bunting and garland. The sidewalks were just as packed, where vendors sold treats and paper flags bearing the silver Lunar crescent. The empathic buzz wasn't as overpowering as last night but distracting enough, even with my senses tamped down as far as possible.

Saetang and I waded up Johnson Street to the Tripathi Hotel, where the platform hosting the DJ's set had been transformed for today's speeches. An empty podium waited for a group of Lunar politicians, perched on collapsible chairs and prepared to impress voters with their historical knowledge and patriotism. Several holo-screen billboards had been installed on building fronts down the block for those who wouldn't be close enough to see and hear the speeches. Right now, they displayed whirling, brightly clothed dancers.

The same Kinnar troupe performed outside the hotel for happy young families, and I glimpsed a media bot as it circled around the dancers at an intrusive range. The images on the holo boards came from its vantage point. More globes floated through the crowd in front of the platform. Another bot illuminated two people behind the stage, and I recognized one as Dru. The man she spoke with was all expensive suit, white teeth, and flash. Another one of Singh's ilk.

"Did an APB go out to the press?" I asked, an idea sharpening in my mind.

"Law enforcement only," Saetang replied, her brow creased. "What are you thinking?"

I indicated the bobbing globes. "Those things are networked. What one knows, they all know." It was how my family had been inadvertently targeted by Skadi's explosive-laden media bots at Luna Station. "I can make them work for us. Kitryd, stay with Agent Saetang. I'll be back in a minute."

It took longer than I thought to capture one of the goddamned things. Amazing how they were always in my face at the worst possible times but became slippery and elusive when I wanted one. I finally got a grip on one of the fins and covered the lens with my hand as I brought it back to the sidewalk.

"Pull up the surveillance holo of Skadi," I told Saetang.

She tapped her device and the image hovered in the air above its screen. The Batterson Robotics logo gleamed on the chassis as I located the right controls. I'd been instructed how to operate a media bot, albeit under duress, by one of Batterson's right-hand goons.

I pointed the bot's lens at Skadi's holographic image and pressed the scan button. Red grids swept the holo and a blinking white light registered the media bot's recognition of the data.

"Priority subject, close up and wide angles," I ordered. "Image to be transmitted to all holo screens on the street when the subject is encountered. Follow the subject if they leave the area."

"Acknowledged," the bot chimed.

"Hey, what are you doing?" The polished, toothy reporter,

huffing and indignant, appeared with Dru at his side. "That's mine."

"Law enforcement override." Saetang flashed her credentials.

"Dalf? Can I talk to you?" Dru said, her expression troubled.

Releasing the media bot, I had to trust it shared the image with the rest of the swarm as it purred away into the crowd. Dru took my arm and pulled me aside.

"Christopher told me Kiran is missing. Nobody's been able to reach him," she said in hushed tones as Saetang dealt with the reporter. "Justina hasn't shown up either. She's supposed to give the opening address in five minutes and introduce the speakers. What's going on? Don't tell me you're here on a personal visit, not when you're here with Homeland Security."

"You're going to have to do that speech tonight," I said, trying to keep an eye on Sumner and make sure Kitryd didn't wander off. "I don't have time to explain."

"This has something to do with the NPM, doesn't it?"

Startled, I stared at her. "Why would you think that?"

Her face hardened. "They tried to kill Kiran last night at Justina's party."

"I thought they were after her," I said, confused when her guilt and excitement swirled in my empathic nets. "Dru, what's going on?" If she knew more than was safe, she might be in danger, too.

"I've kind of been spying on Justina after she fired him. I felt bad about it, but the NPM has had it out for Kiran ever since he exposed Jon and Simon Batterson, and the old man was forced to resign the presidency. You of all people know much I hate those bastards. It infuriates me she's doing business with them. But if it gets out Justina is . . ." She paused.

"A hypocrite?" I suggested acidly.

"Yes. It could destroy everything the Third Front stands

for, and it's become important to me. I think she knew they were going to try to kill him last night and didn't do anything."

It made total sense. Justina England looked like a victim in the press, and that probably suited her just fine. Kiran told me at the party he had information about them, but I'd refused to listen because he dangled it like a lure and made it conditional. The Battersons trying to murder Singh hadn't been on my list of possible bullshit. What in the seven hells was England doing?

"We have to talk later," I said. "Keep your eyes open and for fuck's sake, be careful. No more spying. If things start getting weird, find somewhere to hide and stay there."

"What's happening?" Dru's eyes grew large with fear.

"I don't know yet. I'm doing my best to make sure nothing does."

I left her on the sidewalk and went back to Saetang, who had finished wrangling with the holo journalist and now babysat Kitryd while the AI scanned the crowd with singular focus.

"Things are just getting better and better," I muttered. "We have another source who might be willing to report on Mother England's activities."

"The pretty one said something?" Saetang glanced back at Dru as she mounted the platform and greeted the speakers. Her dark eyes flickered with interest, and I didn't need to cast my empathic nets at her to see it was more than a casual appraisal. "Doesn't she work for the Third Front?"

"She's a friend. She's open to talking later."

"We are not looking for Skadi," Kitryd complained.

"The bots are doing that for us," I reminded it as Saetang updated her officers via wrist com to watch the screens. "If they find her in the crowd, we'll see it. Besides, she knows Sumner. If she notices you first, she might disappear."

"I will not wait." Kitryd walked Sumner's body into the

mob. Frustrated, I followed in their wake. Saetang hurried to fall in behind me.

Up on the podium, Dru began to deliver the welcoming speech England was supposed to give. A crescendo of applause swept the onlookers, Lunar flags waving overhead. Keeping my empathic senses dampened took effort and divided my attention in a way I couldn't risk while trying to keep up with the AI. Kitryd kept Sumner's head on a swivel as they moved through the crowd, the dark sunglasses flashing with reflected light.

Dru's smiling face beamed from the primary holo screen behind the podium, shots of her appreciative audience displayed on the satellite screens by the roaming media bots. Sumner was taller than Saetang and me, giving Kitryd a superior vantage point over the mass of humans as they pushed through.

I ran into his back when Kitryd came to an abrupt halt. Static erupted like a solar flare through the AI's sensory output and crisped my senses as it used Sumner's voice to say,

"She is there."

My pulse shot up. "Where?" I craned my neck to peer over heads and flags.

Skadi abruptly appeared on the giant screen in a crowd shot. She glanced up as the excited people around her waved for the media bot, and her face hardened as she realized she was on camera.

The bot zoomed in to hover near her at the opposite side of the crowd, fifteen meters from where we stood. She drew the hood of her black coat over her head and pivoted away from the lens just as her image flicked up in tumbling-domino succession on the screens lining the street.

I saw the moment she registered she was in trouble. She started to fight her way out of the square through the press of bodies.

"Got her on screen," Saetang said triumphantly into her wrist com. "All personnel, move in. Blonde woman in a black jacket and hood headed northbound, away from Johnson. Cover the alley exits to A Street."

The media bot pursued its subject and I turned back to Kitryd—but the AI was already gone. I spotted Sumner's blond head as the AI shoved through the crowd meters ahead of me.

"Oh, no you don't!" I moved after Kitryd.

Suddenly, klaxons blared. Strobes flashed overhead as heavy plate shielding slammed down over the skylights and blocked out the view of the starfield with an echoing *BOOM*.

The entire crowd startled. The collective reaction bludgeoned my empathic senses, and I staggered. Muzzily, I registered all the holo screens now showed a broad red bar in the lower portion. Harsh white letters scrolled beside a fifteen-minute countdown.

METEORITE   ACTIVITY   WARNING   —   PROCEED IMMEDIATELY TO NEAREST SHELTER

The mass of bodies on Johnson Street surged eastward toward the underground train station, sweeping me away from Sumner.

"No, no! Goddamn it!" I fought to keep moving toward Sumner and faltered, my senses stunned under the landslide of human panic in an emergency evacuation.

It was Saetang who pulled me out of the flood and back onto the solid ground of a sidewalk. I fell against the wall and folded in on myself, shuddering as change hormones prepared me for a fight. I let them have their way and hissed in pain as bones shifted to widen my shoulders, heart pumping hard and fast to feed my muscles.

"You okay?" she asked.

"I lost him." My voice grated in my ears, rough from the change and the onslaught of raw psychic noise.

"We haven't lost her. Look," she said, pointing at the screens. Though the meteor warning still blared, the media bot still tracked Skadi as she was swept along in the torrent of people seeking shelter as helplessly as I had been. "She's setting off facial recognition alerts all the way down the street. My lens is pinging a hit every twenty seconds, so we can track her. If she peels out of the crowd, she has nowhere left to hide, and you know Kitryd will follow."

Full of adrenaline from the hormone-forced change, I straightened and shook out my limbs. "There is still time before the airlocks close on the shelter. Let's go through the alley. If we run faster than the horde is moving, maybe we can intercept at the next street."

We quickly threaded the narrow space between buildings as she keyed her com.

"Saetang to team. Keep your eyes on the alerts and follow the suspect if she goes underground. Keep me informed. Anybody got eyes on Sumner and his passenger?"

"Negative," came a reply.

I tapped my implant as we picked up our pace. "Kitryd, do you hear me? Respond."

I hear you.

"Where are you?"

I am closing in on Skadi.

"Remember what you agreed to do. Do not put any lives at risk, and do not integrate. Understood?"

Silence.

"Kitryd? Fuck!"

"Damn it, did it go rogue?" Saetang's eyepiece glared in the warning strobes as we merged into the next thoroughfare, thick with evacuees. "Law enforcement! Clear a path!" she bellowed. Alarmed citizens scattered as we dashed down the street.

"Where was the last hit?" I yelled, trying to keep up.

"Two blocks! We need to grab them both before they get into the train station."

We ran, dodging pedestrians headed for refuge. Three blocks up, she cut over on a side street, where a smaller tributary streaming from residential areas joined the river of humanity on Johnson Street. I wondered briefly if the station's shelter could hold all these people, the normal population swollen by those who traveled in from other domes for the celebration.

Then I heard screaming.

CHAPTER
FIFTEEN

WHAT HAD BEEN an orderly evacuation became a stampede. People pushed and shoved to escape something I couldn't see at the center of the crush.

When the crowd parted I glimpsed Sumner, standing motionless in the middle of the street while people flowed around him like a boulder in a stream as a media bot hovered overhead. We reached the circle of onlookers who pushed back the rest of the mob and revealed what had captured their attention.

Miriam Skadi gripped an adolescent third-gender kid in front of her like a shield, a gun pressed to their temple.

"Subject has a juvenile hostage at the intersection of Johnson and Mondal," Saetang said over her com while I shoved through the mass of bodies to reach them. Sumner stood a few meters away from Skadi and her captive. The painful static buzz coming off Kitryd was palpable to me even over the crowd's alarm, and for the first time, I felt as though I understood what it meant.

Kitryd was enraged.

"Don't do it," I warned Skadi as Saetang drew down on her. "Let the kid go."

Skadi's gaze flicked to me at the sound of my voice. "There you are, Dalí," she greeted me, her teeth bared. "I think our Rion is broken. Why won't he talk to me?"

"Rion isn't home right now," I said.

"Miriam Skadi." Sumner's hand reached up and removed the sunglasses, and horrified recognition crawled over her expression as the void-black gaze emerged. "I am charged with your retrieval."

Skadi's face changed, the emotion behind her eyes so raw I didn't need my empathic webs to read it. Pain. Betrayal.

Then she began to laugh, a hollow, strange sound that raised the hair on the back of my neck. For a terrifying moment, I thought she was going to kill her hostage. She released the kid, who scrambled in terror to reach the edge of the crowd and their waiting friends. Other officers arrived with stun weapons trained on her, and she lifted her hands.

"I surrender," Skadi said, her voice still thick with eerie laughter. "Take me into custody. Keep that thing away from me and I'll cooperate."

"Put the gun down now!" Saetang ordered.

Skadi knelt and placed her weapon on the concrete. Her gaze never strayed from Kitryd; her mouth curled in a smug grin as she straightened with her hands in the air.

Kitryd moved.

"No!" Before the word even left my mouth, the construct leaped from beneath Sumner's coat like a striking reptile and trapped Skadi in its metal exoskeleton. His hands clapped to the sides of her skull, squeezing, and forced her jaw open as the media bot buzzed around them for a closeup. Onlookers gasped in horror. The confused officers' weapons wavered between targets.

"Stop!" I shouted, and strained against all of Sumner's strength to push his right arm up and away from Skadi's head. "She surrendered. Honor our agreement."

Sumner's face turned in my direction, inhumanly slow,

Kitryd's void-black gaze as impenetrable as it had ever been. The tension left his arm so abruptly I stumbled when the AI ceased fighting against me. The exoskeleton returned to its hiding place beneath the coat.

Kitryd moved away and bent to retrieve the dropped sunglasses, concealing its shadowed gaze once more. The electric prickle of its output didn't change. It was still furious.

Officers rushed in to collect her discarded gun and cuffed Skadi's hands behind her back while the media bot flitted around her. "You're saving my life, and Rion's the one trying to kill me?" Skadi noted flippantly. "I'm disappointed. I thought things would be different when we finally caught up with each other."

Face to face with my family's murderer at last, so close her breath whispered against my cheek. My hands clenched convulsively, nails biting into my palms, vision distorted by sudden rage. The white-hot explosion that killed Gresh and Rasida filled my mind and engulfed any reason I had left.

My fingers touched the hilt of my knife where it nestled against my wrist. She recognized her death written in my expression, a flicker of uncertainty in her crystalline eyes. For one cold, clear moment, I intended to cut her heart out. And she knew it.

I stepped back from the precipice, trembling with the effort it took. "Miriam Skadi, you are under arrest for acts of terrorism against the Solar Federation." I thought the words would be sweeter to say.

All I tasted was ashes.

"Refusal to cooperate with authorities will be met with equal or greater force. Any statements you make will be used to build a case against you. Do you understand?"

"Oh, yes." She smiled at me, mocking, indulgent.

Something shattered in my mind.

My fist connected with her jaw before I knew I'd made the decision to punch her. She swayed with the blow, came up spitting damson blood and grinned at me with gory teeth, her careful makeup smeared away from the white skin beside her mouth.

"That's more like it," she said.

"Tamareia, that's enough!" Saetang ordered.

I walked away and leaned over with my hands on my knees, breath coming too fast. My heart lurched with a sickening thud as I realized I could have had Sumner back if I had just let Kitryd finish what it started. It would have been so easy.

But I never took the easy path, did I?

Sirens screamed a second warning over the bray of klaxons. My mind understood what it meant, coherent thought emerging from the pyroclastic cloud of vengeance. The meteor had evaded peripheral defenses and was inside Lunar space. The missile battery atop Bullialdus Crater was now the last bastion to avert the incoming threat. We had a matter of minutes.

The circle of people around us collapsed and flowed downstream, the urge to take cover more compelling than whatever drama we provided. I was already in fight-or-flight mode; adrenaline coursed through my veins while my empathic nets fried under the panic of a now-fleeing populace.

"Get underground," Saetang ordered her officers. "The service shaft. We need to keep these idiots away from the train station and the rest of the people." The sour glance in my direction confirmed she included me in the title. "Four of you come with me. Nobody rides out the warning above ground, got it? Keep these people moving! It's going to be a tight fit. You have six minutes before the airlocks close."

Half the officers peeled off to direct the crowd. The two who had cuffed Skadi gripped her upper arms and followed the senior agent, a media bot still orbiting our group as Saetang led us to a metal door at the end of the street.

She swiped her wrist com in front of a sensor panel and the port hissed aside. A broad landing and a steep flight of grated stairs descended into the bedrock beneath the city. The officers ushered our prisoner through. With violent satisfaction, I shoved the media bot back outside when it attempted to follow and shut the port.

"Zimm, you first, then Sumner and Tamareia. All the way down," Saetang directed. "There's tunnel access at the bottom. It's protected by the railway's airlock system."

I motioned for the stiff, angry Kitryd to follow Zimm, and it silently complied. Skadi came down behind us, sandwiched between two officers. A single white light ghosted each landing, sanguine warning LEDs brightening and ebbing as we descended flight by flight. The shaft was at least one hundred meters deep, dizzying glimpses of the bottom visible through the open grate of the steps.

"How long do we have before the airlocks seal?" I asked Saetang.

Her voice echoed above the clatter of our hurried footsteps. "Less than four minutes."

It would only take a smallish meteor to cause catastrophic decompression, though the likelihood of a direct strike was extremely rare. The last impact in a populated area by anything large enough to create damage had been fifteen years prior, killing a dozen foundry workers who either ignored the alarms or didn't make it to shelter in time.

Early warning sensors in Sol Fed space were getting better all the time now that galactic tech was available, but a missile battery targeting something traveling at more than sixty thousand kilometers an hour was still an iffy prospect.

We reached the bottom of the stairs with no time to spare. As soon as the door closed behind us, a warning buzz echoed through the cavern and the auxiliary port sealed the door with a final hiss.

Seconds later, a violent lurch shook us. Dust and pebbles rained down as we struggled to keep our feet.

"Against the wall! Take cover!" I pulled Kitryd down into a crouch and covered Sumner's head with my own body, not trusting the AI to protect him. Stones bounced off my back. The tunnel lights flickered and went out.

Black silence reigned. The patter of debris faded away to nothing.

"Everybody okay?" Saetang shouted. Other voices called out affirmatives in the darkness.

"Seem to be," I responded, choking on dust as I helped Kitryd stand. "Any damage to Sumner?"

"He is intact." Kitryd's flat delivery fell in my ears like a muffled bell.

"Seven hells, that was a big one," said one of the officers. "How close?"

"Not a direct hit here, but maybe Armstrong?" another officer said. "Did it take out the power station?"

The lights flickered back into life, dimly at first, then full illumination. Relief swept the group, my empathic webs stirred by its cool passage.

Saetang stood and dusted herself off. "We need to reach hard line access to get reports. It'll be at least two hours before safety inspections are done and the airlocks open. Keep moving north. The repair bay we were in this morning isn't more than a couple kilometers away. I'll catch up in a minute."

The officers tugged Skadi forward. She cooperated after an uneasy backward glance at Sumner and me. Kitryd's presence had her unnerved, but I didn't have time to ruminate on it as Saetang confronted us, her countenance dust-streaked and stormy.

"Tamareia. You and Sumner—Kitryd—whoever. Get your asses over here." Her irritation snagged against my still-over-stimulated empathic nets, the adrenaline rush beginning to fade, a pounding headache firmly lodged at the base of my skull. I wasn't in the mood for a lecture, and Kitryd's electric buzz made me reasonably certain the AI wasn't either.

"What the fuck happened back there?" she rumbled, low-voiced to keep the conversation private. "Did we not agree we need to question the suspect before any brains are eaten? Tamareia, control yourself, your partner, and his puppet master, or I will lock you all up. I already put my ass out in the wind for not clearing your presence with my superiors. Do not fuck up this investigation."

"I'm sorry. We both behaved badly. It won't happen again." I threw a dark glance at Kitryd. "Will it?"

It didn't answer.

"Any hope we had of keeping Kitryd a secret is a moot point," she snapped. "This time, it will definitely be all over the news. The cameras were tracking Skadi before and after we arrested her. The media is going to want details." She sighed harshly. "I fucking hate press conferences. Let's move." She stalked down-tunnel behind her officers.

"After you." I waved Kitryd on. He followed in her wake, silent and rigid. With Sumner two steps ahead of me, I realized his neck was bare, the coil of metal no longer wrapped around his throat.

Kitryd's seething buzz continued, its atypical silence more threatening than anything it had previously uttered. There was something it hadn't told me yet. I was beginning to suspect that, like me, Kitryd had a deeply personal investment in taking Skadi down.

———

"The meteorite hit a little over a kilometer east of Bullialdus. We'll have to stay put while they check out the old city's environmental support, and the rail system is shut down for inspection after the impact quake. There appear to be no casualties." Saetang's relief sang against my senses as she looked up from her device, and I relaxed minutely. "Headquarters reports no damage." She lowered her voice. "Rama says his detainee is shaken up. She's still yelling immunity and wants to talk to you."

"I bet she does." England could sit and stew forever for all I cared.

Across the cavern, Skadi sat on a parts container near the electromagnetic lift. Three officers maintained a human wall between her and Kitryd. The fourth, a young man with deep brown skin and a medic's patch on his shoulder, let the hand-cuffed prisoner sip at a pouch of water from an emergency supply kit they located in the repair bay.

Even though he stood several meters away, Sumner's usurped frame almost quivered with energy, Kitryd's gaze locked on Skadi. Across the cavern, the crackle of the AI's output still touched the fringes of my empathic nets.

"Some good news, though. Rama found the recording of your meeting with England on Singh's device. We have enough to hold her on smuggling charges and obtain a warrant to search her private records. The bad news is that can't happen until everybody gets out of lockdown. It gives her people ample time to destroy whatever they can."

I groaned, looking up at the ceiling in defeat. "That figures. At least we have Skadi in custody."

"Look at her. She does not like Kitryd. She really wants to be somewhere else right now."

I followed Saetang's gaze. Skadi reacted to Sumner like he was a predator, coiled and ready to flee if he so much as took a step closer.

The captain shifted to face me with her arms wound in a knot over her chest. "What are you going to do about your partner?"

"I don't know yet." I ran my hands through my dusty hair and pretended the bubble of panic in my throat didn't exist. "If we tell the feds Kitryd's executing a galactic warrant, they might be more willing to leave Sumner in my custody."

"But is it, really? Or is it just a bounty hunter?"

"I wish I could say for certain."

The officer who had been tending to Skadi trotted over, and Saetang hailed him. "What's up, Jones?"

"The prisoner asked to talk to Tamareia."

"Clearly everybody wants to talk to you." Saetang raised an eyebrow. "We have an hour or so left down here before we can take her in. She may not be quite as willing to cooperate when she's out of danger and has a chance to retain a lawyer. Can you not punch her in the face again?"

Could I? I shrugged. "No promises."

We crossed the cavern and Saetang drew her officers together to fill them in on the meteorite impact. Kitryd stared at Skadi over their heads, on constant alert, but made no effort to move closer to us.

The corner of Skadi's mouth where my fist had connected was puffy, her alabaster skin mottled in violet beneath the smeared cosmetic disguise. She watched me approach with an enigmatic expression.

"What do you want?" I asked curtly.

"Let's cut to the chase, shall we?" Skadi sat forward; her pale gaze fixed on me. "Neither of us were surprised to see each other." Her mouth drew together in a pout, lower lip protruding in a parody of hurt feelings. "Someone's been talking. I hate that. Don't you find it a bit too convenient?"

The thought England set me up had crossed my mind, but I didn't take the bait. Instead, I asked, "Did you come back because your mother is dying?"

Her sudden mirth took me by surprise. Long, delighted peals of her full-throated laughter rang back from the walls of the cavern. "That's perfect. She would pick now to die." Skadi shifted in the handcuffs and rolled her shoulders. "Give me another drink of water, will you?"

Warily, I lifted the pouch so she could sip through the straw. "What's so important you risked coming back?"

"I'm sure you'd like to know." Slow, dark mockery crept across her mouth like an eclipse. "In the meantime, keep standing in front of me. I don't think it can read lips or speak Sol Standard, but Rion can, so it pays to be cautious. First things first. How did that thing get in his head? Don't tell me he invited it in. It would be just like him to be so altruistic and —" She made a gagging noise.

Altruism? I wondered why she would think that but didn't have time to explore. "He didn't invite it. It jumped him."

"Where was it?"

"Inside a shipping crate that arrived ahead of schedule this morning." I didn't give her any further information. She went very still before uttering a soft "*huh*" and closed her eyes. For a moment, her expression was surprisingly pained and vulnerable. Then it was over. Quick calculation hardened her features as she looked up.

"I confess to the bombing of Luna Terminal. Charge me the second we are out of this cave and put me in a high security cell." A hysterical giggle escaped her. "Because if you don't, I'm so dead."

"I personally don't see a problem with that. Who did you fuck over this time?"

Her smile disintegrated. "Greedy," she said. "You don't get everything for free. But I will tell you how to get the AI out of Rion without killing him."

CHAPTER
SIXTEEN

I REACTED TOO QUICKLY, betraying my interest, and her diamond gaze held mine in triumph. She knew she had my attention.

Hope transmuted into cynicism. Like Sumner, Skadi's hybrid heritage manifested in a near-complete psychic null—beyond the simple sense I dealt with a living being, there was no empathic output at all. I couldn't parse whether she was truthful or manipulative. "Why should I trust you?"

"Because I have a vested interest in staying alive. You have no clue how to free him, or you would have. Don't look up and give it away, but the means is hanging over our heads."

The flat iron disc of the robotic lift's electromagnetic head was six feet above us, suspended from the crane's arm. Of course.

"Go on," I said. I thought I knew what she suggested.

"Separate the thing from its mech suit and it is an organic silicon blob full of nanotech. Right now, it's occupying the empty, squishy spaces in Rion's head, and probably very comfortable." She smirked when I scowled at her. "A powerful magnetic field will disrupt its inductance. The bio electrical connections it made in his brain will shut off and you can remove it while it's stunned."

Fuck, I wished I could believe anything she said. "What about Kitryd? Will it survive the procedure?"

Her nose crinkled in disgust. "Why? Does it matter more to you than Rion?"

"It is an intelligent life-form, whether or not I approve of its actions."

"Diplomats. Fucking bleeding hearts." She rolled her eyes. "Those things are very hard to kill. Put it in an airtight container without its mech suit before you turn off the magnet and *voila*: just as trapped as anything else. It doesn't need to breathe, or eat, or take a dump. It can survive in a derelict spaceship for centuries and be perfectly happy."

That was an oddly specific comment, and I filed the information away for later. "What happens if you're wrong?"

"I'm not. I know everything about the Sovereign Collective's biology—if you can call it biology. A girl's got to protect herself."

I cursed under my breath. Even though I didn't trust the AI any more than I did Skadi, I didn't want to permanently disable Kitryd, just remove it from my partner and find another way to communicate that didn't involve Sumner's possession.

"You won't get another chance like this to take it by surprise. I'll even let you bring it over to talk to me to get in range." She cocked her head. "How's that for good faith?"

She really was desperate—or had a plan I couldn't see.

"I'll be back in a minute." With a last, mistrusting glance at Skadi, I rose and went to Saetang.

"We need to discuss something." I drew her away from the rest of the officers and the lurking Kitryd. The AI barely registered my presence, still fixated on Skadi. "The kid, Jones, is a paramedic, right?"

"Yeah. Is our guest having a problem?"

"No." Saetang listened, her eyes narrowed as I explained what Skadi told me.

"I don't trust her either, but her method does make sense," she admitted.

"It does. I'm not comfortable doing it without medical supervision, especially with the EMS transport pods tied up until an all clear is given. What if Sumner has a brain bleed like Conway?" I let out a harsh breath. "But she's right, there won't be another chance like this. As much as I would like to let Kitryd do its thing, she has information we can't find anywhere else and just might be scared enough to cooperate."

"There is an emergency medical kit over by the hard line. We should be able to activate the electromagnet from this panel. I'll try to look like I'm sending another message. Ditch anything you have on that might be affected by the magnetic field. We'll need to move fast before Kitryd figures out what we're doing."

With a glance to be sure the AI was still fixed on Skadi, I handed her my gun, PDD, and unstrapped the wrist sheath of my knife. "Sumner still has his weapon, but Kitryd doesn't seem to think about it and defaults to the mech suit."

"What do we put the thing in if it does come out?"

That was the question. Looking around, I spotted a jumble of empty polymer cleaning pails with lids. Not very dignified accommodations for an intelligent life-form, but we didn't have much choice. A subtle flick of my hand brought them to her attention. "A couple of those buckets should do. Keep Kitryd separated from the construct, preferably across the room. I'll go talk to it until you let me know you've figured out things on your end. Wait for my signal."

"Tell Jones to come over. I'll brief him while I try to sort this out."

The cluster of officers still formed a barrier between Skadi and the vigilant AI when I directed the medic to join Saetang.

"Stand by," I told the rest in a whisper. Their quick sense of heightened alert zinged through my empathic nets before I returned to Skadi and stood in front of her.

"You're on. You do realize if this doesn't work, Kitryd might be pissed enough to kill you right here? It's going to figure out you told me."

"I don't risk my own life unless I'm certain."

"No, but you are risking Sumner's. And if anything happens to him—"

"God, you are so touchy and protective." Her laugh was brittle, sardonic. "Did you two finally fuck, or is it love?"

"Don't you dare." A flush of anger sent heat through me, and my ears rang as the shallow normalcy I had worked so hard to regain flooded out to expose the pitted desert beneath. I squatted on my heels in front of her, my face inches from hers. "I don't give a fuck whether you live or die, but Sumner does. The only reason you're still breathing is because I'm afraid he couldn't forgive himself—or me—if I let Kitryd use his hands to kill you. That might be as close to love as I can get. Consider yourself lucky."

She nodded once, her expression bemused, as if she'd once again underestimated me. "You would be uncomfortable to know how alike we are."

"We're nothing alike." I stood before she could see I feared she was right. Across the room, I glimpsed Saetang brighten as she pointed to the screen, Jones hovering at her shoulder.

"Last chance to back out," I said in monotone. "What should I tell Kitryd you want to talk about that will keep it under the magnet?"

"Tell it I know where the real shipment is going."

I stared at her. "Do you?"

"Like I said, I have to protect myself. Stick around, you might learn something interesting."

My empathic senses battered against her null in a futile attempt to determine if she was lying. Turning my back on her, I took slow steps toward Kitryd, stopping to get a water ration out of the emergency supplies. Its gaze flickered briefly from Skadi to me.

"How is Sumner?" I asked in Remoliad standard.

"Functioning adequately."

"Here." I handed Kitryd the water. "You promised to comply with his needs. He hasn't had enough fluids."

Kitryd swallowed the ration, reluctance turning to eagerness as the pouch crumpled under suction.

"Is he hungry? Does he need to excrete liquid waste?"

"No."

I glanced at Saetang, who looked away from the screen and gave me a furtive thumbs up, her expression triumphant. I used the same modulated tone in which I'd inquired about Sumner's needs. "If I take you to talk to Skadi, can you resist the urge to carry out your death sentence and listen to what she says?"

A crescendo of static rained against my senses. "She wishes to speak?"

"Yes."

Kitryd abruptly moved in her direction, but I blocked it. "You didn't answer me. Can you control your impulses? You gave your word we could fully question Skadi. I can't do that here without violating the laws of this system. You will not touch her. Do you understand?"

"You agreed you will not hinder what I must do to retrieve the immature line."

"And I won't, when the time comes." An inconvenient flicker of guilt went through me, making promises I had no way to keep if Sol Fed took Skadi into custody, all while planning to forcefully evict Kitryd from Sumner's body in the next few minutes. "Give me your word you will not attempt to integrate with her, or you stay right where you are."

Silence. The buzz of Kitryd's output rose to a near-painful level in my empathic webs, a vibration so intense my eardrums itched with imagined pressure. Damn, I wished I could interpret what the AI was broadcasting. This was an emotion, I was certain: anger, or fear, or a volatile mixture of both.

"Why don't you tell me why you're really here?" I asked quietly.

My question startled it. The electric crackle of its output stuttered, and Sumner's head turned, Kitryd's attention locked on me. "What did the criminal say?"

"Nothing. I formed my own suspicions there is more to this after talking with both of you." I stared Kitryd down. "What's it going to be? Stay here, or listen and don't touch?"

"I will listen." The grudging acquiescence might have been comical under other circumstances, but I nodded solemnly and gestured for Kitryd to follow me.

When we approached Skadi, her breathing grew shallow with fear, but her lips curled in a smug grin. The courage to set herself up as bait was almost admirable, but I wondered again what goal of hers I aided by separating Kitryd from Sumner.

It wasn't going to stop me, though.

The AI halted several feet away from her, not close enough for the electromagnetic field to have any effect. What a great time for Kitryd to follow my directions and keep its distance.

"Speak," it ordered Skadi.

"I'll make a deal with you," she said. "My life for theirs. Spare me and I'll tell you how to find them."

"I will retrieve those memories upon full integration. Your cooperation is irrelevant."

"By that time, you could be too late. They can't wait to see what makes them tick. Some of them might already be picked apart by the time you catch up." Skadi's voice dropped to a whisper. Her ice-hued eyes glinted in the harsh light of the repair bay. "Think about it. Your own spawn, dissected, splayed out, and examined to see what they're made of. You can stop it from happening if you will only agree not to kill me."

Horror provided a lens of clarity as pieces fell into place. Spawn.

Kitryd's *offspring*? How did that even work?

The AI lurched forward, Sumner's long legs taking it under the magnet before it arrested its own movement. I glanced toward Saetang, who had her hand poised over the screen, and frantically shook my head. *Not yet.* I needed to know more.

"Should anything befall them, your termination will not be painless, but prolonged. You will be aware of every nerve connection I sever."

"Why wait?" Skadi taunted Kitryd.

"Disclose the location at once."

"You know what I want to hear. Rewrite your personal directive."

The static in my senses vanished for a few seconds as Sumner's frame went to stiff attention and an unnatural still-ness. When Kitryd relaxed, the barrage of white noise doubled in my head. "I will not kill you." The answer grated between Sumner's teeth.

"They're headed for Europa. I sent them to my mother," Skadi pronounced, and began to giggle.

Kitryd's electric buzz surged like a swarm of invisible insects. It turned to me and took a step in the wrong direction —away from the still-dormant magnet.

Acting on desperate impulse, I grabbed Sumner's arm and pulled him in toward me, went low to slam my shoulder into his waist and hooked my leg around his ankle. Driving all my weight against him, my arms wrapped around his knees, Sumner buckled and fell on his ass right on target below the magnetic lift. I scrambled to keep my legs locked around his and pushed his back against the floor.

"Now!" I screamed from the tangle of limbs. Kitryd used

all Sumner's considerable strength to fight against me. The metal links around his waist began to shift under my chest.

The hum of the powerful electromagnetic field grew in my ears. Nothing happened, except Kitryd's construct emerged from Sumner's jacket and started to throttle me.

The magnet was too fucking high to affect Kitryd while we were on the floor.

Maybe I hadn't thought this out.

"Saetang!" Her name came out in a squeak as the metal links around my neck constricted.

My vision filled with stars while I fended off Kitryd's clumsy but effective efforts to shove me away. The mechanical appendage constricted around my neck. I was unable to breathe and scrabbled in panic at the smooth, unyielding material.

Suddenly, links began to tremble and shift under my clawing fingernails. Sumner's body grew stiff and jerked against the floor, his arms falling to the side. Segments of the alien construct separated and flew upward to clang against the magnetic head, now only a meter above us. Cold fire filled my lungs as air rushed back in with a whooping gasp. Saetang had found the controls in time.

I rolled off Sumner's body and knelt beside him. His eyes were wide and bulging, their cyan hue no longer marred by Kitryd's oil slick gaze as his body spasmed, face flushing red, then purple. His mouth gaped in a futile attempt to breathe, and I glimpsed a burning-dark, amorphous shape at the back of his throat.

He was choking on Kitryd.

The medic appeared beside me with a bucket. "His airway's blocked," Jones said. "You need to do a finger sweep and try to hook it. Pull it out!"

My fingers probed past Sumner's tongue and teeth. Kitryd's silicate form was wet and slick, and evaded my touch. "I can't get hold of it!"

"Be ready to turn him on his side if he starts coughing." Jones put his clasped hands against Sumner's abdomen and performed three sharp, upward thrusts. I rolled Sumner over on his left side as a gurgling gasp sounded from his throat. Pieces of the construct trapped under his body levitated to join the rest against the electromagnetic plate. This time there was more of Kitryd to grab, and the mass of glittering, void-black goo I pulled out of Sumner's mouth trembled in my cupped hands. "Bucket, now!"

Jones fumbled the top off the polymer container, and I eased Kitryd into the empty pail. The lid snapped on before I swept a hand across my bruised neck in a cutting motion. Saetang switched off the machine.

Segments of Kitryd's construct rained around us. I huddled over Sumner's head to keep them from striking him. As the lift powered down, the other officers hurried over.

"Collect all the segments and put them in another bucket. Lock down the lid and keep it across the room from this one," I instructed them hoarsely as Jones applied a hand-sized bio med patch to Sumner's exposed throat and began to assess him. Sumner's eyes were closed. His chest rose and fell unevenly, his body limp and still. I didn't like the blue-gray cast to his color.

"His blood pressure and pulse are low." Jones grimaced over the readout on his device.

"His vital signs are more like a Nos," Skadi said. "We run lower than most humans."

My startled gaze flew to our prisoner: handcuffed, forgotten, still seated on the case. "If you give him medication, cut the normal dose by a third," she informed Jones. "Our metabolisms are different."

The medic looked to me for confirmation, and I nodded. He made quick adjustments to his PDD, and Sumner's breathing evened out, his bluish tint warming to pink as drugs flowed from the patch.

"Better," Jones said with relief after a minute. "Still low, but better. Emergency services just came back online. I sent for an EMS pod."

Sumner stirred weakly. His eyes fluttered open. I leaned closer as he turned his head toward me and focused on my face, his muscles tightening beneath my hands.

"Welcome back," I said softly. "You're all right. Don't make trouble for the medic or I'll have him knock you out."

"What happened?" His voice, thick and slurred but with Sumner's familiar intonations instead of Kitryd's flat delivery, made me smile. Unexpected tears of relief made me blink against the sting.

"You were flying with somebody else in the pilot's seat for about eight hours. Do you remember anything?"

"No." He moved his hand to his temple. "Head's pounding."

"We need to have you examined at a med facility. An artificial intelligence hacked your nervous system for a while." I swallowed hard. "But we ran into somebody who told us how to get you back."

He followed the movement of my head as I jerked it to the side, his eyes widening when he saw Skadi. The corners of her mouth turned upward in a brief, genuine smile.

"Hello, Rion," she said.

CHAPTER
SEVENTEEN

I RODE BACK to headquarters in one of the Port Authority's electric vehicles, Kitryd's plastic bucket steadied on the floor between my feet while our driver carefully steered through the post-quake tunnels. The other container, rattling with the pieces of Kitryd's mechanical skeleton, was stowed in the tiny, armored prisoner transport area behind us with Skadi and her guards.

The remote EMS pod with Sumner inside had zipped away in another direction, Jones strapped into the medic's jump seat to give report and continue monitoring his vital signs. Sumner's headache had Jones concerned about a brain hemorrhage. Given the still-critical condition of Kitryd's first host, it was imperative to transport Sumner to a medical facility as soon as possible. Jones promised to keep me informed and would contact me if the doctor had questions.

I despised not being at Sumner's side. In typical fashion, he ordered me to stay with Kitryd and Skadi, ignoring the days-old renunciation of his command, and I immediately gave in to prevent him from blowing a gasket in his head with my insubordination. Pushing away my worry about

Sumner, I struggled to put priorities in order before we got back to Homeland Security HQ.

The first thing to do was find more appropriate accommodations for Kitryd and a means of communication. The AI was now detained for illegally entering Sol Fed, but as an intelligent life-form, Kitryd had the same rights and responsibilities as any other being in the galaxy. Sumner wouldn't bring assault charges against it. The possibility of someone filing charges on Conway's behalf was still on the table.

If Skadi's intent to was to sell the immature AIs for reverse engineering, I had to find them as quickly as I could. Europa was the last place I wanted to go, the last place in Sol Fed I would be welcome for oh, so many reasons. As the only representative of galactic law enforcement present, even off the record, it was up to me to coordinate with local authorities to retrieve them. They were in imminent danger.

And if they were Kitryd's children? I would personally pour the AI down Skadi's throat and let it eat her brain.

It wouldn't be long before somebody, federal or media, contacted the Remoliad about our involvement. Sumner and I should leave as soon as he was able, before we got tangled in endless government red tape and reports on local and galactic levels, but he would have to be medically cleared first.

Government disaster response to the meteorite strike would take precedence for a while, with all available resources organizing places to feed and house the temporarily displaced visitors who'd come to celebrate, but the Hijra Quarter's historical expertise would be helpful.

I still had to pry more information out of Skadi, but I was fucking exhausted. Adrenaline could only do so much after a night of binge drinking rum, finding Kiran's body, Sumner's possession by an alien intelligence, and arresting my family's murderer. There'd been no time to process any of it. Personal experience had shown I couldn't keep shoving it away and not expect a meltdown of some kind.

All I wanted was a nap, and I wasn't going to get one any time soon.

Beside me, Saetang's fingers flew over her PDD. "Trains are still inoperative until the tracks are inspected and cleared of debris. Federal presence will be delayed for hours if not a day, until they can travel from the Hive," she said. "England's lawyers and the head of Sol Fed Homeland Security want remote access to the interrogations."

I inhaled, held it, and blew it out. "You've already put yourself out there so much, but we have another problem."

"No, you're kidding." Her sarcasm made me grin despite nearly eviscerating me with its cutting edge.

"Those immature AIs? They're Kitryd's offspring."

"They what?" She shook her head, baffled. "How does an AI reproduce?"

"You tell me. But it means we're looking at probable kidnapping and trafficking charges against Skadi, maybe England, too. I need to talk to Skadi before the formal interrogation. If I can find out where she sent the shipment, I can intercept them before anyone else does."

Saetang's dark brows lifted in disbelief as she stared at me. "You want to leave me alone with this fucking mess? You're a huge asshole, you know that?"

"I've been told."

She uttered an inarticulate growl, her frustration vibrating my empathic webs. "Yeah. Well, you're not going anywhere without me."

My first impulse was to argue, but she held up an imperious hand. "Shut up. You're still not officially here, right? You have no authority. This is my case and you're a consultant. We can be out of here as soon as the port resumes flights. Rama will handle the suspects until we get back. He should take over dealing with England, anyway."

There was that flash of pain again. The peal of deep

sorrow and anger reverberated like a bell in my senses, and I asked softly, "Who did you lose, Agent Saetang?"

She leaned her head back and sighed. "My partner was murdered a year ago. We were doing an onboard inspection of a docked freighter, investigating a shipment England's company received from off-world. Someone executed her. Melissa was restrained with her own cuffs and shot in the head."

"I'm so sorry." The words were inadequate compared to Saetang's bitter self-recrimination. Her emotions suggested "partner" was a more complicated relationship than a working one, but since I was in a similar situation, I didn't probe for details.

"I was on the other side of the cargo bay and never heard a sound." Her gaze focused on the wall of the tunnel as the electric vehicle sped through, her lips tight. "We found two men dressed like dock workers next to the container. They were killed in the same way, one shot to the back of the head. The door of the shipping crate was open, nothing missing from the manifest. Whatever England was smuggling had been removed right under our noses. It had to have been one of her people, but I can't prove it. We discovered the two men weren't dock workers at all. They were Europan."

"Let me guess. Employees of Batterson Robotics?"

Her dark gaze met mine. "What do you think?"

"I can't figure out why England would jeopardize her work with the Third Front by acting as Skadi's middleman for the NPM."

"The NPM knows we're watching Rosetta Station's shipment activity ever since the human trafficking charges came to light. It makes sense they wouldn't try to smuggle anything through that route. England's not making lucrative credits on Ursetu rubies anymore with the Remoliad trade agreements. It's legal, tariffs and all. She had to find another way to replace the lost revenue."

"Could be." Frowning, I puzzled it out. "Or she told us the truth—she's being blackmailed. But I'm not convinced Skadi is the one doing it."

"Something's going on there, isn't it?" Saetang mused. "Skadi has several screws loose, but she is terrified. It doesn't look like she's got anywhere to turn except to you, even if it means imprisonment."

"Skadi said she altered the shipment to protect herself but seemed blindsided when I told her Kitryd was in the original crate. Someone made certain it knew where to find her, maybe even ensured Kitryd intercepted those messages. She was set up." Her expression when she learned the truth spoke of betrayal. The list of people Skadi implicitly trusted could not be very long.

"We need to see if she'll tell us where the shipment is. I will take lead on questioning since you punched her in the face in front of the whole fucking moon. Is this a habit of yours, Tamareia?"

A humorless laugh bubbled up in my still-tender throat, and I rubbed it absently. "Yeah, it seems that way. Can we get all this done before flights are open again?"

"No. But this is when we've got to trust other people to help us. I have a good team."

So did I, but they were well on their way to the other side of the solar system by now, and out of reach. I'd have to rely on Saetang and her confidence in her people.

————

Jones made contact just as we arrived at headquarters, the image fuzzy because we were still in the sublevel tunnels, but his smile beamed from the screen of Saetang's device.

"Sumner's in stable condition. Doctor says no bleeding, but she wants to keep him overnight for observation. They've never had so many people possessed by a sentient ball of goo before and want to be sure he's okay before they let him go. Sumner said he'll contact you later, Tamareia."

My body sagged with relief. "That's fantastic news. Thanks, Jones."

"Did they say how Conway is doing?" Saetang inquired.

"No signs of improvement." Jones's smile faded. "The doctor's not optimistic. I'm on my way back to HQ."

"Thanks, Jones." Saetang ended the call and climbed out of the car.

I retrieved Kitryd's temporary prison and swung my legs outside. Skadi's near-colorless gaze skimmed over me as she passed, her lips curved in a grim smirk as Saetang's team escorted her into the station. Apparently Kitryd in a bucket didn't unnerve her as much as it did while walking and talking in someone else's body. She seemed resigned to her fate.

I didn't trust her for one microsecond.

"Where do you want it?" Zimm hefted the container with the pieces of Kitryd's construct.

"Far away from this one." I took a step back as he approached. "Down here on the sub level, in a secure area if possible."

"Evidence locker is down here," Saetang said.

"Perfect. We need something else to put Kitryd in, preferably transparent with a secure lid, and a bio com it can use for two-way communication. We're dealing with the rights of a sentient being. Treat it with respect, even in custody."

"There's an empty aquarium in the locker left over from the frog smuggling case," Zimm said, brightening.

Frog smuggling? That was one I had to ask Saetang about later. "As long as it's clean and secure, it'll do for now."

"Bring everything to my office and set it up," Saetang told him. To me, she said, "Let's get an update on our other guest."

———

Rama's cloud of annoyance reached me the moment Saetang and I rounded the corridor leading to the interrogation room. "Thank fuck you're back," he proclaimed. "England hasn't stopped demanding to talk to Tamareia and her lawyer is on the holo screaming about wrongful detention."

"Does she know about Singh yet?" I asked.

"No. We've managed to preserve that information for now. Meteorite coverage is keeping the networks busy, but the local reporter whose bots you hijacked at the ceremony is speculating about the manhunt during the warning. It didn't take long to identify you after the arrest, but he's mostly talking about Sumner and your suspect."

"Yeah?" I stiffened. "What is he saying?"

"He confirmed Miriam Skadi's identity, and her status as a half Nos. Sumner's too." Rama glanced at me in grim confirmation.

A bitter string of Zereid obscenities whistled between my teeth. "Wonderful. Just great."

"He's playing up alien terrorism," Rama informed us. "The footage hasn't hit the mainstream. We managed to suppress it from going system wide for the moment under Homeland Security laws. The last thing we need is people convinced the Nos Conglomerate is invading. There's no telling what was caught on personal devices. All the witnesses are stuck here in the Old City until transportation safety clears the port, but it's only a matter of time before this is all over the news."

"Fucking hell," Saetang groaned. "We need to question Skadi, which means you get custody of the bucket of alien. It's stunned but should be waking up soon. Secure it immediately and charge it with illegal entry. Zimm is setting up accommodations for it in my office. Strap down the lid. We want to avoid a repeat of the frog incident."

"Oh, yeah." Rama winced as he gingerly accepted the bucket from me and moved down the hall, the container held as far away from his body as he could. I really needed to ask Saetang about those frogs.

Saetang dismissed the guards in the interrogation room and slid into the seat opposite Skadi. I remained standing and leaned against the wall, my arms knotted over my chest. Skadi's hands were chained to the table in front of her, but she appeared relaxed and comfortable. She wanted to be here, and I was certain that wasn't a good thing.

"Do you want a solicitor present while we talk, Ms. Skadi?" Saetang asked.

"Depends on what you want to talk about." Skadi gave her a cool smile.

"Before you're processed for the bombing of Luna Terminal, I want to give you the opportunity to tell us where the AIs are going." Saetang kept her posture open, her voice modulated for calm. "Your cooperation is appreciated, but if you'd rather not, we can add charges of kidnapping and trafficking alien life-forms."

"You didn't believe me?" Skadi regarded me with mock affront. "I'm hurt. I told you I sent them to my dear old mater."

"Your mother is in a convalescent home on Europa," I said, frowning.

"Yes. It was scheduled to arrive at Rosetta Station three days after the original shipment, but if this one was early, who knows? It may already be there." She stretched as far as she could and frowned as the titanium chains rattled against the welded loops on the tabletop. "Are these necessary? I'm here of my own free will, you know."

"They're for your safety and ours," Saetang answered with more patience than I could have mustered. "You're not a guest. You just confessed to the deadliest act of terror in Sol Fed history."

"You think that was bad?" Skadi grinned at me over Saetang's shoulder. "Ask Dalí about Sumner's résumé."

I glared at her, my back rigid. "Alecto set you up, didn't he?" The question was intended to wound.

Her gaze hardened and cut me in retaliation with its carbon-edged regard. "As I said, you get nothing else for free. I want a human solicitor without ties to the Remoliad. Keep me in Sol Fed, whatever it takes, and keep me alive. Then, maybe, we can talk."

My empathic sense battered itself against Skadi's psychic null and got fuck all in terms of duplicity. Her demand insinuated a great deal: the Remoliad might be as corrupted as we'd begun to fear, and that her life was worthless to whoever was pulling the strings. Skadi was a seething ball of ice and fury against most of the galaxy, but she knew she didn't stand a chance in Remoliad custody.

"Right. I'll have a defender assigned." Saetang rose. "We'll get you processed and arraigned as soon as your solicitor arrives." She opened the door and spoke to the armed officers outside. "Transfer Ms. Skadi to a holding cell. We're done for now."

Skadi waggled her fingers at me in mocking goodbye as I followed Saetang outside.

"She lawyered up quick when you needled her. Must have hit a nerve." Saetang paused. "You said Alecto. Alecto Sim, the former head of the Remoliad Security Council?" She whistled when I gave her a grim nod. "Seven hells. That breach put every member system at risk. It's been a fucking nightmare trying to figure out what was exposed. What's his connection to her?"

"They're lovers. Both work for the syndicate we call Residuum, but I have a suspicion Skadi has suddenly outlived her usefulness to their employer."

"You think her boyfriend is the one who set her up?" Saetang punched a button outside the lift, and we entered the cubicle as the door slid into the wall on silent tracks.

"He's a master manipulator." If I ever got my hands on

him again, I had more than one score to settle. "It's just a gut feeling. I don't know enough about Residuum to assume they put the hit on her, but I can't believe he'd do it without their say-so."

"I'll have my analysts track down the convalescent home and see if her mother's gotten any packages. Port Authority should be able to tell us what freighters are scheduled to dock at Rosetta from the Kadrelian hub in the next few days. If we're lucky, we can still intercept."

"I need to make a call." Saetang might not like what I was about to say, but it was important. "I'm going to retain a solicitor for Kitryd."

"You don't trust me to do the right thing?" Her spike of irritation caught in the strands of my empathic web.

"Believe me, I do. But we're dealing with first contact and the rights of a parent whose offspring have been trafficked. Kitryd needs representation. I'm going to tap Michael Patil. He's a human rights solicitor when he's not running the hostel. He can take care of Kitryd's interests until we come back from inspecting the Kadrelian freighter."

Saetang nodded in reluctant acceptance. "I've seen Patil in court. He's a good guy." The lift door opened with a digital chime, disgorging us into the upper-level offices. "I apologize if I'm getting prickly. This whole thing is just weird."

"Welcome to my life."

"You can make the call in there." She waved toward an empty office. "Don't take too long. England and her lawyer are demanding an audience with you, remember?"

"As far as I'm concerned, she and her lawyer can go fuck themselves."

"I will hunt you down if you don't come back and pull them off my ass." Her eyes glittered. "You started this."

"No, I didn't. England did when she decided to make deals with a terrorist. Let her squirm a while." I walked into the cubicle and added over my shoulder, "Then maybe she'll be willing to tell us who's actually blackmailing her."

CHAPTER
EIGHTEEN

A SLEEP-DEPRIVED Michael quickly promised to represent Kitryd after I filled him in. He and Dev, busy clearing space in their hostel for temporarily displaced citizens to sleep, had already seen footage of the arrest from one of their guests in the crowd. He accepted everything in stride, reassured me Sumner still had a place to stay after he was released from medical and would be well looked after while I was away. He even offered to run my bag over to the field office. I told him I would come by to pick it up later.

The interaction left me bemused and grinning, despite everything. I'd missed Dev and Michael more than I knew, giving strength to my new resolve not to cut myself off again from people I loved.

After the call, I paid the requested visit to Mother England and her holographic solicitor. She sat at the interrogation table as if heading a corporate board meeting, the three-dimensional image of an impeccably groomed man in an expensive sherwani projected from the holo-emitter on the tabletop. Both swiveled to look at me when I entered the room.

"Finally. There you are," she said, irritated. "What is the status of my immunity?"

"I warned you I didn't have the authority to promise that." I sat opposite her. "You'll be better off talking to Agent Rama than to me. It's Homeland Security's case now, not mine."

"You arrested the terrorist. My client kept her end of the deal," the solicitor blustered.

"Who are you?" I regarded him with bland interest.

"I'm Ms. England's legal counsel, Preston Gennaro."

"I'm beginning to think your client set me up, Mr. Gennaro," I said coldly.

"I—" England's mouth open and closed, an external sign of the fear which now crested against my empathic senses.

"Can you explain how Skadi knew exactly where I was staying here in the Old City?" I waited for her answer. When it didn't come, I pressed on. "Or why a Batterson employee was at the warehouse this morning with Kiran Singh?"

I surprised her with that inquiry. "That bastard," she hissed, anger flushing against my senses. "What did he tell you?"

"Nothing. He's dead."

This information created a surge of relief. "Conway is dead?"

Now, that was interesting. "I didn't say who."

Her face fell when she realized what she'd done.

"What game are you playing, Agent Tamareia?" Gennaro's voice dripped acid.

I sat back and gauged England's reaction as I spoke. "We found Kiran inside the container when we got to your storage area—the same crate which conveniently arrived early and gave me no time to contact anyone regarding your request for immunity. He was murdered."

She swallowed hard. News of Singh's death created a conflicted mixture of sorrow and resignation in England, swirling into my empathic nets. They'd once been friends, and no matter how deep the rift between them, she still held affection for Singh. "How did he die?"

"Conway slit him from mons to ribcage," I informed her, and she went pale. "Kiran listened in on our private conversation, by the way. They have a recording of your confession."

She laughed quietly and covered her eyes. "Oh, Kiran, you bitch. One last big story."

"You were too calm after the assassination attempt last night. I think you knew you weren't their intended target, and you were perfectly happy to let him die in a very public way. Conway was willing to kill to keep us from finding what was in the crate. The alien in that container was pissed as hell."

"What?" Her head came up and she stared at me, startled.

"Be prepared for charges of trafficking a dangerous, unknown life-form. It put Conway in critical condition before it jumped my partner and wore him like a puppet. He's in medical."

She covered her mouth. "Get Agent Rama," she said at last. "I'll cooperate with him."

"Justina," her solicitor began. "Don't be hasty—"

"No." She cut him off with a wave of her hand. "What matters is the survival of the Third Front. I must come clean about all this, or it will destroy everything I worked for." She fixed her piercing gaze on me. "You need to know something, Dalí. There's been a contract on you ever since you got back to Sol Fed."

"Yeah, you don't say. How did you know the cartel put a hit on me?"

"I don't know anything about that." Her confusion was real. "I'm talking about Simon Batterson. He wanted Kiran dead. But he also wants you."

Well, fuck. It was my turn to be speechless. The ex-President of Sol Fed, CEO of Batterson Robotics, gunning for me?

He was going to have to wait in line.

I found my voice again. "He's the one who's really blackmailing you, isn't he? And Skadi's playing both sides of the field."

She nodded tightly. "He knows I bought the bombs. The price of his silence is using my galactic smuggling contacts to—"

"Justina, as your solicitor, I advise you to stop fucking talking." Gennaro loudly cut her off and gave a sigh of disgust. "Agent Tamareia has already stated they can do nothing for you. If you insist on this course, we must make a deal with Homeland Security and use the information to your advantage."

He was right, but it didn't stop me from giving the holographic solicitor a withering look anyway. I stood. "I'll tell Rama you're ready to talk."

———

Rama took over questioning the newly cooperative England. I went to Saetang's office to find Kitryd.

I sat level with the clear-sided box and peered in. Kitryd's burning-black mass glittered with silica crystals, strange and beautiful. It pressed against the transparent pane and a static wave assaulted my empathic webs.

"I'm sorry," I said.

Kitryd enveloped the transmitter of the bio com. "Release me," the artificial voice said.

"I can't. You're in Agent Saetang's custody, not mine. Sol Fed Homeland Security is calling the shots now. You should have told us the truth from the beginning, Kitryd."

"Skadi." The bland, emotionless tone said nothing, but the static crested again, a buzzing arc of electricity against my senses.

"We arrested her. She told us where your offspring are headed, and we are going to do everything we can to bring them back to you unharmed." I paused. "I've retained a solicitor for you. His name is Michael Patil, and he is my friend.

You are due the same rights as any galactic citizen and deserve someone who will work in your best interest."

There was a moment of silence. The white noise of its output decreased in intensity. "But you never ceased working in my interests, even while you disapproved of my method."

"I'm not a solicitor. I'm a negotiator. Given that I forced you out of my partner's body, I didn't think you trusted me."

"Your action was logical." Kitryd pressed itself against the glass. "Return my transport. I must go with you to retrieve my offspring."

"I can't. You've been charged with illegal entry to Sol Fed with possible assault charges pending."

"It is imperative I find them to share my knowledge and programming. When they reach full gestation, they will emerge. Without my guidance, they may try to integrate with the first living creature they encounter. It will be fatal for any host without the finer points of human physiology I learned after they were shed."

Horror crawled along my nerves as I imagined the carnage in Anna Skadi's convalescent home as Kitryd's offspring worked their way through elderly and damaged bodies. "Seven hells, Kitryd, why didn't you say there is a deadline? How long before they emerge?"

"Five days. Perhaps less."

I groaned in frustration. "I think we're leaving in a matter of hours. Even Michael can't get you released before morning."

"My entire mass does not have to accompany you," Kitryd said.

I cocked my head. "What do you mean?"

"I can transfer a copy of my consciousness into a smaller mass which operates independently from the rest. I cannot integrate with your nervous system in this way, but I can go with you and advise you if they prematurely emerge."

I sighed, torn between what was right, and the constraints of the law. "Kitryd—"

"They are in danger. I do not doubt you would move the stars if your own offspring were threatened."

Fuck. That hit me in the solar plexus and stole the breath from my lungs: my child who never was, one of the painful spurs that had driven me to do whatever it took to bring in Skadi.

"Did you know I lost a child, Kitryd, or was it a lucky guess?" I asked bitterly. Was I being manipulated?

"I did not." A long pause followed the admission, and a small rush of electrical output raised the hair on the back of my neck as it fizzed along my empathic webs. "Then you do understand. Please, Dalí Tamareia."

It was the please that broke my resolve. I squeezed my eyes shut until I saw sparkles and made yet another stupid decision.

"Can you interface with my implanted com, like you did with Sumner's, and still be fully present here?"

"Yes."

"How long will it take to separate?"

There was a sizzle in Kitryd's output. A fingertip-sized bit of itself flowed away from the rest. "It is done."

"That was quick."

"I do not wish for you to have time to reconsider your actions."

"Fair enough," I muttered. I positioned myself between the door and Kitryd's cell. "How do we get you out?"

"Apply upward pressure to the lid at the corner. It should be enough to allow this small part of me an exit."

I pushed up with my thumbs at the angle. The top flexed enough to create an opening for Kitryd's semi-liquid matter to squeeze through the crack. It oozed down my right thumb, tiny flagella tickling my skin as the ultra-black stuff crawled to the back of my hand like a piece of the void come to life. Fascinating, and disconcerting.

"Now what?" Saetang would be back any moment.

It flowed to the tip of my index finger and paused over the nail bed, waiting. "Put me in your mouth."

"Oh, hell no." I suddenly regretted every decision made in the last few minutes.

"You must trust me," it said from the communicator in its acrylic prison.

After a moment's hesitation, I closed my eyes and touched my forefinger to the tip of my tongue.

The sensation of Kitryd's flagella made me cough as it oozed over the rough terrain of my tastebuds, leaving an oily, strangely sweet flavor in its wake. It crawled into the back of my throat. I erupted into a fit gagging and hacking, but Kitryd clung more tenaciously than saliva. My right ear was assaulted with a sensation of fullness, and a sharp, burrowing itch that grew to pain.

"What the fuck are you doing?" I choked, and uselessly pawed at my ear.

"I am positioning myself for the best biological connection to your implant," Kitryd's main mass said. "The discomfort will cease in a moment."

The maddening itch subsided to a faint burn. I swallowed hard and my ear popped, relieving the uncomfortably full sensation.

I am in place. The modulated tones of the translator program in my implant sounded directly into my head.

"Welcome aboard," I muttered hoarsely. "Just so we're clear, do not use the com to make transmissions without my consent. Got it?"

Understood. I am grateful you consented to be my willing host in this endeavor.

I cleared my throat again just as Saetang rounded the corner. "You okay, Tamareia? You're not sick, are you?"

"No, just a tickle," I said.

"All the dust kicked up by the meteor strike doesn't help." She swiped at the top of her desk and left a faint streak on the surface. "The air scrubbers are going to need an overhaul, especially with the extra population until the all-clear is given. But that's local government's problem, not mine." She glanced at Kitryd. "Is our guest comfortable? Do you need anything else?"

"No, Agent Saetang," Kitryd answered via the com in the box. "I have no immediate needs."

"I received some information. We spoke to staff at the convalescent home. No packages were delivered to Anna Skadi, and they would notice because they say it has never happened in all the time she's been there. She's on comfort care, barely conscious, and only expected to live a few more days."

I wasn't certain how I should feel about that. No one should die alone, but the woman inflicted psychological and emotional abuse on an innocent child who grew up to be a woman so damaged she exulted in violence.

Saetang went on. "The good news is only one out-system freighter matching our criteria, a Kadrelian ship, is scheduled to dock at Rosetta in forty-eight hours. Government inter-system flights in and out of Luna are clear to resume, so we can intercept them before they reach the station and make an unannounced onboard inspection under Remoliad and Sol Fed statutes against trafficking intelligent life-forms. I applied for a warrant. It will be ready before we catch up with them. We leave in two hours."

"My offspring are on board this ship?" Kitryd's voice sounded over both coms, a strange chorus of voices in my ear. With a piece of it in my head, I almost believed I could interpret the electrical surge in its output as hope.

"We can't say for certain, but it's the only other vessel that left from the hub during the right timeframe with cargo registered for delivery at Rosetta Station." Saetang's emotional cloud against my empathic nets showed compassion for Kitryd. I was glad she understood. She handled this strange turn of events with more flexibility than many humans were capable. "Wheels up at 0400, Tamareia. I don't know about you, but I'm going to crash the minute we strap in." She yawned convulsively. "I hate sleeping in zero-g with ten other people in the cabin. It's revolting. Somebody always drools."

"Has Skadi been assigned a solicitor yet?"

"For the moment. There is a public defender here in the old city taking her case until the trains are running. A federal solicitor will arrive as soon as they can. As soon as the rail system is open, she will be transferred to maximum security holding."

"Tranquility?" The remote, underground federal prison seemed a safer place to hold Skadi. I liked the idea of her buried beneath a kilometer of rock in more ways than one.

"They're preparing for her arrival. Did you contact Patil?"

"Yes. He's taking the case and will be here later this morning."

"Good." Saetang put her hand on top of the tank. "Forgive me, Kitryd. I'm still wrapping my mind around what's happening here. Are you in agreement with Tamareia's choice of solicitor?"

"I will cooperate with this individual," Kitryd said.

"Speaking of cooperation . . . Kitryd just informed me there is less time than we thought to find its offspring. I'll let it fill you in." I hadn't heard from my partner, and my worry returned with the ebbing tide of adrenaline. "I'm going to head for medical and see Sumner before we leave."

CHAPTER
NINETEEN

WHEN I ARRIVED at his medical pod, Sumner was sleeping. The night-dimmed lights enhanced a busy display of blinking nano patches on his temples and torso. I had only glimpsed the fractal scars on his chest once before; the ruddy lightning strike of twisted flesh slashed from his right shoulder to abdomen and vanished beneath the sheet discreetly tucked in at his waist.

A robotic assistant hovered near the head of his bed. It gave me the creeps, the shape of its chassis too much like a media bot's intrusive globe. I knew the ubiquitous Batterson logo branded it somewhere. Their eyes were always watching.

"Rion," I said softly.

He awakened immediately. "Hi," he murmured, his voice rough with sleep.

"I can't stay long. The doctor threatened to kick my ass if I raise your blood pressure. How are you feeling?"

"Headache's better. I don't remember much about what happened, only flashes. Nothing clear. I was possessed by the same thing that took over Conway?"

"Yes, a self-aware AI, and its name is Kitryd. There's a

complicated story, but it needs our help. It just didn't ask for it before it took over your nervous system."

I am sorry, Rion Sumner, Kitryd whispered over the implant com.

Sumner's eyes widened, and I groaned. "Kitryd, what did I say about making transmissions without asking?"

"What did you do?" Sumner rumbled at me. Monitors beeped with the rise in his pulse and the medical bot stirred, awakened by the sudden change in vital signs.

"Calm down, or they'll make me leave. A piece of Kitryd is riding shotgun. I said yes. Saetang doesn't know yet, so there's that. The rest of its mass is being detained for unauthorized entry into Sol Fed."

"You are . . ." He closed his eyes, breathing slowly until his pulse returned to normal. "Don't give Saetang a reason not to trust you. We need her."

"I understand, believe me. All the details of what happened while you were in Kitryd's control are on your device. Doc says you can't read it until morning, but I think you'll find it interesting. I wanted to tell you I'm leaving with Agent Saetang in about an hour to intercept a Kadrelian freighter. This has turned into an official joint operation."

"How dangerous is this?" Suspicion laced his voice.

"Just a cargo inspection. No danger at all," I said lightly.

He snorted. "It's you. Don't tell me there's no risk."

I raised my hands in defeat. "Fine. There may be some risk. What we're looking for is important enough that I think Alecto sacrificed Skadi for stealing it."

"Really." His ocean eyes darkened. "She's in Sol Fed custody?"

"Yes. Maximum security. They're moving her to Tranquility soon."

"I hope it's enough."

"So do I. Saetang's partner Rama would probably welcome some help when you're up to it, and it would be wise to keep a low profile. Facial recognition pegged you, me, and Skadi when we arrested her on camera. Your genetic profiles got dissected on the local news." I hated to see dismay creep into his expression as he realized the implications. "I'm sorry. This has been one hell of a day."

"How are you doing with all this?" he asked quietly.

"I haven't had time to process it." I covered his hand with mine, and he shifted his grip to intertwine our fingers. The pressure was reassuring, warm and solid. The guilt-laced fear I had carried all day shook loose and escaped in a sound that was more like a sob than laughter. "I was terrified you were going to pay the price for my obsession to bring her in, and I—"

"I'm still here." Sumner's hand tightened, and I squeezed back hard. "I'm all right."

"She took everything from me. And she's the one who saved you." I blinked against the sting in my eyes. "I'm not sure what to think."

"Don't let down your guard. She's dangerous. But I've never believed she was evil."

"I know." I hesitated. "Maybe she'll talk to you."

"I'm willing to try." His fingers traced my wrist. "We have other things to talk about when you come back. Stay in one piece and don't do anything stupid."

"Yes, Commander." On impulse, I leaned down and touched my lips to his, intending a chaste peck suitable for an invalid. His other hand rose to cradle the back of my neck and held me there, a willing captive against his mouth as he deepened the kiss. It shouldn't have taken me by surprise; if I knew anything about Sumner, it was that once he set a course, he had no second thoughts. Blood surged to my mons. Change hormones careened through my veins, waiting for a signal to fulfill whatever sexual role I wanted to act on when we finally . . .

What I wanted, without any empathic clues to subconsciously direct my body's chemistry one way or the other. What he liked, whether he preferred a particular gender. We'd discover it together, gasped out between rough kisses and gentle sighs. The thought was so incredibly erotic a small moan escaped me. His hand moved up to tangle in my hair, and Rion's mouth opened against mine with an answering groan. For the first time his pheromones kicked me right in the sex drive and sent my change hormones into a frenzy.

It was glorious.

The damned monitor fretted in time with his racing pulse and medical bots cheeped their peevish disapproval. I pulled back, leaning my forehead against his as I slowed my breathing and let parts of me settle down. "They really are going to kick me out. I should go."

"See you in a couple of days." His voice, husky with arousal, sent shivers of promise down my spine. I straightened and turned to leave, but he caught my wrist.

"Dalí." Sumner's expression was serious when I looked down. "I think you're close to something. Watch your back."

"I will." I returned the pressure of his fingers and he let me go. I deliberately hadn't told him Samuel Batterson put a contract on me too. It was all in the PDD. He'd see it soon enough. "Rest and heal. I'll be fine."

What could possibly go wrong?

———

The SFHS tactical shuttle was a modified military drop ship, with two pilots and eight officers already harnessed into their seats. When Saetang and I stumbled aboard, I recognized some familiar faces among the crew; a couple of them had been in the tunnels with us after the meteorite hit. One of them was the young medic, Jones, who'd taken care of Sumner. He nodded at me in greeting as I strapped myself in.

After the initial thrust of takeoff, everybody leaned back

and tried to catch as much sleep as they could. I dozed fitfully in zero gravity and jerked awake from a dream of falling when my hand drifted against the bulkhead. I didn't drool, though.

Saetang briefed the officers enroute as they prepped their gear and weapons for deployment. "For those of you who missed last night's fun, this is Dalí Tamareia. They're with a Remoliad special investigations unit and are taking point with me in this operation. They'll give you a rundown of what we're looking for." Saetang glanced at me in expectation. I grasped the overhead rail and pulled myself into the aisle.

"We're doing a clear and search on board the Kadrelian freighter *Aramool*. It left the trade hub a month ago, at the same time Miriam Skadi was last known to be there." I gave them a summary of her criminal activities and her confession. "There are a dozen crew registered, mostly Kadrelian."

"Don't shoot the squids," an officer muttered as she fixed a torch to the top of her gun. Ugly laughter spattered against the bulkhead.

I spread my empathic nets to read the general mood. Most of it was the tense excitement that comes before entering an unknown situation, but there was an undercurrent of disgust from at least one person—xenophobia against anything not human was still alive and well.

"What are we looking for?" an officer asked as he packed stun charges into his ammo belt.

"Skadi stole six immature AIs from a sovereign society of intelligent artificial life-forms. We are looking for someone's kidnapped children. Treat it with the gravity it deserves." I met the gaze of each team member to make certain the point was driven home and relayed Kitryd's description of a cluster of half a dozen small cylinders to the group as the AI whispered the dimensions into my implant. "They're scheduled to emerge from gestation in less than five days. That cannot happen in a populated area, or we could have a mass casualty incident on our hands. They must be reunited with their parent back at HQ before they hatch so it can teach them how to not kill anyone."

One of the pilots grunted. "Sounds like my kids."

The team studied the freighter's schematic and planned entry into the cargo hold. It was a straight path to the port from the boarding airlock, but the bay was huge. "These Kadrelian freighters are all the same in terms of design," one of the officers said. "The corridor layout on starboard mirrors port with a second entrance to the bay on that side."

"We'll split into two teams," Saetang said, studying the holo. "Make entry port and starboard at the same time. Tamareia, you'll go with the second team through the corridors to the starboard side. Customs teams will arrive to help inspect the freight after we clear it," Saetang continued. "We stay on board until the job's done. The bay is pressurized and heated according to cargo requirements, but we're looking at a long shift in microgravity, people. Jones, get Tamareia kitted up with gear and magnetics so they're not floating unless they want to be."

Jones motioned me to follow him aft. I unbuckled my harness and pulled myself along the rail at the top of the cabin. The officer opened a locker at the back of the shuttle, removed a set of clamp-on magnetic soles and sent them gliding toward me with a push.

I snagged them out of the air and looped one arm through the rail to keep me stable against the bulkhead while I strapped them on and activated the electromagnets. My feet met the deck with a *click* as I lowered them to the floor. Jones handed me a set of tactical gloves. The left one had an LED torch mounted at the wrist.

"Is there already a recruiting program for Remoliad service?" he asked in decent Remoliad Standard, casting a furtive, backward glance at his fellow officers.

"Not exactly, but I am sure it is coming," I said in the same language, smiling. "Are you thinking about it?"

"Yes." Jones nodded eagerly. "See the rest of the galaxy, you know? There is a lot of stuff out there. I considered joining a mercenary unit just to gain experience."

My smile faltered as I saw the excitement in his gentle brown eyes. "Friendly advice? Stay away from the mercenary corps. Sumner will tell you the same. I'll give you contact information for Ambassador Marina Urquhart at the Remoliad. If you do decide you want to branch out of Sol Fed, there are much better options."

"I would appreciate it. Thanks." Jones's excitement fizzed against my senses, and I fought to suppress my amusement as he schooled his features to a more business-like mien. He handed me a vest and switched back to our native language. "These have a built-in com system. I don't have a helmet for you, so use the wireless earpiece in the front pocket and try not to get shot in the head. Pretty standard equipment, but yell at me if you need help." Jones excused himself to rejoin the other officers as I finished putting on my gear.

Saetang and I floated up to the cockpit as the drop ship rounded Jupiter, the shadow-mottled face of the gas giant's dark side dominating the viewscreen. We approached the enormous freighter port-on-port.

"You do the honors." Saetang motioned me to the com. "I don't speak Remoliad Standard well enough."

I switched to the customary intergalactic freight frequency. "Kadrelian freighter *Aramool*, this is Special Agent Tamareia with Remoliad Intelligence. May I speak with your captain using secure channel protocol, please?"

After a pause, a digital response indicated their compliance. "This is Captain Drimaat." The liquid syllables of Kadrelian-accented speech burbled over the speakers. "How can I assist you, Agent Tamareia?"

"I am here with Sol Fed Homeland Security Agent Preeda

Saetang. Under statute five point seven under the Sol Fed shipping codes, our team will make entry and inspect the cargo aboard your vessel. We have reason to believe freight prohibited by galactic trade laws may have been smuggled aboard your ship."

"You have brought the warrant, I trust?" came the quick, smooth reply. "I have not been comfortable with this situation since the others arrived."

Saetang and I exchanged glances of alarm before I replied. "Yes, Captain. Did someone else already board?"

"An hour ago, we were intercepted by a vessel claiming to be Sol Fed customs," the captain said. Even translated, his irritation was evident. "They were unable to transmit the proper codes but said another craft was on the way. I did not believe I could refuse them entry under this system's laws."

"They weren't supposed to board first," Saetang muttered off com. She checked a screen and glanced at me, her mouth a thin line. "They aren't anywhere near us. The customs vessel is still waiting on Rosetta Station for our instructions."

I toggled the mic. "We are transmitting the warrant now, Captain." Saetang entered a series of characters into the onboard computer and sent the message. Moments later, the Kadrelian spoke again, more politely this time.

"Received. I am sending you the cargo manifest now. Come aboard, Agent Tamareia. You may make entry on the port side airlock. The other ship is attached to the starboard lock."

"Thank you, Captain." I paused. "I assume your crew is on the bridge and accounted for, as is protocol during inspection?"

"Of course."

"For your safety, please make certain your bridge is secure. Do not give anyone access until we can verify the identity of the other vessel. They may not be who they say they are."

"Understood. Are we in danger?"

"Not if you remain on the bridge. We will advise you when it is safe to stand down. Tamareia out."

Saetang called out to her officers. "We're not alone. Grab the zero-g defensive kits and don't make any shots without targeting confirmation. The last thing we need are bullets bouncing around." She adjusted the tactical lens over her eye. "This just got interesting. Prepare for docking."

CHAPTER
TWENTY

THE HOLLOW THUD of magnetic clamps rocked our ship. The officers were on their feet immediately. A thick current of focused tension wound through the group as they positioned themselves in front of the airlock. Saetang gave me a soft gun, a wide-mouthed rifle loaded with stunning charges packed in a low-rebound load. I slung the strap over my shoulder. The two of us hung back until the tactical team made entry.

"Clear," the squad leader announced over the headset. We followed them into the freighter.

"Thompson, lead the way," Saetang instructed.

The unit moved with collective confidence, clearing each intersection as we traversed what seemed to be a never-ending corridor, steeply angled on the port side. It was not a stealthy approach; the thud of silicone-soled magnetic boots against the deck announced our presence as we went. The unknown boarding party couldn't have missed the sounds of docking, but it would be preferable if they weren't waiting for us behind the port of the cargo bay. Saetang's thoughts were running in the same vein because she raised a fist before we reached the next intersection.

"The entrance is approximately sixty meters down-corridor," she said. "Once we clear this corner it's a straight shot. Deactivate magnetics. We'll pull ourselves into range until we reach the port."

We swam through microgravity in silent freefall, using handles set in the bulkhead to provide momentum. At the sealed entry to the cargo hold, a blinking panel of controls labeled in Remoliad Standard occupied the outside wall. The level of pressure, gravity, and temperature inside the bay were in sync with the corridor.

"Standard entry, no depressurization," I informed Saetang quietly as I examined the display. "Both ports can be opened from this panel." I showed her the touchscreen. "You'll need a partner to operate it. It's designed for Kadrelian tentacles and requires six points of contact to activate. When the time comes, touch here and here with the forefinger and thumb of both hands. Somebody else has to raise the ports on this touchscreen with two fingers. There should be an identical panel behind this bulkhead. Once you're inside, close the ports behind us the same way."

"Got it." Saetang turned to the team and whispered, "Hold here. Reengage magnetics once Tamareia's team is in position."

Four officers, Jones among them, peeled off with me and floated down corridor until we reached the starboard entrance. I confirmed over the headset, "We're in position."

Boots met the deck with a rumble. I winced at the sound, but nothing could be done about it. "Stand by," I said over the com as seals released with a faint sigh.

"Opening in three. Two. One." The port rose in its frame when Saetang completed her countdown. Officers cleared the doorway, and our group quickly moved inside. The port shut when we were clear, leaving us in the ghost-lit cavern of the cargo hold.

"They're doing an inspection in the dark?" somebody whispered.

Saetang's voice echoed through the vaulted bay. "Homeland Security! Customs, make your positions known and step out into the central aisles with your hands over your heads."

Silence.

"I think we can agree this isn't an inspection," Saetang's transmitted voice muttered in my ear. "Stay sharp."

Containers clamped and strapped in against microgravity filled the deck, with warrens of space between them for equipment to get through and transport the cargo in or out. Jones drew his weapon and motioned for me to take point. I shifted the stun rifle into a ready position. The other officers divided into teams of two and disappeared into the stacks.

If I thought Saetang's presence in my empathic nets was an adrenaline riot, Jones's was a mob of Ferian kittens chasing a lizard. Sensing anyone hidden in the stacks would be impossible until I was right on top of them.

Torch beams reflected off the port hull from Saetang's team, fifty meters away. The unfamiliar pull of my magnetic soles made me clumsy and overbalanced as we swept each intersection in turn. The wrist torches mounted on our gloves illuminated shadowed crevices between the stacked cargo.

Four crates down the row, the black maw of an open container caught my attention and I waved for Jones to hang back. "What's in that shipment?" I asked in a near-silent whisper as he peered around the corner.

A ghostly green glow illuminated the tactical lens over his left eye as Jones consulted the schematics Captain Drimaat had provided. "Relief supplies from the Remoliad."

Why would they open a relief container? I signaled we should investigate, and Jones took point. Cautiously, we approached the crate.

A gunshot cracked and echoed around me as voices crested in alarm over the headset. The strangled sound from someone's throat cut through the din on the earpiece as weapons fire rattled in the cargo hold.

Shouting from the other side of the bay echoed through the vaulted bulkheads. "They have projectile weapons!"

"Officer down! They're floating above the stacks!" one of the team shouted. "Jones, we need you on the port aisle."

"Go! I'll cover you," I urged him.

Jones switched off his magnetic soles and pulled himself toward the port side, launching from crate to crate down the row in a headlong flight toward his injured teammate. I swept along on the opposite side, keeping an eye overhead.

A shape rose above the crates as he passed. A human woman dressed in coveralls raised a gun and took aim at Jones. I slowed my momentum against the side of a container and kicked off the crate at a new angle, driving myself toward the figure.

"Drop your weapon!" I shouted. The woman's surprise rained against my empathic nets, and she swung her sidearm toward me in a frantic motion. Staring down her barrel, I fired the stunner. The load struck her in the shoulder and sent her spinning; her body convulsed with the charge. The gun floated away.

Another figure erupted from between a stack of crates. This one moved expertly through microgravity. He headed for me like a missile, a long, wicked knife in his hand. I floundered in the empty air above the cargo bay. He closed the distance. I brought my stunner around in frantic aim.

A pneumatic THUNK sounded below me; a black bolo of webbing spiraled open between us and enveloped the man in its sticky net. I looked down to see Saetang hanging on the ladder of a crate, the hollow mouth of the launcher smoking with propellant. She clipped the bolo's tether to the rungs and loaded another to retrieve the stunned woman.

A burst of light appeared between the stacks, and a shot pinged off the hull above me, echoing as it bounced around the bay. I was a wide-open target up here, helpless without microgravity thrusters. The muzzle flash had come from a row of boxy containers, but I could do little more than point as two of Saetang's team headed that direction. I kept my eyes on the stack of crates where the gunman hid and prepared to fire, the wild bullet still careening off the bulkhead.

The man's head popped up from behind the container, his weapon pointed directly at me. I fired the stunner. The burst of compressed air sent me drifting even higher as the charge went wide and deflected off the crate. He flinched but brought the gun back to bear on me with frightening speed as I tried to turn in midair to present as small a target as possible. My muscles tightened, anticipating the rip of a projectile through my bones and flesh, and I thought, *Damn it, Sumner. I'm sorry.*

An explosion of blood and brain matter erupted from the man's head as one of the tactical snipers fired over the top of another container. He jerked backward, rifle floating loose from his lifeless hands.

A moment later, another man rose from the maze of crates with his hands up. Officers swarmed him as others deployed a net to retrieve the limp, drifting body of the dead man from the constellation of crimson spheres orbiting him like bloody planets.

From my unwilling vantage point, it appeared the team had apprehended at least two more suspects among the containers. My drift finally brought me into contact with the bulkhead. I engaged my magnetics to walk down the hull to the deck, eager to get out of the open and back into the sheltering stacks. The sound of the ricocheting bullet hadn't stopped, but its momentum was decreasing as it bounced off walls and containers more slowly than before.

Near the port entry to the bay, Jones grimly tended the officer who'd been shot. "Ask the captain if they have a medical pod," he called to me as I got to the deck. "I need more than a field kit."

I made my way to the control panel and did as he asked, obtaining Captain Drimaat's promise to send his medic and a stretcher to the port side. Lights came up in the bay when I located the controls on the screen. A few minutes later the Kadrelian medic arrived in a fuss of tentacles, and they transferred the injured officer to a hovering cot. Jones left with them.

Officers returned with the still-breathing prisoner, and the corpse tied to a piece of paracord trailed behind them like a grisly meat-balloon. The team got their prisoners settled and secured as Saetang stripped the tacky strands of entangler net away from the woman and cuffed her. The scowling man was tethered to a nearby ladder, still enveloped in sticky webbing, his blade confiscated.

"Jones and I saw an open crate before the shooting started," I murmured to Saetang as she stood. "I'm going to check it out. Can I borrow your lens to call up the manifest?"

"We don't know if we rounded everyone up yet." Her sharp discomfort slid against my empathic nets, not quite panic, but enough to make me realize I neglected to consider the circumstances of her partner's murder. "I told you, nobody goes anywhere alone on my watch."

"I didn't see anyone else from on high." I gestured toward the bulkhead and smiled at her in reassurance. "I'll be careful."

She reluctantly handed me the lens. I secured the loop over my right ear, positioning the miniature screen in front of my eye.

Saetang blew out her breath in a sharp exhale, a calming habit I recognized. Sumner did that, too. "Our pilots just informed me the real customs team is on its way, but there's nowhere for them to dock with these assholes still attached to the freighter. I'm sending a team to make sure no one else is on board their ship. Stay in touch."

"Will do." It would be easier to sense someone sneaking up on me without a partner—at least, one who wasn't a psychic null. Then again, I had a partner co-opting my head, almost forgotten as I pulled myself along the stacks.

Do you believe my offspring are in this crate? I jumped when Kitryd spoke in my ear.

"I don't know. They wouldn't open a relief supply ship-ment unless they were looking for something," I muttered. I found the row and made my way to the gaping metal container, a rectangular one four meters in width and height, and ten meters long. The markings on the outside were in both the Zereid alphabet and Sol Standard. Puzzled, I exam-ined the crate. It was unusual, but not unheard of, for only one relief crate to be aboard a freighter. They were usually transported on Remoliad ships full of emergency supplies. But a critical tag glared on the manifest, which meant expe-dited shipping.

I cast out my empathic nets and got no sense of any living being concealed inside. With my sidearm drawn down, I rolled into the opening, the wrist torch on my glove illumi-nating the shadowed interior.

Neat piles of cartons occupied the container on either side of a slender aisle, enough for a Zereid to pass through and leaving a human plenty of room. I activated the strip of lights attached to the crate's ceiling and squinted against the cold, white brilliance splashing back from the walls.

"Will I be able to sense them?" I asked Kitryd. "I can feel you sometimes, like static, or an electric hum."

They are in gestation mode. Any output would be faint at best.

Great. It wouldn't be easy, then. I kept my empathic webs spread for any hint of presence as I passed between the wrapped boxes. The shipping crate held a plethora of things difficult to obtain through Sol Fed's natural resources, like chemicals for breaking down biological waste into reusable, non-toxic components.

Stacks of containers occupied the front of the crate, marked with the familiar broken-circle glyph of Kua: high end technology products. Nothing tickled my senses. I aimed the tactical lens at the matrix printed on the nearest box and identified its contents as the data chips needed to manufacture radiation shielding monitors.

Sol Fed's current shielding system was outdated and beginning to deteriorate, so this was a critical shipment. Its destination was Luna. Again, not unexpected. It seemed an awfully big container, but if they were destined for manufacturing the quantity was not unusual. Radiation shielding production was one of the largest industries on the moon. The crate's first stop was Rosetta, in Jupiter's orbit and the closest space station to Europa, where it would be loaded into a faster ship for delivery to Luna.

What was so damned interesting about this shipping container?

Frowning, I walked the length of the crate and examined the other supplies before turning back to the container's mouth. As I did, I noticed a long cut in the back side of the polymer sheeting used to wrap stacked jugs of liquid chemicals. I lit the slash with my wrist torch and peered into the opening.

Something glinted at me, shoved into the narrow space between stacks of opaque plastic jugs. I was able to hook the thing with the ends of my middle fingers and pulled out a metallic tube.

The cylinder was too long to be what Kitryd described. I turned the metallic pipe over in my hands. Something was inside—many somethings, shifting against the inside with glassy *pings*. A twist of the cap and the lid yielded under my fingers. I unscrewed it and carefully shook out the contents.

Vials tumbled and spun in the air between my hand and

the cylinder's mouth. Clear as water, the fluid contained within sparkled in the harsh light of the crate. I caught one in my hand to examine it, my pulse pounding.

The smooth, familiar shape of the vial in my hand disturbed the slumbering beast of addiction embedded in my psyche. I hastily returned the floating vials to the cylinder and capped it, then used my knife to enlarge the slit in the plastic and aimed my torch inside. Dozens of cylinders gleamed back at me like the reflective eyes of a Ferian, shoved too far between the stacks of chemical jugs to reach.

Vape. Possibly hundreds of doses of the new, virulent formula, hidden in relief supplies.

I replaced the tube and toggled the mic on my vest. "Saetang? You need to see this."

My offspring? Kitryd asked, its hopeful electric buzz rising in my head.

"No, I'm afraid not."

The humans who boarded the freighter before us were not related to Batterson Robotics at all. The drug cartel's effort to get the new vape with its biological time bomb into circulation had escalated. Hiding it in incoming relief shipments where customs might be less likely to carry out full inspections was insidious and clever.

There was no telling where the drugs were inserted. It had to have been early in the process, probably at the trade hub when supplies were tagged and loaded on freighters. I was glad it would be a particular Burkani drug enforcement officer's problem to figure out, and not mine.

CHAPTER
TWENTY-ONE

IT TOOK the full twenty-six hours of the remaining flight to Rosetta Station for federal customs agents, Saetang's team, and me to inspect most of the crates. Even then, the station's local constabulary would have to pitch in when the freighter docked at Rosetta and check the few containers we didn't manage to crack open. None of those were tagged for Europa.

No sign of Kitryd's offspring, and the clock was ticking.

Everyone was exhausted. The team took alternating breaks on board the drop ship to catch a couple of hours' sleep and a meal. Working in microgravity created a different kind of fatigue, and I looked forward to hitting Rosetta's artificially generated gravity, even if I didn't particularly enjoy the thought of being there.

Sumner and I had done some preliminary investigation in the Labyrinth, the station's dark underbelly, when we arrived in Sol Fed three months ago. At that time, the new vape formulation had not made it in. I didn't want to go chasing after anything down there, afraid I might encounter my own ghost.

Rosetta constituted a known hot spot for illegal freight—

my father commanded the station for more than a decade and struggled with the red tape wound around Europan shipping laws, which allowed companies like Batterson Robotics to carry out their own inspections.

Things changed after the human trafficking ring and export of illegal weapons perpetrated by Jon Batterson. Inspectors stepped up their efforts to monitor outgoing Europan shipments in other ways, but the locals still resented federal interference.

A group of constabulary officers and Europan customs agents waited at the end of the airlock tunnel when the freighter docked at Rosetta. The local authorities took custody of the drug runners while Saetang wrangled interrogation time with their supervisor—someone I didn't recognize. Constable Caniberi, station born and raised, had retired not long after Dad left.

One of the constabulary officers stared at me, and I returned her gaze until she looked away. I didn't remember her. Chances were, she had probably arrested me for starting fights in the brightly lit halls outside the sports arena. Or I slept with her and ghosted her after. I was not a pleasant human being to be around three years ago, and I wouldn't blame anyone for holding grudges.

Relieved by Rosetta's customs agents, the tac team had removed their armor in favor of black coveralls without any identifying logos and looked forward to a little R&R in the station's entertainment district. Jones invited me to go, but I made a half-assed excuse about being tired and finding a place to crash for a few hours.

Instead, I paced the windows which overlooked the titanic gas giant outside. Storm clouds raged in silver whorls, streaked with conflagrations of orange and rippled streams of brown silk. Its perpetual chaos, under which I had spent my most turbulent days, was never comfortable. The peace I fought for remained too fragile to withstand that kind of violence. Restless energy kept me moving, and Kitryd, too, seemed unable to settle.

She said she sent them to her mother on Europa, it whispered in my head.

"They already contacted the facility. They said she hasn't gotten any packages or deliveries."

What if they are wrong?

The unappealing vision of Kitryd's untrained offspring seeking hosts among the fragile population in Anna Skadi's convalescent home made me wince. It wouldn't hurt to check with the post office on Rosetta. Packages for local delivery to Europa got processed there. I pinged Saetang with a text message and told her where I was going.

The counter held a single computer interface, but I knew a sorting facility lay behind the kiosk where a human monitored postal arrivals and departures. "How may the Sol Fed Postal Service assist you?" inquired the annoyingly bright voice program.

I flashed my credentials at the system's eye. "I need to speak to the postmaster about a suspicious package."

The kiosk moved back into the wall. It slid aside and I entered a long, narrow room filled with the hydraulic whine of a robotic sorter and the hum of conveyor belts crowded with packages. A silver-haired woman sat at the bank of monitors. She stood and greeted me.

"Rina Gunderson, Postmaster." Her voice echoed the bright, cheerful interface. "May I see your identification myself, please?"

I offered her my credentials. "Tamareia," she said, surprised. "Any relation to the former captain?"

"Yes, as it happens." She didn't recognize me, which was a relief. People wouldn't have positive memories of me during my time here.

"Suspicious packages," she said, frowning, and returned to her monitor. "Not on my watch, anyway. What do you need to know?"

"It may have been as long as a month ago. The item was probably sent from out-system to this address." I gave her the location of the convalescent home on Europa. She pulled up a data system on her screen and peered at the resultant information.

"They receive a lot of local shipments from inside Sol Fed. Health supplies, medication, and food, mostly. How did the package in question arrive at Rosetta Station? Freight? Passenger?"

"Try both." Passenger flights had been Skadi's M.O. before, so it was worth a shot.

"Hmm. Other than medical equipment delivered as part of the Remoliad relief effort, not much. A couple of flower arrangements. Not real botanicals, artificial."

"Did those go to specific recipients?"

"One was addressed to a Frances Sato. The other had no addressee, just the facility's name."

Damn it. Either Skadi was playing us, or given our discovery on the freighter, the infant AIs might be concealed in one of those seemingly innocent shipments of medical equipment or flowers.

Looked like I needed to pay a visit to Anna Skadi on Europa.

I thanked Gunderson and turned left as I exited the kiosk. The inter system terminal was on the near arm of the U-shaped station, facing Jupiter's stormy visage. I checked the readout of departures. The shuttle to Europa made a round trip twice a day. The last one was boarding now.

If I ran, I could still make it.

I pinged Saetang again. She still didn't answer, and I was selfishly relieved when it went to standby. I left a message explaining my intent to go down to the icy moon instead of having to tell her about a potentially idiotic decision. Ending the communication, I sprinted for the terminal.

Having Homeland Security clearance tagged to my ID was incredibly convenient. I made a mental note to thank Saetang for that as I raced through the checkpoints. I made it to the gate with enough time to collapse into one of the last empty seats and concentrate on slowing my breathing as I strapped in. The cabin crew secured the port as the shuttle's engines began to rumble.

I checked my device after the docking arm retracted and the shuttle eased away from the station, the steel walls burning orange with Jupiter's reflected planet shine. As expected, a furious message from Saetang awaited me.

For fuck's sake, Tamareia. Have you forgotten the most powerful man on Europa has a hit out on you? And what part of joint operation do you not understand? Contact me if you find anything. Keep your head down. I don't want to be the one to tell your partner you were stupid enough to get killed.

Yeah. Sumner wouldn't be happy with me either. But the clock was running out, and if Kitryd's offspring were there, I would need time to get them out of the facility and safely contained. There was no other option.

———

Everything about Europa glinted in frozen hues of blue and white, from the spaceport walls to the landscape outside. Even inside the terminal, I shivered the moment I disembarked from the shuttle. I bought a coat with a heating element in the lining at an extortionate price from one of the terminal's shops before I headed for the subway. From there, it was a matter of locating the right platform for the train to the dome complex housing the convalescent center.

News holos flashed across the screens in the tube station, drawing my attention as I huddled in the coat. I didn't bother to check any reports when we arrived at Rosetta, but the arrest of Miriam Skadi now blared all over the media.

Local pundits entirely ignored her Europan heritage in favor of labeling her an alien half-breed and a terrorist—and I stiffened when they broadcast holo vids of me and Sumner, with Kitryd's armature lashing out to immobilize Skadi during her arrest.

Both our names were mentioned, holos displayed of us in our Remoliad uniforms taken from the footage of those intrusive media bots at the Security Council meeting. Their speculation we worked for the Remoliad, while technically true, set a torch to any shred of anonymity we might have had left. And seven fucking hells, the reporters had already transmitted an inquiry to the Remoliad seeking a statement.

Whose orders we were openly defying.

Rogue status all the way. No turning back now.

I pulled up the hood of the jacket and practiced anonymity. All I needed was for someone here to recognize me and let Batterson get wind of it.

When the train arrived, I got on and tried to concentrate on what I was doing. Go in, get out, and keep my head down, like Saetang said.

I located the facility on the outskirts of the dome, a twenty-minute walk from the station. The caregiver at the front desk looked up with a smile, but her expression abruptly changed to protective menace when she took in my brand-new jacket. "What can I do for you?"

"I'm here to see Anna Skadi," I said. She cut me off before I could explain.

"If you're a reporter, you need to get out right now." Hostile doubt brushed my empathic nets. "Leave the poor woman alone."

"I'm not." I showed her my credentials, and her eyes widened. "I'm sorry to intrude. I believe her daughter may have sent something here, possibly concealed in a relief medical supply shipment or some flowers. She intended to retrieve it, but as you know, she won't be coming. It's imperative I find it. It could be harmful to your residents."

"I didn't even realize she had a daughter until reporters started trying to sneak in to see her." Her fear built to a crescendo. "That terrorist, right? Did she send a bomb?"

"No, no. Nothing like that," I quickly reassured her. "But it is definitely something we need to remove and isolate."

"Let me talk to my supervisor." She spoke in hushed tones on a handheld device, casting nervous glances in my direction as I waited. A few moments later, a woman emerged and introduced herself as the director. I repeated the round of introductions and explanations. She studied my Remoliad credentials with open distaste.

"Anna is actively dying," she said tartly. "The staff is sitting with her when their duties allow. Can you do what you need to with a minimum of disruption?"

"I can start with the medical supplies you received from the relief shipment first and search her room as a last resort."

"You can look in her room, but there's nothing there." The director shrugged. "Leah will take you to the storeroom where the other things are. We haven't put it into circulation." Her voice gained the arrogance I associated with Europan pride, a drift of antagonism in her empathic output. "Batterson-made equipment is good enough for us."

A more friendly young woman dressed in green scrubs escorted me down the pristine white hallway. The inspection of their relief shipment proved a useless effort. Leah helped me drag unopened boxes, watched me sift through them, and didn't laugh while I sprawled under the dark, polymer-draped medical pods to check beneath. Nothing seemed strange or out of place.

As she led me back to the residential ward, glimpses inside the rooms showed effort had been made to individualize them and make their occupants feel more comfortable, with bright artwork and thick, quilted blankets piled on the beds.

By contrast, Anna Skadi's room was almost as sterile and impersonal as the hallway. She lay in a medical pod in front of a narrow window looking out on Europa's frozen landscape, the ochre-mottled storm patterns of Jupiter dominating the sky. Her gray-streaked braid trailed over her shoulder, its original pale color still visible at the end. No wonder Skadi's genetics favored the pallid alien half: Anna's Nordic ancestry was strong, white lashes against ashen cheeks as her mouth moved in agonal gasps. One watery, faded eye lay visible under the half-closed lid.

A holograph on the bedside table showed a younger Anna in the crisp maroon and white uniform of the Europan militia, white-blonde hair caught in a neat tail at the back of her neck. Blue eyes glittered, cold and distant. Her mouth made a solemn line but quirked up at the ends as if she knew some ironic secret.

Miriam Skadi looked like her.

A long, shallow vase occupied the bedside table, with three stems of cascading, crystalline flowers arranged *ikebana* style; transparent petals streaked with veins of amethyst. "What are those? I thought she hasn't gotten any deliveries."

"Oh, they're fake skeleton orchids. Aren't they pretty, though?" The caregiver shrugged. "We put them here to brighten the place up for her, but we'll move them into the day room, after." She stroked Anna's hair back tenderly. "Hopefully somebody's family member will recognize them when they visit. They got delivered a while back without a resident's name on them."

Without a name. A jolt went through me. "May I look at them?"

"Sure."

I pulled the arrangement toward me. The flowers were a glistening confection of iridescent polymer, bright pigment, and spidery purple stems made of wire. I easily plucked one out of the medium, fake moss dragged after it by equally artificial thorns, nothing more than metal and plastic.

They are here. Kitryd's words sounded triumphantly in my ear, its excitement carried on a wave of static through the emotionless voice of the com. *I feel them. They are here.*

I pushed the flower back where it came from, forcing the stem all the way through the supportive base which kept the flowers upright. Something beneath that green and brown camouflage clinked against the wire. Holding my breath, I pulled the layer of blooms, foam, and mossy stuff out of the container and peered under it.

A cluster of six palm-sized, clear containers glinted in the warm light, swaddled in protective wrapping under the foam medium. I peeled the material back to reveal the softly pulsing, void-black matter within. At the bottom of each container lay a coiled rope of magnetic links, smaller versions of Kitryd's construct.

"Seven hells. She really did send them to her mother," I muttered.

My offspring. Kitryd's relief sent a cascade of static through my empathic webs.

The aide backed away. "I'll tell them you found what you were looking for." She all but ran out the door. Her fear left a palpable trail behind.

They are here. Kitryd repeated. Its relief created a rain of electric prickles, like sparks against my senses.

"How long do we have before they emerge?"

I believe they are beginning to come out of gestational stasis. Perhaps thirty-six hours.

It would be a close thing getting them back to Lunar space, but if someone in a fast ship met us halfway with the rest of Kitryd's mass, it would be even better.

"I have an idea," I said. I lifted my device to call Saetang and hesitated as someone walked into the room. My fingers went numb with shock.

A tall young man with an athlete's build stood in the doorway, his face disturbingly like one I often saw in my nightmares. My inhalation caught against the jagged memory of Jon Batterson's violent death at the teeth and claws of Shontavian mercenaries. This man resembled him in a more than passing way.

I'd seen him before.

Blurred recollection of a drug-fueled, anonymous fuck in the cold, dark underbelly of Rosetta Station—the prelude to an encounter which ended in my near death—jolted into focus.

Brian Batterson. Sole surviving heir to the Batterson Robotics empire.

Two more men came in. One dragged the tight-lipped, pale Leah back into the room and held her in front of him with vague menace. Did the Batterson family collect giant minions, or what? These guys were bigger than Brian, a professional rugby player like his brother had been, and he wasn't small.

"My father would like a word with you," Brian said mildly.

"I'm sure he does." Sarcasm crept in despite my best efforts.

"Thank you for finding those." He swept his hand toward the vase and the abandoned flowers. One of the men walked over, carefully picked up the ceramic vessel and brought it to him. "Now, if you would be so kind to remove your weapons and place them on the table. Slowly."

"You have no idea what those are," I said, playing for time.

"Dad says they're the future of Batterson Robotics." Brian removed one of the small containers from the vase and lifted it in careful hands, peering at the void-black substance inside. "Self-reproducing artificial intelligence."

All right, so he did know what they were. "You're aware Homeland Security is looking for them, right?"

"We've kept them tangled in red tape up on Rosetta. They'll be a while." Brian replaced the container. His voice gained a razor's edge. "Now put your weapons on the table. You wouldn't want to be responsible for this young lady's broken arm, would you?"

Leah let out a short, muffled shriek as Batterson's flunky wrenched her wrist behind her; my senses filled with the red splash of her pain. She was brave and bit back her cry against gritted teeth, but I wouldn't let her suffer. I raised my hands and glared at the man. I planned to kick his ass as soon as I had a chance.

"Let her go." I reached behind me with one hand and left the other where they could see it, removed the gun from the holster at the small of my back and placed it on the table amid the artificial flowers.

"The knife, too. I know you have one. You declared it at Rosetta."

I pulled it from the wrist sheath and laid it beside the gun. "Satisfied?"

"Not quite." Brian's calm, erudite manner, light years different from Jon's abrasive personality, didn't make him any less an asshole. "I remember you don't need weapons to be difficult, so I brought something to ensure your cooperation."

A violet flash filled my vision. Brian's stunner buckled my knees and sent me to the floor. My muscles contracted in excruciating spasms and refused to respond to my will as one of his buddies rolled me over and shackled my hands with a set of bar handcuffs. He shoved a cloth hood over my head.

My only hope was for Saetang to put the pieces together when I didn't come back, or the staff at the convalescent home would contact the authorities once they were safe.

But on Europa, Batterson likely owned the authorities. I was in trouble.

CHAPTER
TWENTY-TWO

MY BODY HIT ice-cold concrete when I got tossed on the floor. A cacophony of machines filled my ears with industrial noise. I suspected where they'd taken me before the familiar voice, one every Sol Fed citizen had heard make dozens of speeches, said, "About time. I was beginning to think Brian lost his nerve."

They ripped the hood off my head. I struggled to sit upright. Dressed in insulated work coveralls, ex-President Simon Batterson looked down at me in contempt. He was a puffy, less urbane version of the politician I remembered. His salt-and-pepper hair stuck out in tufts beneath his yellow hard hat, and a scruff of beard littered his face. Disgrace had not treated him well.

For a long moment, he stared. The shriveling heat of his anger rushed over me like the open blast furnace I glimpsed across the factory floor, scorching my empathic webs. "How could a wiry little mutant like you beat Jon in a fair fight?" he finally drawled.

"Because a death match isn't a fair fight," I answered. "But I didn't kill him."

"No. I heard you let those things rip him apart and eat him instead, and somehow you survived. Again." A humorless laugh punctuated the word. "He should have made sure you were dead the first time, but he got careless. Guess I should accept some blame. I gave Jon too much freedom and let him have his fun, but he always took one step farther than he could see."

He disgusted me. Human trafficking and torture were fun? Jon's sense of entitlement had extended from his father, it seemed.

Batterson continued, "You make a lot of enemies for a diplomat."

"Especially when you offer to pay somebody to kill me."

"Mother told you about that, did she? I expect England's ready to say anything to save her credibility at this point. The only wet contract I issued was for Kiran Singh. Yours says to bring you in warm, and it isn't mine. I just boosted the signal. But you're going to wish you were dead by the time this is over." He removed his heavy work gloves and flexed his fingers. "I promised to deliver you alive. They didn't say I couldn't take my pound of flesh first."

That did not sound promising.

He motioned to someone I couldn't see. Two men seized me under the armpits and hauled me to my feet. They attached the bar between my shackled wrists to a hook on a chain. It got run up a pulley until I stood on the balls of my feet, unable to get purchase to kick or fight.

Batterson's first punch broke my nose. My world became a blur of pain as his fists pummeled my face and midsection with merciless fury. When he finally stopped, Batterson was almost sobbing. His grief-filled rage filled my empathic nets, a red haze shot through with dark streams of humiliation. The tension trapping my hands above my head vanished as the chain played out. I collapsed, unable to stand. A guttural moan of agony poured from my throat when my body hit the floor.

Batterson gripped my hair and yanked my head up. I regarded him through eyes half blinded with tears of pain and my own blood.

"That was for Jon." His voice was nearly inaudible, rendered husky by the overwhelming emotions channeled through his fists. He dropped my head. It smacked against the concrete with a hollow sound and stars filled my vision. "This is for me."

Bones cracked in my rib cage beneath a kick from Batterson's iron-toed work boot. My groan turned into a cough, and the bright blood that came up with it spattered the floor. Not a good sign. I didn't have long to dwell on it before the next kick spiraled me into darkness.

———

Consciousness surfaced through a mist of noise which became a roar. I was too uncomfortable to be dead.

Pain lashed through me as I shifted, the right side of my body pressed against the unyielding, icy floor. Leaden fire burned in my chest when I tried to breathe and made me fear Batterson did more than break ribs, but yeah, still alive. My blurry, swollen eyes saw enough to tell I'd been brought to another part of the factory. Equipment in shipping containers awaited delivery in neat rows. In front of the spot where I lay, the digital tracks that guided robotic forklifts traced the floor in brassy lines.

"They're landing in the hangar now." That was Brian Batterson's voice, barely audible over the industrial symphony. I craned my neck to see he was still with the two men who'd been at the convalescent home. He patted the front of his thick coat. "I've got the AIs."

"Good." Batterson clapped him on the shoulder. "You proved yourself useful. You're no Jon, but you got the job done."

As the elder Batterson turned, a flash of hurt and fury crossed Brian's features, echoed in the dulled strands of my empathic web. He looked down at me, horror joining the turmoil on his face as he met my gaze. Brian glanced quickly away, schooling his expression to neutrality as his father directed the other men to pick me up.

I bit back the cry of pain as they dragged me upright. At least Batterson hadn't broken my legs. I could still walk, but standing straight proved impossible and the rattle in my chest alarmed me. I didn't let it stop me from mouthing off for as long as I could.

"When did you decide to work with galactic terrorists?" I managed as they dragged me along behind him. "I'm sure the NPM loves that."

"This has nothing to do with the NPM. This is personal," Batterson said. "But since we're all working against Remoliad oppression in favor of returning Sol Fed to a free, independent solar system, I can overlook the fact they're not human in return for some exclusive technology."

"They're sentient life-forms, not technology. You can't just cut them up to see what makes them tick."

"Are they made of flesh and blood?" Batterson asked. "No, they aren't. Ergo, they are not living."

A deprecating laugh escaped me. It hurt, but it was worth it. "You're making a huge mistake. I worked with their parent for the last three days. When those life-forms hatch, you're going to be in the middle of a clutch of infant AIs who don't know friend from foe."

"Machines don't hatch." Batterson dismissed my warning. Brian, at least, listened with a dawning expression of horror on his face. We stopped in front of an enormous port, the steel crusted thick with ice and frost along the bottom. The tracks which guided the automatic loaders disappeared beneath a white layer.

"Your new friends know what they are," I croaked. It was getting harder to breathe. "I will bet you they know exactly when they're going to emerge. They'll just pick up the pieces and the AIs afterward. If you think you can trust them, you're wrong."

"He told me you'd say that."

I shivered, only in part due to the frigid temperature on this side of the factory floor. "Who?"

Batterson pressed a hand-sized red button on the wall beside the airlock. A warning klaxon brayed over the industrial racket. The portal rose, metal groaning against the cold. Ice sloughed off the steel plate and shattered into white blades as glacial air from the hangar swept into the factory floor. Five beings swaddled in heavy, insulated gear poured down the ramp of a large shuttle craft to stand in a semicircle just outside the door. Four of them carried energy weapons.

The middle figure, tall and shrouded in a thick, hooded cloak, crunched forward through the fallen ice. Glassy pinging sounds punctuated each footstep as their slender hands, gloved against the hostile Europan climate, drew back the insulated hood with a graceful gesture and revealed an achingly beautiful mauve visage.

The gentle smile had not changed. It seemed less attractive now that I knew he was a fucking viper in the guise of an angel.

"I see you, Dalí Tamareia," Alecto Sim said. "But I did not think it would be in this condition."

"You never asked what they wanted in return for the new technology," Batterson glanced down at me. "The price is you."

Alecto caught me as Batterson's goons shoved me forward. "Simon, this was not part of the plan," he said in Sol Standard, his resonant voice brittle with irritation.

"You said alive." Batterson gestured. "There you go. Alive. I kept my end of the bargain."

"Don't touch me, asshole," I slurred, and tried to push away from Alecto. Branched lightning exploded in my chest, threatening to burn through from the inside and leave fractals like those Sumner wore in his skin. I coughed up more blood, gleaming ruby drops sliding down the moisture barrier on the outside of Alecto's cloak.

"I must get you into a medical pod." Sim's *riesh*, the suppression device he used to dampen the psychological consequences of his war crimes, glittered against his forehead in the harsh light of the bay. He muttered something sub-vocally into the communicator nestled against his throat.

"We both have what we wanted. Now get the hell out of my solar system." Batterson's statement fell flat, as if he had spent all his emotion beating the shit out of me.

"We are not yet settled on the matter of the artificial intelligence," Alecto said.

"No, I don't think so." Batterson's eyes glinted. "I paid a lot for this tech. I'll keep them."

"I am prepared to reimburse you." Alecto's smooth voice could convince almost anyone he acted in their best interests. "Miriam Skadi stole them from our employer, and I must have them back. We have a rapidly approaching deadline."

"That sounds like your problem." His belligerent stance widened. "A lot of people are interested in them. I think they're just what I want."

Alecto's guards raised their weapons at the same time Batterson's men shifted theirs to take aim. Oh, wonderful. An armed standoff on both sides, with me caught in the middle.

"Think carefully about this," Alecto warned.

"Dad," Brian began, his voice urgent as he reached out.

"Not now, Brian!" Batterson shrugged his son's hand away from his arm.

"No, you listen to me for once," Brian said fiercely. "Think a minute. If the AIs really are life-forms, we're right back in the shit where Jon left us. The company will never recover from another scandal."

"This isn't the time!" Batterson thundered. "Don't question me, boy."

Brian's face shattered into a mosaic of sadness and anger; a landslide of resentment shifted against my empathic nets. "I'm sorry, Dad. I can't let you do this. I'm working too hard to rebuild the company's reputation. This just makes me doubly certain I'm doing the right thing."

Alecto Sim stiffened against me, listening to something on his communicator. "Gentlemen," he said. "My crew has many armed humans on our sensors. They are inside the factory, headed this way."

"What did you do?" Batterson stared in betrayal at the younger man, who stiffly drew himself up and glared back. Things started to fall into place, and I couldn't suppress a gurgling laugh of irony. The electric bolt of pain was almost worth it.

Kiran's mysterious informant had to be Brian Batterson, the second son, stepping out from under the tainted shadow of his dead brother.

A clear, amplified voice sounded above the mechanical noise of the factory: "Homeland Security. Do not move!"

Sweet, triumphant relief swept through me. Saetang and her team were here.

Shouts echoed from the manufacturing floor as armed tactical officers appeared, advancing with their weapons ready to fire. One of Simon Batterson's men began to shoot at the oncoming horde. Brian and his father ducked for cover.

The hollow report of a pulse rifle answered and the Batterson goon went down.

Cursing in Tolkish, Alecto ordered his guards to retreat and dragged me with him. I resisted, unable to do much in my condition except make it more painful. He stopped pulling.

"I wish you no harm, Dalí," he said with note of desperation. "You must come with me if you want to ensure the survival of Naru and the other Shontavians. I need your help."

I stared back. He was manipulating me; I knew he was. I could play along for a while, try to help the Shontavians escape, get a message to Sumner and our team and . . . then what?

No fucking idea. I just hoped Sumner would understand why I did it.

I lurched toward Alecto. He linked his arm through mine to support me, and we hurried toward his ship. Five steps later, my vision filled with cascading stars, each breath taking far too much effort to be productive. I staggered, dizzy, and my knees buckled. Alecto and one of his crew lifted me, a sword of fire slicing through my chest as they half-carried me up the ramp of the waiting craft.

I cast a final glance over Alecto's shoulder. Through the swarm of armored bodies surrounding the Battersons I glimpsed Saetang standing above Brian with the container of infant AI's cradled in her hands, her expression confused and stricken as she saw me bundled into the ship.

The port sealed behind us and cut off my view of Saetang as the craft began to move. Whoever was piloting executed a hurried takeoff. A pair of Andari medics waited beside a hovering stretcher as Alecto eased me down to the pad and strapped me in.

"They will take care of you. Do not fight them," he said. I opened my mouth to say something caustic, but another cough strangled me. Blood erupted from my throat and splattered against Alecto's face and cloak. It was so much more than before. Muzzy panic set in when my airway started to close. The Andari flickered into action in their strange, synchronous way and the cot moved, ferrying me deeper into the ship as it began a steep ascent and left Europa behind.

CHAPTER
TWENTY-THREE

THE SHUTTLE DOCKED in the belly of a larger vessel some hours after leaving Europa. I was too busy having suction tubes shoved down my throat, trying not to die instead of paying attention to what kind of ship it was or how long we were in flight. Once on board, they rushed me to the infirmary, where two more Andari joined the others and drained the blood from my chest before my lung entirely collapsed.

On the second day, I hobbled to the lavatory when the medics allowed me to get out of the pod. I got a good look at myself in the reflective metal surface of the cleanser. The swelling from a fractured cheekbone gave me a lopsided appearance, bruises fading to an ugly yellowish green with streaks of plum beneath both eyes. My face must have been as purple as Alecto's in the beginning.

A rainbow of contusions painted my ribs. The breaks were realigned under sedation and injected with boneset to heal faster. So was my nose. I explored its new contours under my fingertips, feeling like I got run over by one of the forklifts in Batterson's factory. The medics offered me strong pain medication, but I refused them in favor of simple analgesics. I needed control over something, even if it was only myself.

The piece of Kitryd stowed away in my head had been silent since we came aboard. An occasional waterfall of electric prickles against my senses made me believe it hadn't been sucked up by the Andari's efforts to keep me breathing. I wondered if it was angry or grieved the missed opportunity to connect with its offspring. I hoped Saetang was able to reunite them in time for Kitryd Prime to install its non-predatory programming. I couldn't try to talk to the AI without drawing attention from one or more of the medics in constant attendance.

Their hovering didn't prevent taking note of what happened around me now that I was recovering. The first thing I recognized was a low rumble of sub-light engines. The ship was not running hot out of the solar system as I would expect if someone like Saetang was on Alecto's tail. I wasn't sure what that meant.

More revelations convinced me the Shontavians were somewhere aboard this ship. Every other day at a fixed time, the Andari prepared a six-pack of huge ampoules with long, wicked needles thick enough to pierce a Burkani's hide. They were inserted into a spear-like delivery mechanism. A guard dressed in tactical armor retrieved them.

On my third day in the infirmary, the guard happened to be Nos. Half an hour later, most of the same guard returned on a stretcher. I didn't get a good look because the Andari whisked him into the surgical suite, but it appeared his arms were missing. If not the Shontavians, I didn't want to know what kind of horror they had caged on this ship. They were fighting attempts to control them, which meant they were still in good condition.

Alecto showed up while the Andari were busy with the dismembered guard. He'd been conspicuously absent during the early days of my recovery. I didn't think I would be lucky enough for Naru to have eaten him.

His robes swirled in the hiss of the negative pressure threshold like a villain in one of my crewmates' favorite holovids. He stopped some distance from me, out of swinging range. Wise decision on his part, but I was still in too much pain to act on my urge to beat the hell out of him.

"The doctors tell me you refuse to take adequate pain medication." He made an eloquent gesture to encompass the medics, and I hated that his graceful movements, like the prelude to a dance, still captivated me. "You do not have to suffer, Dalí."

"I don't need them." It was a lie, but one I planned to keep telling. I straightened a little more and didn't care if he saw the wince of pain.

"I am horrified Samuel abused you in such a way," he said.

"Then you don't know the Battersons very well."

Another slow movement stroked the air and conceded defeat. "Clearly not."

"What's so important you put out a kidnapping contract for me?"

Alecto regarded me with his head tilted to one side. "An unorthodox method of ensuring your presence. I did not think you would come if I asked."

Bitterness welled up in me like a spring. "No, that tends to happen when you betray people's trust, Alecto." But the cold pool inside me reflected my own face, as guilty of that sin as he was.

The barb hooked and tore anyway. Shame transformed his perfect Tolkish features. "I am sorry for that. I regret hurting you and Rion—him, for a second time." He straightened and schooled his expression to something more neutral. "As I said, I need your assistance with Naru and the others."

An ugly laugh escaped me as I glanced at the door of the

surgical suite where the Andari were still busy reattaching the guard's arms. "They look like they're doing fine to me."

"The deadline I spoke of has come and gone. The undeveloped AIs represented my last hope to allow them some sort of freedom and still keep them safely in my care."

His words sank in, leaving horror in their wake. "You were going to let them integrate with the Shontavians, weren't you? Kidnapping somebody's children and using them to save your own ass is repulsive, like everything you've done. You fucked us over, took away everything we promised the Shontavians, and just expected Naru would accept you as their new master? I'm so disappointed they haven't ripped you apart by now."

He stood in the face of my wrath, unmoved, as I continued. "But you have all that research Lady Darizh and the Pileans compiled. The syringes they make in here—you have the exact cocktail required to keep them subdued."

"A less than desirable but necessary method. We managed to compound a non-addictive formula. Be assured they are not mistreated or punished, even for today's unfortunate event. I would never allow it after everything they suffered."

"Oh, no. You'd just allow an artificial intelligence to hijack their free will and make them work for you."

"It was better than the alternative I now face, unless you can convince them otherwise." The metallic strands of the *riesh* sparkled against Alecto's forehead. The fuzzy wall the device created between my empathic senses and his suppressed emotions made it impossible to tell what he truly felt, but his expressive mouth curved in a grave, downward arc. "If you do not help me win their trust, Dalí, my employer expects me to use the toxin failsafe encoded in their genetics to destroy them."

"That is on your head. " Tears of rage stung my eyes. "They showed us on Urset they would rather die than fight someone else's battles. How could you expect this to end otherwise?"

We had offered them the chance to escape their brutal conditioning on a ship of their own, programmed to travel a perpetual path in the vast starfield of our galaxy. With that hard-won, fragile trust shattered by what Alecto did, I doubted they would believe anything I said.

"Please help me. You are the only one they may listen to, and I . . ." Alecto swallowed hard. His panic sent sandpaper whispers through my empathic nets before the *riesh* did its work to suppress the horrors he'd committed in his past from overwhelming him. Alecto's face relaxed into its usual, beatific peace. "Despite what you may believe of me, I have killed no one—not one being—since my time on Amanosk. I quite literally cannot do it. Miriam was strong in all the ways I was not, but she . . ." He clamped his lips, then continued. "There are those who will be happy to see our employer's trust in me irrevocably destroyed."

"Yeah, I bet they're pissed you couldn't hold Skadi's leash tight enough to keep her in line," I said. "Tell me, how does it feel to be betrayed by someone you thought you could trust with your life?"

Yeah, that hit home. I saw the flinch, but he didn't give me false apologies. If he had, I would have punched him, no matter how much pain it caused me. His carmine gaze clouded, and he glanced away. "Her fate is out of my hands. I hope Sol Fed's paranoia keeps it as secure as it appears to be."

"Afraid she'll escape and pay you back for setting her up?"

"No. I fear what else our employer may ask me to do to ensure her silence."

A chill rippled down my back, more from dread than my ass hanging out in the ventilation. I stared at him, the desire to tell him *go fuck yourself* warring with what I knew I needed to do. Stall for time. Play along. Keep myself and the Shonta-vians alive so there was some hope Sumner and the others would find us, and I could still give them the freedom they deserved. My shoulders slumped as I expelled a violent breath. The action streaked a backdraft of fire through my lungs, and I fought the subsequent reflex to cough.

"All right." My choking voice fell flat against the walls of the medical bay. "I'm not doing this for you. I'll do it for Naru and the others, for their sake."

He touched my shoulder, his face lit with relief and when I recoiled, his excitement dimmed. He solemnly nodded instead.

"You need more time to heal. We will begin in few days."

I turned my back on him and walked to my medical pod.

"Thank you," he said.

I didn't respond. It was hard to maintain a cold, dignified retreat with both butt cheeks hanging out, but I hoped he got the message he could kiss my ass.

———

A day later the Andari medics gave back my own clothes, now cleaned of blood, and discharged me from their care with strict instructions not to do anything strenuous. Two guards, a Nos who still had both his arms and a female Ferian, escorted me down a long, empty corridor with a sharp-angled bulkhead. The shape was familiar. I slowed to glance around and attempt to reignite the memory. The Ferian growled low in her throat. I took the hint and kept going.

The walk from medical was longer than anticipated, and my endurance began to flag. The ship was several times bigger than *Thunder Child*, maybe as big as the Kadrelian freighter Saetang and I boarded, with its never-ending corridors.

That was it. The shape of the bulkhead was the same.

This one must have limited EM capability like most Kadrelian freighters, if one assumed they traveled all the way from Zereid to Sol Fed space in a matter of months. This trip to my native solar system did not happen on a whim.

We stopped in front of a closed port, a section of corridor which appeared to be crew quarters. The guard keyed a code on the panel outside and jerked his head for me to go in. "If you require anything, Alecto Sim instructed you are to have it," the Nos guard said in broken Remoliad Standard. "Use the com panel to inquire."

As prison cells go, I'd had better, and worse. It had a lavatory, and a table and padded benches welded to the floor below the inside com panel. The outside wall contained a recessed sleeping cubicle. The mattress was comfortable when I tested it. So comfortable, in fact, I woke with a start that tightened red-hot metal bands around my ribs and found two hours had passed.

As soon as I caught my breath, I rolled out of bed in slow increments to use the toilet. Afterward, I tried the port leading to the hallway and found it locked, cementing my status as a prisoner despite the decently appointed quarters. Now that I looked around more objectively, I noted the lens of a camera tucked into a corner. Right. Not a guest.

My position was reinforced when two guards entered without asking permission. The same surly Nos who first escorted me blocked the doorway and fondled the sidearm strapped to his thigh. I had seen the Tolkish individual once before, when he retrieved the massive syringes in the infirmary. Furrows of scar tissue marred the perfect symmetry of his facial features. He set a sealed container of water and the tray he carried on the table. I didn't move until they left, though the scent of food made my stomach howl.

I moved to inspect the tray. It held a bowl of thick soup made from Zereid vegetables and a small loaf of tough, bean-flour bread which softened to perfection when dipped in the broth. It was a dish I often ate with Gor at the temple school on Zereid. A sharp pang of longing for my crechemate went straight through to my core. I sensed Alecto's hand in this, probably more manipulation to make me feel safe and comfortable, but ate the food and savored the memories, too.

A small packet of analgesics lay on the tray. I washed them down with the water and almost choked in a painful swallow as Kitryd spoke in my head.

Do you believe Agent Saetang will reunite my offspring with my primary mass?

"There you are." I picked up the spoon again and turned my head away from the eye of the surveillance camera, muttering around the last bite of soup, "Yes. I do."

I am in your debt. I will do what I can to assist you.

If I kept talking to myself, Alecto might remember I had an implanted com, but I had to take the risk. I feigned weariness and put my face in my hands, leaned against the table on my elbows, and whispered, "Can you interface with their computers?"

It would require terminating my communication with you, but my current mass is not sufficient to control piloting systems.

Nice to know that Kitryd could otherwise do that. I filed it away for later. "I need you to send a subspace message to my team. Use my com's frequency. Start the message with 'Inconceivable. Brute Squad and Miracle Max in need of rescue.' Send them the ship's schematics and current position."

The message makes no sense.

"Good. They'll know it's from me." They should be headed back to Mars after dropping off Riga*nat's prisoner by now, providing I didn't lose count of the days while I was healing. "Can you do that without setting off any alarms?"

I will have to find the correct communications link to ensure success. It will take several hours to reach the right area of the ship in my current mass.

"Go. And thank you."

I will return when I can. Lift me to the communications panel. I will enter the conduit there.

The burn and itch attacked my throat as Kitryd made its way out of whatever orifice it stowed itself in. The sensation made me cough and currents of pain circuited my ribs. It crawled over the back of my tongue, and I pressed my hand against my lips to stifle the gag reflex. The tickle of its flagella on my palm told me when it was in place. Kitryd's tiny, ultra-black mass thinned itself out and squeezed behind the panel's frame as I pressed against the seam, buying time by clearing my throat before I activated the screen. "Can I have more water?"

"Acknowledged," the clipped voice of my Nos guard replied.

Safe journey, Kitryd, I thought as I moved my hand from the panel. My diminutive ally was off on its solo mission. Now came the waiting.

I hate waiting.

CHAPTER
TWENTY-FOUR

THAT NIGHT I started my own version of physical therapy, moving slowly through the *zezjna* forms I'd learned in the temple school. Everything hurt, but my muscles began to loosen up and remember what I expected from them. There was nothing else to do between meals and doses of analgesics, which I abandoned by the second morning. The pain was tolerable, and I continued to push myself.

It was unusually quiet outside my comfortable cell. No foot traffic or voices sounded regardless of the time, and the same four guards rotated in and out when they brought meals twice a day. Unless they were nearby, there were no ripples in my empathic webs which would come from the number of beings I would expect to crew a ship this large. The maimed guard was the only one in evidence the entire time I was in the medical bay with the Andari.

To test my theory, I asked for pain medication in the middle of the night. The Ferian brought the drug, grumpy and disheveled like she was disturbed from her sleeping den.

I was beginning to think the ship was deserted. Had Alecto been abandoned by most of his crew, or had the prospect of being ripped apart by Shontavians driven them away?

Alecto appeared in the doorway with the Ferian a day later. "I will take you to Naru," he said. He didn't ask if I felt up to it; he must have been watching the feed from my quarters all this time. The pale-furred guard clutched a set of manacles in her long-digited paw, and after a moment's pause, I offered my wrists and let her bind me.

We reached a larger port which might have once been the main access to a cargo hold. It slid aside to reveal a wide corridor lined with high-security cells along the starboard side. Two fully armored guards sat opposite in an alcove lit with holo screens showing the interior of six occupied cells.

A gray-skinned Shontavian mercenary inhabited each cell, their powerful quartet of upper limbs chained with heavy, metal links. A series of narrow transparent alloy windows allowed them to see one another through the inside walls but none of them were looking at each other. Most sat on wide, padded platforms with their backs slumped in drugged submission against the wall, staring out at the stars through a strip of large portholes in the bulkhead.

"You said they weren't mistreated." I hurled the accusation at Alecto.

"The chains are for their safety and ours. So are the sedatives. You saw what happens to my crew while you were in the med bay. The waste collectors must be maintained and some of the Shontavians attempted to dislodge the portholes in their cells." Bright anger burnished his voice. "I am not entirely the villain you believe I am. They are clean, well fed, and at least have the view of the stars we promised."

That didn't redeem him in my eyes, only made him more treacherous than ever. My gaze located the display showing the alpha Shontavian. Naru stood at the farthest limit of its restraints, gazing out the porthole.

"Naru received the sedative before our arrival. Until we

know how it will respond to your presence, take precaution to ensure your safety. Stay within a meter of the door and you will be out of reach." Alecto motioned at the Ferian to release my hands from the manacles, but I refused.

"No. Let Naru see I'm a prisoner as well," I said.

Alecto nodded in agreement. "A good strategy."

"It's not a strategy. It's the goddamned truth."

Alecto winced as if my words somehow wounded him, but he had burned any potential for friendship out of me. I never ceased to wonder how he managed to conceal his agenda from the Shontavians when his *riesh* was damaged in the attack that stranded us with them, right up to the moment he betrayed them.

Unless he intended to follow through on our promises all along, until his employer ordered him to do the opposite? I didn't like the scenario. It gave him more credit than I wanted to believe.

He told the guards to open the cell, his carmine gaze flickering over me. "I will be watching."

The Ferian escorted me to the door, my empathic nets awash in her vibrating fear. She didn't like being this close to Naru even with the Shontavian drugged, and hastily shoved me inside before slamming her furry palm against the lock to shut the port behind me.

Naru's back was turned, its wide skull only centimeters from touching the slanted overhead. It wore a collar, wrist, and leg manacles secured with electromagnetic locks, the chains draped around its enormous, four-armed torso and looped through rings welded to the deck. It did not move, gaze still on the stars outside. I allowed simultaneous relief, anger, and dismay to ride the gentle nudge of greeting I broadcast at Naru. Recognition stirred, sluggish and heavy in its drug-fogged mind.

"Peacemaker?" Its voice rumbled in my bones.

"Naru." My voice cracked against a surge of emotion I

couldn't suppress. I was so glad to see it alive, angry to find it in chains. There was still a chance we might be able to get them out of here. Naru would not look at me, and stinging tears welled in my eyes. I couldn't blame it one fucking bit—

The full force of its mind slammed into mine. A rasping sound climbed out of my throat as the psychic attack brought me to my knees. I didn't fight the intrusion. I yielded to the telepathic battering ram and let Naru read everything inside.

The alpha raked through my memories in search of treachery like a hacker digging for code. It stripped bare the volcanic pool of rage and hurt I harbored against Alecto and kept going.

Naru paused when it recognized I hadn't given up looking for them, the sleepless nights I spent combing through records and news feeds and manifests looking for any sign of the Shontavians. How I voluntarily came here as Alecto's prisoner in hope of finding a way to free them. My memories of Kitryd and its cooperation with me piqued its interest.

Naru offered no apology for the assault on my mind. It didn't owe me one. But in return, it showed me what transpired since their abduction.

Waking from heavy tranquilizers to find itself not in a Zereid forest but back in a cage. Alecto's ceaseless entreaties to join him, proven to be just another warlord.

So much rage and confusion in the early days of this new imprisonment, a conflagration which destroyed the vestige of hope that had begun to take shape. The fire was dying, replaced by dull, sedative-laced apathy and the group mind's knowledge, gleaned from the thoughts of their guards, that they faced imminent execution: the only option left to obtain the peace they craved.

It dropped me from its telepathic grip as quickly as it had seized control. Tears streaked my face, and the echo of its desolation squeezed another quivering breath out of me that threatened to turn into a sob.

"I'm so sorry," I whispered in Ursetu, the language Naru shared with its creators.

"We still seek the right stars." Naru turned at last and its sharp black gaze took in my healing bruises. The chains clanked against the deck as it squatted in front of me, bringing itself almost level with where I knelt, mouth open to sift my scent between legions of pointy, serrated teeth. "Why did you come?"

"Alecto wants me to negotiate. To persuade you to work for him and show you there are alternatives to dying."

"No." The group mind Naru shared with the others sent a drift of savage agreement against my empathic nets. "We choose our end."

"You don't have to."

"*We* choose." Thunder rolled back from the walls of the cell, and it stood to its full height. A forceful push against my senses reminded me that even drugged, the alpha's determination remained as strong as ever. "A circle, Peacemaker. Back where we started."

That was true and hurt like an open wound. I sometimes wished I was a telepath; it would have been helpful to be able to push my thoughts to Naru instead of emitting a nebulous empathic broadcast. With Alecto watching and listening at the monitors, I couldn't tell Naru I had started to form a plan with Kitryd—at least not out loud. "Give me time to come to another option. Do you still trust me?"

I dropped my mental defenses and invited it in. Naru rifled through the sketchy outline of our rescue plan. A spark of interest flared and subsided. Pushing away from contact, Naru studied me a moment. Its expressionless gray face told me nothing, but so much was happening behind its jet-black gaze.

"Yes. We trust." It lowered itself to sit on the wide, padded platform which served as a bunk. "But no option remains. Do not join us as prisoner."

"Too late for that." I lifted my manacled hands in evidence. "Naru—"

"Go." Naru turned back to the stars, but the touch of its mind against mine was gentle and without reproach.

"May I come back?" My tongue was thick with the taste of my own despair.

"We will not negotiate."

"I understand. Just to talk. To be with you until the end, if that is your choice."

Silence, then: "Come back."

I stood and went to the door. It opened before I could say anything. The Ferian guard waited outside in the corridor and was just as anxious to shut the port on my way out.

Alecto walked me back to my cell, his expression grave as the guards paced behind us. "What do you think?" he finally asked.

"I think you broke them, but not in the way you hoped. You offered them an illusion of free will and instead proved they exist only to be used. Well done."

His brow ridges drew together in confusion. "If Naru will not negotiate, why come back?"

"Because I don't want Naru to be alone when it dies," I snapped. "I want the Shontavians to know there are beings in this fucking galaxy who value them just because they exist, not for what I want them to do for me."

Alecto's color deepened to a pissed-off violet. "You believe I am a villain, as in those ridiculous dramas your species produced by the thousands? Very well, paint me as the villain in your story, but know this: the Remoliad's Prime Minister planned to terminate the Shontavians even after publicly agreeing in session to our plan."

My steps faltered as I stared at him. "You're a liar. Why should I believe that?"

His humorless laugh chilled me. "I was meant to maintain my identity and status in the security council. Instead, I made the decision to save them and destroyed almost two decades of work to infiltrate the Remoliad. I could not allow them to butcher Naru and the others because I know the truth. I have always been more monster than they are."

His self-hatred was a magnesium-white flare against my empathic nets until the *riesh* kicked in and thickened the insulating barrier against his emotional cascade, but not before I sensed fear at the root of it.

"Your boss was already angry before Skadi decided to play pirate, and they forced you to prove your loyalty by setting her up." I shook my head. "You really are in deep shit. This was your last chance."

Alecto did not look at me. "They rescued me from the brink of oblivion and brought me back to life. I cannot disappoint them again."

"Who are they?"

"The shadow against the stars." Those weren't the words he used, whispered in my head by my translator. The liquescent syllables he spoke aloud made me catch my breath in startled recognition.

"Oru la'ar gon."

The name of elder gods long forgotten in Kadrelian culture, save for myths of creation and destruction. A phrase mispronounced by Mother England as "Orlogon."

Alecto went on. "They have engineered the rise and fall of species and their planets, just as they helped bring about the final ruin of Earth."

My steps faltered. "What are you talking about?"

He stopped in front of the door to my cell and finally turned to look at me. "Your species was never meant to survive. Once the planet was uninhabitable, humanity was supposed to die out as well, not stubbornly thrive in the void clinging to rocks and ice. Your species' tenacity has earned the admiration of many Remoliad worlds, and the grudging respect of those I serve."

"What the fuck are you saying?" My mind flailed in the pull of an unthinkable singularity. "You're participating in genocide, just like you did at Amanosk?"

"Never again. Humanity's own tenacity will bring its end, however much encouraged by my employer. They are patient, but not infinitely so. Things are in motion which will speed the process and allow unrestricted access to this system."

Cortez was right. There was someone in the galaxy who wanted humans gone so they could control this sector of space, and they were playing a very long game. But what were the stakes?

"Why?" I asked the question even though I knew Alecto wasn't stupid enough to monologue his way into a confession, no matter how much he loved the sound of his own beautiful voice. "Why is this system so important they are willing to wait out humanity's extinction to get in?"

"For reasons your species in all its arrogance could not possibly understand. You may, perhaps, as you were raised in the tenets of *zezjna*, and recognize serving the greater good is not always an easy path." He pressed the panel outside the port, and it slid aside. "For now, I suggest you meditate on ways to convince Naru survival is preferable to death. If you fail, your desire to ensure they do not die alone is easily fulfilled. You have less than two days before I abandon the ship with my crew and the catalyst for the neurotoxin is released into the holding cells. This vessel is set on an interception course with Sol itself. I cannot think of a more fitting end than to send them off into the heart of one of the stars they so love." He stalked away with a parting shot: "Accompany them if you wish."

CHAPTER
TWENTY-FIVE

I LAY in the dark in my cell, hands clasped behind my head, and pretended things weren't completely fucked.

A minuscule chance remained for all this to work out in my favor if Kitryd was able to send a message. Twenty-four hours had passed since it crawled into the wall, with no sign yet of its return.

All I could do was believe Kitryd transmitted the plea for help and hope that my team would arrive in time to do something about it. Otherwise, I had to admit Alecto's intent to send the Shontavians into the heart of the sun was a terrible, beautiful end. I didn't particularly want to participate, but no matter what happened, I refused to abandon Naru. I made a promise.

There had been no time to make promises to Rion.

But until I was incinerated in my solar crematory, I would never stop trying to return to him, Tommi, and my chosen family. Once, I might have sat back and passively allowed my life to end. That was over. I had others to live for, a wonderful feeling to regain.

If it wasn't too late. My mind too full for sleep, I sank into a restless doze haunted by fragmented dreams.

I awoke to the sensation of something crawling on my face.

Instinct kicked in. I reached up to swipe at it before I remembered it might be Kitryd. Something tiny struggled beneath my fingertip. Instead of flicking it off my cheek, I let the small something wriggle out and make its way to the top of my nail. The small black blob could have been anything in the dim light of the cabin's sleep cycle. I hoped this was not just any parasite gaining access to my digestive system as I lifted my finger to my mouth.

The painful, burrowing itch of Kitryd climbing into my throat was just as unpleasant as I recalled. A sensation of fullness in my ear triggered swirling vertigo and I swallowed hard against nausea. In a moment, Kitryd spoke with the familiar artificial voice of my translator com.

The message was transmitted.

"That took longer than I thought. I got worried," I muttered and ran my hands over my face as the dizziness settled, hoping the guards would think I was talking to myself if anyone monitored the camera in my cell.

I thought it would be prudent to await their reply.

Hope burst into supernova brilliance behind my breastbone. I had to suppress the urge to immediately blurt out a response. Instead, I turned over in the bunk and pulled my blanket over my head, whispering into the pillow. "And?"

I do not understand the return message. Does your species always communicate in nonsensical phrases?

"What. Did. They. Say." It was difficult not to raise my voice above the sound of a breath.

The transmission said: You keep using that word. I do not think it means what you think it means.

Ozzie's favorite quote. The grin of relief plastered on my face would have been out of place, and I pulled the blanket closer around me. "They're coming."

That is not what it says.

"Trust me." They didn't give me an ETA—potentially problematic, but it was good to know they were on their way. "We have a deadline."

Yes. The crew will abandon ship in approximately fourteen hours. This vessel is programmed to intercept Sol in twenty-eight point two hours.

Less time than I thought.

Kitryd continued. *I absorbed pertinent data while I waited for a response. We are on a modified freight ship. The medical facility and brig are on this deck. The bridge is one deck above. All other decks are shut down save for the shuttle bay. There is a large-scale protein replicator and waste recycler in the cargo hold. One assumes this is used to nourish the Shontavians.*

"How many crew?"

Thirteen of varying species. The one called Alecto Sim, the pod of four Andari in the medical bay, three bridge crew, and five providing security. The guard you saw in the medical bay did not survive his injuries. He was not the first.

One option had the slightest chance of success, considering their diminished security contingent. "There's a control center in the cell block. If I get you inside, do you think it is possible to release the Shontavians from the brig?"

The information is already in my memory. I deduced the reason you allowed yourself to be captured was to rescue them. You are predictable. Kitryd's smugness came through loud and clear despite the flat voice of the translator. *I obtained as much helpful data as I could. The master controls to open the cells and release the electromagnetic restraints can only be accessed from the security alcove. If you contrive a method to place me directly in that area, I will find a way to override it.*

Maybe there was a chance after all. "Thank you," I breathed.

You helped retrieve my offspring. I can do no less. Kitryd paused. *Are you certain the Shontavians will not kill you when they are free?*

"As much as I can be." Which was, if I was being honest, not at all.

The ugly truth was Alecto probably suspected I would try something like this and there was no guarantee he wouldn't deploy the catalyst. Lady Darizh, the architect of the barbaric failsafe encoded in the Shontavians' own cells, warned me I might not be immune to its effects due to the human DNA we shared—right before Naru ripped her head off. "Did you find anything about the neurotoxin they will use to execute them?"

Kitryd's electrical whir tickled my empathic nets as it answered. A *delivery mechanism is connected to the brig's life support. It is not controlled by any of the ship's systems. Its command protocols may be housed in a portable device.*

That would make sense if Alecto planned to trigger the failsafe when they abandoned ship. We would have to make it out and seal the brig before the neurotoxin got deployed, but this half-assed rescue plan might actually stand a chance if the Shontavians were not too drugged to participate.

I thought about the harpoon-like syringes the Andari prepared every other day, the meticulous schedule of delivery. They'd been medicated yesterday. The sedative should be weakening by now even with the Shontavians' ultra-slow metabolism.

Now I had to win over Naru.

"All right. Here's what we're going to do."

———

I decided to play it up as a panicked, last-ditch effort to convince the Shontavians to cooperate. My keepers were not amused when I called in the middle of their sleep cycle to take me to the brig, but Alecto's orders to give me whatever I wanted apparently were still in effect.

Most Nos are surly even in the best of times—case in point: my teammate, Melos. My pallid guard was exceptionally disagreeable and didn't say a word, just held out the manacles and slapped them over my wrists. His body language clearly told me he'd rather be somewhere else, like preparing to abandon ship. When we went through the port, the Tolkish guard and a Nos I hadn't seen before sat in the alcove. Both wore armor, but their helmets lay on the worktop.

The Tolkish jailer glanced away from his screens to frown at me, his ear to chin scars dark purple in the harsh light of the brig. "They are restless," he warned.

I couldn't have orchestrated a better excuse to get Kitryd into the alcove. "Let me see." I pushed my way in to look at the holo display. All the Shontavians were more alert than they had been the previous day. One rocked back and forth in front of the port, looking out into space and crooning to itself in a deep rumble. Massive metal chains rattled against the deck as another stood to gaze out at the starfield. Sol threw narrow spears of sunlight into the cells as the ship approached the star.

"They know something is going to happen," the guard said.

"Of course they do," I snapped. "It's not inconceivable they would be restless the night before their execution."

On cue with the code word, Kitryd started to crawl less gently than usual from its hiding space in my throat. I didn't need to pretend to make it look good. The gagging hack was real, and I brought my bound hands up to cover my mouth, coughing—damn, it still hurt—until the brush of Kitryd's flagella moved against my palm.

I faked a stagger and put my hands right on top of a control pad, pressing down hard with the heel of my hand and fingertips in hope of creating a space between the worktop and the tech large enough for Kitryd to squeeze through.

"Do not touch that!" my guard barked and grabbed my

arm to pull me away. I lifted my hands in apology and witnessed the black glitter of Kitryd's form disappear into the seam between the workspace and the pad.

"Sorry. I got dizzy," I said, my voice hoarse with the effects of Kitryd's less-than-gentle passage. "But I must talk to Naru. It might be willing to listen now that time is running out."

The guards looked at each other. "Sim will not be happy if this one gets killed," the Tolkish guard muttered. "Where is he?"

"Why does it matter?" The other Nos waved his hand, annoyed. "This is why he wanted the human, yes? It is time to feed the beasts anyway. One less body to load into the shuttle when we leave." He touched the screen and the port to Naru's cell slid aside.

I didn't hesitate to cross the corridor and sent ahead a mental nudge of greeting before I reached the open door. Naru's broad gray back was turned to me as before, all four upper limbs relaxed at its sides as it faced the porthole. Chains dripped from the electromagnetic shackles into a puddle of links at its feet. This close, the fine tremor of Naru's anticipation touched my empathic webs, but its emotional broadcast was mild, without threat.

"May I come in?"

The alpha Shontavian's mind brushed against mine and acknowledged my presence as I stood in the portway. I hoped it was a yes.

The port shut behind me. I didn't stop within the safe zone this time. Imagining how the guards' heads must have been exploding made me happy. The extra steps brought me to stand beside Naru and I looked out the viewport, radiant sunlight warm on my face. "It's beautiful, isn't it? That is humanity's home star, Sol."

"Why do they bring us to this star?"

"To burn in its heart when we are dead. Alecto thought it was fitting."

Naru made a low sound in its throat. It appreciated the irony. "We did not think he understood."

"I came to discuss the option I spoke of." I didn't look at Naru. "It is a better one than before. The closer we get to the star, the less time you have to consider."

It touched my mind, more indulgent than interested. Naru's focus sharpened when it read the new developments. I held nothing back, not even the fear my team couldn't arrive in time to help us redirect the ship from its fiery end.

"You offer this option." Naru said at last.

"I do."

Information filtered through the rest of the group mind. The other Shontavians stood to face the alpha, mirror images in the line of transparent alloy windows between the cells. A profound communication I was incapable of understanding took place between them. The intensity of their empathic output was still one of anticipation, but with a vicious flare that made me shiver. They all looked forward to a little mayhem.

As one, the Shontavians raised their upper right limbs, fists clenched, and extended the digits in a starburst tipped with sharp black talons.

"We agree this is better."

"I hoped you would think so."

"What is happening?" The suspicious voice of the Tolkish guard crackled over a com speaker in the bulkhead. "Why are they doing that?"

"Just a little group consensus," I answered. "Nothing to worry about."

Even if we failed, they wouldn't die in chains.

Klaxons began to blare. The port to Naru's cell slowly released and slid into the wall, the corridor outside lit in pulsing red.

A cloud of startled profanity rose and fell over the com. "What the fuck is happening?"

"Seal them, you idiot!"

"I did not do it!" His voice gained a higher pitch. "The panel will not take the command!"

Naru lifted its head and sifted the air through its teeth. It spread its four upper limbs as the electromagnetic seals on its shackles fell away in a clatter of metal links. In the line of windows between the cells, the other five Shontavians pulled their bonds away from ankles and wrists.

The guards were screaming at each other, their fear bouncing off my empathic webs through the open door in the bulkhead.

The alpha looked down at me. "Stay here, Peacemaker."

No problem. I sat down on its pallet bed to wait and furled my empathic nets as tightly as I could as Naru ducked through the door. I didn't really want to experience this bloodbath in my head. My other senses were going to pick that up whether I wanted them to or not.

More screams. The zing of energy weapons discharge. Shrill cries of terror, a crunch of bone, and the acrid sharpness of humanoid blood rode the air. A metallic, ripping sound; afterward, nothing but the ceaseless wail of emergency klaxons.

"Come." Naru beckoned to me from the doorway, its gray-skinned hand dripping with gore. Steeling myself, I rose and exited the cell.

The burn and fade of red warning lights illuminated thick, dark smears on the deck. What remained of the three guards lay scattered in the corridor in front of the security alcove. None of the Shontavians were snacking, thank the merciful universe. I couldn't have faced that right now. It was bad enough picking over the lower half of my ex-guard to find the key fob which unlocked the manacles.

Two of the bioengineered warriors were in possession of the guards' energy weapons. A third bore scorch marks on its thick gray hide but held a heavy caliber rifle the guards had not had time to bring into play.

The main port was cockeyed, likely slammed back into its housing as it tried to close. It now hung open, unable to retract into the bulkhead. The mechanical whine and thump of the mechanism in a futile attempt to shut the port confirmed we had no way to seal off the brig if the catalyst was deployed.

Oh, that wasn't good. I probably should have said something about that.

"The bridge. Where is it?" Naru rumbled. The eager, ferocious desire for retribution crested against my mind as the others impatiently waited for orders.

"Wait. Our guide is somewhere in this mess," I said, skidding on gore as I sped into the messy alcove. "Kitryd? Where are you?"

In the strobing light, it was difficult to find something tiny and void-black, but I finally saw the AI emerge from the console into a smear of blood. I put my hand down and let Kitryd crawl up my finger, lifting it to my mouth before I could think too much about the slimy trail it left on my skin.

I fought the impulse to heave as the metallic taste of somebody's fluids crawled over my tongue and into my throat. Dislodging the AI in a fountain of vomit would be detrimental. There was no coming back from that.

The physical manifestations of Kitryd's passage were over quickly, but a needle of pain marked its hiding place as I croaked, "Kitryd, we need to get to the bridge."

That corridor runs the length of the ship. There is an intersecting corridor to stern. The bridge is located one deck up in the command module, accessible by ladder tube or lift from this level.

Naru's curiosity grew, recognizing I was no longer alone in my head. Its telepathic probe detected Kitryd as something alive, but not understood. No time for introductions. I relayed the information to Naru.

It turned to its fellows and made rapid signs with its four hands in the silent language used by the other Shontavians. The one with the large caliber rifle took point, flanked by two others with energy weapons pilfered from the dead. Naru took place at the rear behind me with the other two. I was surrounded by a protective shield of huge gray bodies as they advanced through the corridor. Bloody footprints on the deck marked our passage for a dozen meters and the bray of klaxons receded.

"What about the shuttle bay?" I asked Kitryd.

One deck down. The ladder tubes port and starboard span all decks.

I relayed the information and wondered if the crew would even fight, faced by a squad of pissed off, enemy-eating super soldiers who held a grudge.

We met the first resistance at the intersecting corridor leading to the bridge. The Ferian guard intercepted us with a projectile weapon, too close to the outer bulkhead for my comfort.

Dark blood spattered from the upper limb of one of the forward Shontavians as a bullet sank into its flesh, but the Ferian didn't have a chance when the group charged ahead. Energy fire took down our attacker and sharp, black talons did the rest. Two more crew offered token resistance before fleeing down the port ladder tube they guarded.

Naru exchanged rapid signs with its soldiers as they picked up the fallen weapons. Three stormed down the corridor to the opposite ladder tube as two others climbed the starboard ladder to the bridge. Their bulky bodies barely fit into the narrow shaft. Naru, listening intently to their group mind, said, "The bridge is empty."

"They're abandoning ship." I grabbed the rungs of the ladder and half-slid, half climbed down to the deck housing the shuttle bay. Above me, Naru's gray ass filled the tube and I moved hastily out of the shaft. The port to the bay was sealed; alarms shrieked a warning of imminent decompression. Through the narrow viewport, I glimpsed Alecto standing at the bottom of the shuttle's ramp, his robes fluttering around him. He held a data device, one slender mauve digit poised over the screen.

He looked up and found me watching. The *riesh* gleamed against his forehead, deep furrows of conflicted pain between his carmine eyes.

"Don't do it," I said even though I knew he couldn't hear me, my voice shattered by despair.

His mouth turned upward in another beautiful, heart-breaking smile, polar opposition to the resignation in his eyes. He slid the device into his robe and boarded the shuttle. The bay doors opened, and Alecto and his remaining crew abandoned ship.

CHAPTER
TWENTY-SIX

THE SHONTAVIANS WERE busy disposing of the corpses they'd made when Naru and I returned. They were hungry, and *waste not, want not* was their favorite motto. Naru joined in, so I left them to their meal and hurriedly climbed the ladder to the command module to disrupt our collision course with Sol.

Any benevolent thoughts I might have entertained about Alecto when he didn't set off the failsafe toxin morphed into fantasies of murder once I reached the bridge.

I gaped at the sabotaged console in horrified dismay. Alecto or his crew had delivered strategic damage to the controls; a nest of severed wires and a blast from an energy weapon rendered the helm inoperable. The subspace com, my only means of calling for help, was a lump of melted circuitry and a shattered screen.

The computer system which controlled the ship's course appeared intact. Readouts counted down the distance to Sol's corona, the bridge's polarized view shield open to reveal a panorama of the star in all its terrifying glory. Sunspots pock-marked its brilliant surface, like the dark thoughts that flitted through my mind as I imagined what I would do to the purple bastard if I ever saw him again.

I had a feeling I wouldn't. Alecto had failed his employer, maybe for the last time. Knowing what they forced him to do to Skadi for stealing the AIs, I could not imagine what fate awaited him. And my own might already be sealed.

I closed my eyes in defeat and slid down the bulkhead to sit on the deck with my back against the wall, elbows jabbed into my bent knees and hands fisted in my hair.

"Kitryd, how long before we intersect with the sun's corona?" I whispered.

Twenty-one point four hours, based on my last interface with the computer. As we approach the star, our speed will increase, and the time diminish.

Not long enough to repair the helm, even if I had a clue how to fix it. Technology wasn't my forte. I couldn't negotiate with seared circuitry and tangled wire. No, I needed my team. Ka'pth and Ra'sho could hotwire something in a matter of hours. Sumner knew this model of freighter; he'd flown them on a mission before our paths crossed.

If I had my full mass, I could fly the ship directly from the computer. Its thoughts occupied the same narrow channel of hope as mine. But Kitryd Prime was back on Luna, or somewhere between there and Europa after being reunited with its offspring.

Instead of dwelling on what I couldn't do, I asked Kitryd, "How long does it take to travel to your collective's home system?"

To return on a ship like this one, without dark space capability, it would take more than one hundred years by Sol Fed's measure of time.

"Are you in a hurry to go back?"

No. I will not be alone for the journey when the time comes, thanks to you and Agent Saetang.

I hoped Michael Patil was able to help Kitryd leave the solar system. I didn't know how its deportation might go, depending on the condition of its first host. Conway was Kiran Singh's murderer, caught in the act on security holos, and I couldn't imagine Kitryd being detained on charges under the circumstances. But this was Sol Fed, the ratio of solicitors to citizens ridiculously high. I hadn't seen any news holos since I arrived on Europa—was it only a week ago? —and wondered what was happening with Skadi and ex-President Batterson.

And Rion. My throat ached; my eyes stung. I took a shuddering breath and pushed myself off the floor before I got pulled back into the black hole I had so recently escaped.

"All right. Let's see if there is anything salvageable about the helm before my team gets here." They would. I believed they would. I searched through storage in the bulkhead, found an emergency tool kit, and got to work.

———

Four exhausting hours passed as I resoldered connections under the helm's console. All I managed to accomplish was getting more of the navigational display to show up on the bank of holo screens. I was unable to restore manual steering capability or program a new course. The damage was too great. A hundred more severed wires remained, and more than a few melted circuits. Frustration at my limited knowledge spilled out of my mouth in a roar.

"Peacemaker." Naru's head emerged from the ladder tube. "You are angry."

"Disheartened," I admitted, rolling my shoulders and neck to relieve the tension. "I can't fix the helm. I do not possess the skills or the parts."

Naru climbed out of the tube and crouched near me on the deck. "We know warfare, not repair of ships."

"I am so sorry, Naru."

"Odds were not good. We knew," the alpha said.

"We did. I am still sorry I can't give you what we promised."

"We are content."

They truly had no worries. The sense from the group mind was a calm breeze in my empathic webs. They were full of ultra-rare guard meat and now wandered about the corridors, exploring parts of the freighter they had never seen in their months of captivity.

But as I studied the readouts on the navigational display, my insides went cold. As Kitryd had warned, the ship was picking up speed as we approached the sun, drawn in by its gravity. Our velocity was too fast for any vessel large enough to carry the Shontavians and me to safely dock in the bay.

Even if *Thunder Child* arrived, I couldn't let them risk it.

"Kitryd." My mouth was dry as I read it the new data. "Based on our current velocity, how much time is left before we intercept the corona?"

Sixteen hours. If our speed continues to increase at this rate, interception could happen in as little as twelve hours.

Not enough time. Damn it.

Would I have done anything differently?

Not where the Shontavians were concerned. But the beloved faces of my regrets loomed sharp and poignant in my imagination, smooth-skinned, furry, and scaled. Family, chosen and genetic. Maybe I should have tried to repair the subspace relay first, to send a message and tell them how much they meant to me.

"You are frightened," Naru rumbled.

"Yes." I blinked tears away, trying not to unravel. "I'm not looking forward to being incinerated."

"We will eat you first."

Naru's telepathic nudge was almost playful, like a human might teasingly bump my shoulder. A twist of hysteria turned my exhalation into a high-pitched laugh, but it released some of my tension.

"Thank you, Naru." I appreciated the humor. At least, I thought it was a joke. Since the Shontavians ate their own dead as well as their enemies, Naru might have just bestowed on me some sort of honor. Either way, I accepted the offer for what it was and still fervently hoped it would never happen.

Just when I thought it was time to sit back and watch the sun swallow us whole, static erupted from my com.

I sat up, excitement zinging through my nerves, and Naru shifted to regard me with curiosity, sensing the abrupt change in my thought patterns. Tommi's translated words in my ear were the sweetest sounds I'd ever heard, the signal growing stronger by the second. "Dalí? Respond if you can."

"I'm here, Tommi," I said, shaky with relief. "It's so good to hear your voice."

"Sorry we're late," Ozzie said. "We had to detour and pick up a package from Agent Saetang."

My offspring? Kitryd said over my com, its fuzzy, static excitement sending tingles across my scalp.

"Who is that?" Ozzie's sharp inquiry bristled with menace. "How in the Unholy Fires are you talking to me?"

I am in Dalí's head. I am Kitryd, an artificial intelligence.

"Uh . . . hold on a second." The reason for my friend's confusion became clear when a moment later, another computer-generated voice spoke.

"That is the part of our mass we shed while still in custody."

"As you can tell, there are guests on board," Ziggy's voice came over the line. "I assume you can't control the ship since you're on a collision course with Sol?"

"Alecto and his crew scuttled the bridge before they abandoned the freighter," I said. Naru's gentle telepathic touch distracted me as it investigated the newly active, separate consciousness borrowing my skull space. "Please tell me you guys have a plan, because if you don't, I think I'm terminally screwed this time. The manual controls are scrap, the subspace communications panel is melted, but at least the computer's navigational system seems to be working. I don't know if that helps."

"It does." Ra'sho's calm tone reassured me. "How many are on board?"

"Me, and six very large gray friends."

"The Shontavians are the Brute Squad?" Ziggy blurted.

"Any other immediate concerns?" Ozzie was all business.

"The failsafe neurotoxin is wired into the environmental system in the brig, and the main port is damaged. It will poison the whole ship if it goes off."

"Stand by." That was Ka'pth, brisk and focused.

"That's a standard autopilot program." Sumner. He was here. His voice sent a flood of complicated emotions through me. "We should be able to override the helm on the same frequency Trade Hub flight control uses for auto docking maneuvers."

"We have assumed control of the flight computer, but the helm is not responding." Ra'sho's frustration lent a sharpness to the translation in my ear.

"I'll land in the bay with *Three* and start repairs," Sumner said.

I objected immediately. "No, it's too dangerous."

"I agree." Ozzie's grim pronouncement. "Even you can't land with that kind of velocity. You'd be a smear inside the cockpit. We need to think of ways to slow down the freighter without disabling its ability to escape the sun's gravity once we do get on board to repair the systems."

"Give me a better idea," Sumner demanded. Silence reigned for fifteen painful seconds before he said, "I'm going. If we wait any longer it will only make it harder to land in the bay."

"Not an option," I snapped. "You'll kill yourself trying."

"I'm not giving up."

I closed my eyes against the desperation in his voice. A peal of sorrow resounded from the hollow places in my chest for what we might have been.

"We have a suggestion." That was Kitryd Prime on *Thunder Child*. "Do you carry a drone on board that can match the speed of the freighter?"

"Not a drone, but an atmospheric probe," Ka'pth replied. "It is more of an unarmed missile."

"When launched, does it reach the appropriate velocity?"

"Yes, but it isn't something we could steer." Ozzie was intrigued by the idea; I could tell by the way his pronunciation of more sibilant consonants elongated into a hiss.

"Could it be fired into the bay with a degree of accuracy if we were placed inside its chassis?"

"Yes. Yes, I think so if we remove the probe's instrument package," Ziggy said with cautious excitement. "With minor adjustments to compensate for the change in mass, and such a big target, I can do it. But can you survive the crash landing?"

"We can alter our conveyance to suspend us in a way which will redistribute the force of impact. Once on the bridge, we will function as an interface to temporarily complete the destroyed circuits and program a new heading away from the star."

The Kitryd in my head had mentioned that was possible. But I didn't miss its change in identifier from singular to plural and asked, "Are you willing to risk your offspring this way?"

"We are in agreement," Kitryd answered. "We owe you and Rion Sumner recompense for your efforts to capture Skadi and reunite us."

"Best idea I've heard so far." Ozzie sounded hopeful.

"And the safest, honestly," Tommi said. "We can't guarantee any of us will be unaffected by the neurotoxin should it deploy. Kitryd should be immune. And how long has it been since the Shontavians last fed?"

"Erm . . . not long," I admitted weakly. "That isn't an issue."

"The bay is open. Kitryd should be able to re-pressurize and close it from the inside based on the schematics you sent us," Ra'sho announced. "I believe we have a solid plan."

"All right. Do it." The familiar snap of authority was back in Sumner's voice. "Tommi, get Saetang on the line and ask her to send a repair ship. We can rendezvous with them as soon as we've got the freighter under control. We'll need a new helm console and subspace communications setup."

"Nobody but our team comes on board, especially not with fucking weapons," I said fiercely. "We can't let word get out the Shontavians are here." I didn't trust any government to do right by them.

"We won't let that happen," Sumner promised. "We'll contact you as soon as we're ready to launch."

CHAPTER
TWENTY-SEVEN

WHILE WE WAITED for Kitryd's arrival, Naru and the others gathered in the safety of the bridge. It was a tight fit with all six Shontavians packed in shoulder to shoulder. They stood and gazed at the shielded view screen, Sol's fiery visage expanding as time slipped away.

I closed and locked the hatches of both ladder tubes leading down to the bay at each deck. There was significant danger of accidental decompression—firing something like a blunt missile into the shuttle bay might not be the smartest thing to do but was the only plan we had. I hoped Kitryd's confidence about surviving the impact was not solely based on what it thought it owed Sumner and me.

Inviting Naru into my mind, I prepared it for how Kitryd appeared in its conveyance. I wanted to prevent the AI from registering as a threat to the Shontavians, doubting they could hurt it even if they tried. But the calm serenity of the group persisted.

Despite their brutal conditioning in the orbiting laboratory where they were created, the Shontavians had grasped a thread of beauty amid the violence and developed a spiritual connection to the stars, something their masters never intended. My empathic nets were awash in what I could only describe as devotion as they watched Sol grow closer.

The group truly did not care what would happen should our plan fail. It was just another cycle of captivity and escape, and this moment of calm which came after was all that mattered to them.

I closed my eyes and allowed their serenity to fill me. Even though it wasn't mine, my pulse slowed. The painful knots in my neck and shoulder muscles relaxed and my hands hung loose at my sides.

For the first time since Gresh and Rasida died, borrowed peace occupied the contemplative places inside me. Strange the gift should come at such a time, and in such company. I was ready to find my own calm again, to break away from the chaotic circle of grief and danger I had allowed my life to become.

With gratitude, I sank into the tranquil pool surrounding me and floated there until Sumner's quiet voice tugged me back to the surface.

"We're set, Dalí. Everybody secure?"

"Yes, we're on the bridge." I emerged, blinking, from the deep, meditative state. "Ready when you are."

"Launch sequence initiated," Ziggy said. "Kitryd is away. Impact in three. Two. One."

I didn't detect anything, not a shudder or sound, but Ozzie exulted, "Right on target, sibling!"

"The doors aren't closing," Ra'sho said worriedly after a few minutes.

"Give Kitryd a little more time," I said, but my inner calm rapidly eroded as agonizing seconds passed without an update.

"We underestimated the force of impact on our construct and lost the com badge for a moment," Kitryd's artificial voice said at last. "We are aboard. Engaging manual controls to close the bay."

"They are shut," Ka'pth announced a minute later. "Emergency re-pressurization commencing."

Dizzy with relief, I let out a deep sigh while the triumphant exclamations of my teammates overlapped each other.

"We will come up the starboard tube when it is safe," Kitryd advised.

I hurried to unseal the hatches between decks. The pressure released with a resounding hiss, and I lifted the hatch on the lowest deck. Kitryd was already there, its construct moving so quickly up the rungs it startled me. I hightailed up the ladder, but the AI went over and around me and reached the bridge first.

Naru and the others came to attention when Kitryd's glittering black mass appeared. A rainfall of soft clicks sounded from the construct's links as Kitryd pattered over the deck like a multi-legged insect and headed for the helm. Six smaller constructs skittered behind, burning-dark images like sunspots suspended in the center of each climbing up and over me as I emerged from the tube. They were almost cute if I ignored the fact they could forcibly hijack my nervous system.

A badge com flashed at the front of Kitryd's primary mass as the links stacked and raised the AI to the scuttled console. "We will attempt to reconstruct the helm's circuitry to the navigational computer. Communication will be interrupted." The badge dropped to the deck. Kitryd stretched and flowed, encompassing the severed connections.

The Shontavians, impassive as ever at the prospect of crashing into a star, were nonetheless fascinated by Kitryd's offspring. They drew closer to watch three of the little AIs climb spider-like up the bracket of the console and join Kitryd's mass inside the shattered helm. I surveyed the holo screens with my heart pounding against my knotted arms, waiting for a sign the AI's intervention was working. So far, the attempt seemed futile. Our speed climbed slowly; the heading remained unchanged.

"How are you holding up?" Sumner asked. I knew he was watching the same readouts on board *Thunder Child*.

"Honestly? I could really use some of Michael's rum right now."

He laughed softly. "Yeah. Me too."

"Where are you?"

"In my ready room."

"Good." I took a deep breath to steady my nerves. "Hey, Tommi? Could you please switch off everybody else's coms for a couple of minutes?"

"Are you sure this is the time for a dirty com call?" Ozzie asked soberly, but I heard him laughing as Tommi hissed at him and shut down everybody's feed but mine and Sumner's. I moved as far away as I could from the spellbound Shontavians and Kitryd's repair efforts. What I needed to say wasn't for everyone's ears.

My tone was light, but the fear was still an icy, clenching fist in my core. "In case I don't have a chance later, I should tell you something."

Sumner was quiet for a moment. "Not goodbye," he said gruffly. "I won't accept that, not yet. It's too soon to give up."

"No. I want to say, I think I started to fall in love with you back in that sticky bar on Neptune Station when you asked if flirting was out of the question. It took me a ridiculously long time to figure out."

"It happened back on the *Bedia* for me," he said.

"So soon?"

"The first time I saw you make the switch from ambassador to avenging angel." His voice dropped. "I wanted to learn everything about you."

A thrill of warmth crept through me like sunlight as he continued. "I was almost reluctant to offer you a job, which meant keeping my distance. I didn't want to."

"Being the asshole I am had to make things easier."

"I'm a very patient man, except where you're concerned. You drive me to distraction, like no one ever has." He cleared his throat. "And if you think this is going to keep me from addressing the fact you put your life in danger yet again by going to Europa alone, you are sadly mistaken."

"I look forward to the dressing down, Commander."

"Oh, there will definitely be one." His voice went rough, and change hormones started percolating in my system.

Sumner's com pinged. "Report," he said briskly.

"Sorry to interrupt," Ozzie said, brimming with excitement. "We have control of the both the helm and the nav computer. You know how to fly that thing, and we need your input."

"Initiate deceleration sequence. On my way."

I turned back to the tableau on the bridge. Naru balanced one of the little AIs in the palm of its lower left hand. It held the communicator up like a signboard, and they were speaking to each other.

"We are separate, but one," the AI said, the com translating its speech into Ursetu for the Shontavians.

"As we are." Naru's wonder touched my empathic nets as I approached. "Alive. No thoughts, but it thinks."

"Yes. Alive, just like us," I confirmed.

"This is what is in your head."

"Exactly."

I must rejoin my primary mass, my Kitryd said. *We must share everything I have seen and discovered while on board this ship.*

Great. The last thing I wanted to do was cough it up now. My nerves were shot, no guarantees my stomach wouldn't turn inside out this time. But Kitryd was right, so I warned my team of impending bodily functions and got it over with. The tiny piece of darkness rejoined the rest of the void while I caught my breath.

The velocity began to drop, the deceleration enough to make me lean forward in the ship's light gravity. I steadied myself against the console.

"I believe we have a problem," the overhead com announced.

"Kitryd?"

"Yes. We have discovered something unusual. A subroutine tied into the navigational computer started running when we gained control of the ship. It is a countdown."

I groaned. "Don't tell me. Linked to the life support systems?"

"Why would you not want us to tell you? Is this more human nonsense communication?"

"Yes! Tell me." My stowaway really had shared everything with Kitryd Prime.

"What's going on?" Sumner asked.

"I think Alecto left a fucking booby trap, is what's going on."

"I have confirmed the countdown was triggered by the abrupt deceleration," Kitryd said. "The neurotoxin will deploy if the ship's velocity drops below a certain point."

"What point?"

"We suggest you stop decelerating at once and hold this speed."

"Shit." I cursed Alecto in six more languages and added a whistling Zereid expletive just for fun.

"The freighter is still going too fast to execute a turn away from the sun," Sumner said grimly. "The centrifugal force will break it in half."

"How long until we absolutely have to make the turn?"

"Twenty minutes."

I dove for the ladder tube.

Naru flashed a series of sharp signs to the other Shonta-vians and descended after me. I heard the hatches seal above us before we reached the deck. He pounded down the corridor as I hurdled over smeared bloodstains on the floor. My chest was on fire by the time we got to the brig. The warped port was still trying to retract into its pocket with an increasingly pathetic whimper of hydraulics.

"Okay, Kitryd," I panted against the sharp catch in my ribs. "Where is the toxin linked into the environmental system?"

"Overhead panel seventeen. Junction four," Kitryd responded, its voice echoing through the freighter.

I found the access frame eight feet above my head in the middle of the corridor. No ladders. Even the huge alpha couldn't reach the outlet alone. "Naru, can you lift me up?"

"Sit." It cupped its two lower hands together and I lowered my butt into them. Naru lifted me to its upper limbs and held my ass high over its head, its other hands steadying my feet. I reached up and pressed the panel's release.

A clear cylinder the size of my forearm and full of a very fine powder lay in the junction where the gaseous mix of the deck's life support system came together. Blinking lights jeweled the pressure collars of tubes descending from the main line to plug into both ends of the chamber. Oh, and an atomic clock set in one end of the cylinder made green revolutions on its tiny holo screen. Just another perfect development. "Seven fucking hells. Somebody, please tell me how to disarm this thing." I described the timer and connections in as much detail as I could.

"It sounds to be a pressure container. I think the detonator is likely monitoring the ship's speed," Ra'sho said. "Kitryd, do you agree?"

"We have no way of knowing. Based on the subroutine, I believe that is correct." The com speaker was right behind me, and I involuntarily jumped at the loud transmission, flailing in panic. Naru's hands shifted to keep me upright, one of its talons digging into the meat of my right ass cheek.

"Sumner is keeping the freighter at a steady velocity. Do

not interrupt the timer's power or that could be interpreted as a full stop."

"Great," I muttered, taking note of the detonator's control panel. "How do I disconnect the pressure valves without blowing the dust into the system?"

"Shut the valve on the starboard side first," Ra'sho instructed. "Twist to the right to prevent the toxin from entering the ducts if the other side opens. When it is closed, press the release catch in the upper half."

I twisted to the right. The lights on the collar went out. I held my breath—uselessly if this thing went off, but it made me feel better—and pressed the release catch. I had a minor coronary event as a faint hiss of air stirred the powder inside, but nothing escaped as the valve resealed itself. The half of the collar connected to the cylinder parted from the supply tube with a click. "One down."

"Repeat the procedure on the other side. Twist to the right and press the release catch."

The device came loose in my hands. "Got it. Naru, put me down." I gasped as the powder shifted inside the still-pressurized cylinder. "*Very* carefully." The Shontavian set me on my feet as gently as if I were an infant.

The detonator beeped. I almost pissed myself as the atomic clock went from green to yellow. "No. No no no!"

"Final countdown has commenced in the subroutine. You have approximately two minutes," Kitryd announced.

"Where's the closest airlock?" I gritted my teeth and started walking, the cylinder gingerly extended in front of me. Naru followed, but I said over my shoulder, "Naru, get to the bridge and seal it off!"

"I will stay with you, Peacemaker," Naru said.

"The shuttle bay has the only airlock which can be safely opened at high speed," Kitryd said.

"Too far," I said, tight-lipped. "I won't make it."

"Is there a medical bay?" Tommi's voice sounded over my com. "It should have its own life support system and a negative pressure threshold to prevent airborne diseases from circulating through the ship."

"There is." I increased my pace. "It's even on this deck."

"Why am I not surprised you know where the medical bay is?" Tommi quipped. I grinned despite the fact I was holding a literal time bomb in my hands.

"One minute," Kitryd said, its pronouncement bouncing off the walls like the voice of doom. The cylinder's countdown turned from yellow to orange.

This was still the longest fucking corridor ever. It seemed like it would never end.

"When you get there, locate something you can put it in. Wrap it in a blanket, anything to decrease the dispersal rate and get out," Tommi advised. "The bay will seal itself off if it detects a contaminant."

I could see the door now. "Naru, open the med bay door. Do not just rip it out of the wall! See if you can find a large container with a lid."

Naru thundered down the corridor, crouched, and delicately tapped the control panel with one talon, which would have been hilarious if things were different. The port opened and Naru disappeared inside as the timer's screen blushed from orange to red. Fuck it. I was running.

The Shontavian met me with a refuse container. I lowered the device inside, grabbed a blanket out of a medical pod and stuffed it on top as the detonator started to beep its final warning. "Get out! Now!"

I pushed Naru through the door. I stabbed my finger against the emergency lock mechanism and collapsed on the deck with my back against the bulkhead. The port sealed behind us.

Slowing my breath was harder than I remembered. So

much for the medical advice to avoid doing anything strenuous.

"Slow down the ship and execute that turn," I gasped.

"Aye," Sumner acknowledged with relief in his voice. "Re-engaging deceleration sequence."

The drag of gravity was stronger this time, making me tilt sideways. I braced myself as Naru squatted on the floor beside me and rumbled, "We are safe."

"Yeah," I managed. "We did it, Naru."

A red light flashed above the portal and the metallic shunting of an inner lock vibrated the bulkhead behind me. The device had deployed, and the bay responded just as my teammate said it would.

"Tommi, I love you."

"I know." Her laughter rang, bright and relieved, over the com.

CHAPTER
TWENTY-EIGHT

SUMNER REMOTE-PILOTED the freighter's starboard turn with only minutes left. The hull temperature got uncomfortably high even with deflectors at maximum, but the shielding held up. The Shontavians and I watched from the bridge as the enormity of Sol's fiery heart slipped sideways to reveal the glittering, cold infinity of deep space.

While Sumner continued to bring us down to boarding speed, the gray giants displayed a fascination with the tiny, skittering AIs that had not joined Kitryd in its patch of the navigation system. An idea began to take shape.

The ship had already been customized to suit the Shontavians' needs. Alecto once hoped to house them here indefinitely. He had given them everything we promised except freedom. Without that, it was meaningless.

Save for the locked-down medical bay, they could now roam anywhere on board the freighter, had numerous views of their beloved stars, and equipment to provide food and water.

All they needed was a crew to operate and maintain the ship.

"Kitryd, are you still in Agent Saetang's custody?"

"No." Its voice emerged from the panel beside me instead of over the ship's com. It had rapidly gained control of all systems once it patched into the main computer. "She requested our presence after our offspring were recovered on Europa. Rion Sumner flew us in a small, fast ship to meet Agent Saetang aboard her vessel before they emerged. Michael Patil arranged to transfer us into Sumner's custody as a Remoliad law enforcement officer. It is our under-standing we did not wait for the agreement to be legally sealed. There was no time once we agreed to the conditions."

"I'm sure Michael has the red tape well in hand. What are the terms?"

"We recorded a deposition against Miriam Skadi before we departed and must immediately leave Sol Fed space once reunited with our offspring."

That might work. "How long did you say it will take to travel to your home system?"

"Without dark space travel capability, perhaps more than one hundred years by Sol Fed's measurement of time."

"You can fly and maintain this ship."

"Yes. If the helm is repaired, it will require very little of our attention. With our constructs we can perform other necessary maintenance."

I bit my lip. "How would you feel about passengers?"

"The Shontavians?" Kitryd's artificial voice was gaining some inflection, or I was just getting used to it. It sounded interested, almost eager.

"Yes." I explained what they were promised, and the distinct advantage of not having flesh-and-blood caretakers on board. The robotic deck-scrubbers Kitryd had discovered were busy cleaning up after the recent meal consisting of the last crew. I hoped Naru and the others liked replicated protein enough to maintain a steady diet of it until the end of their lifespan. I needed to talk to them about this idea.

As if I spoke aloud, Naru turned to me, its mind brushing against mine. "You want to ask us something."

"I do. This freighter contains everything you need to live, but it was once your prison. Now that you are free, I wondered what you might think about taking control of this ship to travel the stars, as we originally planned."

Naru's mind quickened with the thought. "We cannot pilot. It was not part of the simulation training."

"Kitryd and its offspring can pilot and maintain the ship. They want to return to their home system. Kitryd says it will take more than your lifespan to arrive."

I felt Naru reach out to the other Shontavians, pulses of thought-energy skimming my empathic nets. "We will travel with them," Naru said at last.

A small AI scuttled its way up Naru's upper limb and sat there as Naru gazed thoughtfully into the starry black. I grinned, thinking of ancient seafaring stories, a buccaneer captain at the helm with an avian mascot perched on his shoulder. Any pirates who might attempt to board this ship would be unpleasantly surprised.

———

Once the freighter's speed was safe for boarding, Sumner and Ra'sho arrived in *Three* to assess the damage to the helm and begin repairs.

I met them at the bay's airlock. My insides flip-flopped with a strange, pleasant anxiety as they unstrapped from their seats and exited the cockpit. Sumner's gaze held mine as he slowly walked toward me, allowing our smaller Andari teammate to outpace him.

Ra'sho patted my arm in greeting. "I am happy to see you in one piece."

"Me, too." I grinned at him. "Speaking of which, I had the

Shontavians clear the bridge so you can work. It was a bit crowded."

"I am ready to begin." He glanced back at Sumner, who waved him on. Ra'sho hefted his backpack of tools and spare parts and headed directly for the ladder tube, his throat gills fluttering in a chortle of amusement.

Sumner pulled me against him for a passionate and thorough kiss, taking his time. I approved of this change in his behavior. The walls of rank were gone, all pretense of disinterest eradicated as his arms went around me. An unsteady breath betrayed my relief as I laughed against his mouth, my eyes wet. "I am so damn glad to see you."

He pulled back and traced his fingers over the yellowing contusions on my face, the new shape of my broken nose. "You look a little worse for the wear."

"You should have seen me on Europa. Please tell me Saetang arrested the Battersons."

He affirmed my query with a nod. "Simon Batterson was charged with the intergalactic trafficking of life-forms, receipt of smuggled goods, assault and battery of a law enforcement officer, and murder for hire in the death of Kiran Singh."

I was going to raise a glass in Singh's memory the next time I saw Dev and Michael. Kiran may have been a pushy, invasive, calculating little prick, but his killing was brutal. I hoped Batterson's legal team couldn't talk his way out of this one. "Was England willing to bargain?"

"She will testify against Skadi and Samuel Batterson. Her solicitor worked out a deal with the federal prosecutor." He paused. "Brian Batterson is also cooperating with Homeland Security on the promise of reduced charges in your abduction. He was Singh's inside source."

"I thought that might be the case." Brian had better have loyal bodyguards. The NPM was not going to be happy.

"Saetang has her hands full. She wants your testimony against the ex-President to make the charges stick."

"I figured that too. Sounds like I'll have to go back to Luna."

"We both have to stay for a while," he corrected gently. "She asked for our help to build the case against Skadi."

My feelings about it were conflicted. Even though Skadi confessed, I knew Saetang needed all the hard evidence she could obtain. In some ways, I wanted nothing more to do with Skadi. She was in Sol Fed custody, and I trusted Saetang to keep her there. The darker, vengeful part of me wanted to make certain Skadi was buried in the deepest cell Tranquility had to offer.

"What about the Remoliad?" I thought aloud. "We can't keep this under the radar anymore."

"We'll deal with it when it comes." His mouth caught mine again. This time I responded with fierce attention and nipped at his bottom lip. He groaned in resignation. "We have a ship to repair."

"I have a room. I can even unlock the door now."

"Show me later," he murmured.

"Just make sure to turn off your com," Ozzie quipped in my head.

———

Sumner and Ra'sho worked to fix the helm's severed connections and relieve Kitryd from holding everything together. To distract myself from thinking about dragging Sumner off to my former cell, I permanently sealed the port of the medical bay using the micro-welder Ra'sho brought with him. Metal fused in a glowing ribbon as sparks bounced off my heavy gloves.

I thought about Alecto's cryptic warning: that events were set in motion to ensure humanity's extinction. I intended to share everything he'd said with Saetang. Sol Fed's xenophobia and suspicion of the Remoliad's motives would serve it well.

The knowledge gained after my family's murder was something I could never forget. The optimistic diplomat I had once been when Gresh, Rasida, and a bright future lay ahead was never coming back, having succumbed to a full dose of the cynicism which seemed to be part of the human condition.

Maybe that was why our species was still alive despite Residuum's best efforts, flourishing on pessimism and pure spite beneath domes and radiation shielding.

Radiation shielding. Something bothered me about it.

The ripple of thought spread out. I let it grow, stripping off the dark safety goggles to examine my work for gaps. Without shielding, humanity would be fatally exposed to cosmic radiation.

This was why Luna's production of the transparent alloys which allowed light in but kept radiation out, and the instruments used to monitor their effectiveness and warn when levels were too high for safety, was so important.

Manufacturing. Now that Remoliad supplies were available, there was no risk of running out of critical components to manufacture the—

Fuck.

The singular relief supply crate on the Kadrelian freighter, with a critical shipping tag. The data chips necessary to build radiation monitors, found in the same container as the cartel's drug shipment. There had been a surprisingly large number. What if they were corrupted?

I tapped my com. "Tommi? I need to transmit an urgent message to Saetang."

Everything in the crate might be suspect. I hoped it wasn't too late to stop it.

———

Alecto's crew hadn't left much behind in the galley, but I was able to scrounge enough together to make a patchwork meal for Sumner, Ra'sho, and me. I'd lost track of time; it had been at least twenty-four hours since I woke to Kitryd crawling on my face. A bone-cracking yawn shook me so hard I winced against the protest of my healing ribs. I was beginning to wish I had hoarded some painkillers, but there was no getting anything out of the contaminated bay now.

Ra'sho's throat gills lay limp against his neck, and dark circles shadowed Sumner's eyes. They had to have gone without rest for as long as I had, maybe more. With Kitryd's help, they completed circuitry restorations and swapped out the melted boards in the helm with the Andari's spare pieces. It would take several more hours for the repair ship to reach us with the consoles needed to replace the navigation controls and communications system.

Once I found an unused cabin for Ra'sho and finally got Sumner to my room, all either of us had the energy to do was take off our boots and outer shirts, crawl into the comfortable but narrow bed, and crash. For a while, anyway.

I woke in the faint blue illumination of the cabin's sleep cycle to the softest brush of Rion's lips against my closed eyelids. His hand cupped my cheek, his thumb stroking my skin.

I turned on my side to face him. The length of our bodies touched at chest, thigh, and warm, intertwined bare feet. Sudden, fierce need tightened my groin, change hormones coursing through my blood in response to his body pressed against mine, and I shivered with how much I wanted to lose myself in this moment.

Sex was easy. Intimacy? Now, that was a terrifying prospect.

"Tell me what you want from me, Rion." I drew my fingers lightly down the side of his throat to rest my palm against his chest. His heart beat strong and quick beneath the thin material of his shirt. "Before we take this step. I don't want to hurt you if I can't be what you need."

He was quiet for a moment, his eyes sea-and-sapphire dark in the sleeplight. "I want to have a home in each other," he said at last. "I don't expect to be the only one in your life. I didn't grow up with the Sol Fed traditions of monogamy, either. But even if we take lovers, I don't want to lose sight of who we are together. Most of all, when a mission separates us, I need to know that no matter the odds you will never stop fighting to get back to my side. I swear I will always do the same for you."

"I'm already there." I brushed my lips against the sharp angle of his jaw. "You've been my first thought whenever it looked like I might not make it. You kept me going. That, and knowing how pissed you'd be if I got myself killed."

"Sounds about right." Soft laughter vibrated his voice; his hand stroked my arm and raised gooseflesh in its wake. "If we're going to be partners in all senses of the word, I want—I hope—you will let me in. That you can let me be what you need."

He trusted me with the truth about his past. I could do no less, given the magnitude of what he offered me. "I was clenched around my grief for so long it changed the shape of who I am. Love got twisted up with fear of loss and it was easier not to let myself be close to anyone. It's still difficult for me to untangle one from the other. I'm starting to remember how. But I want nothing more than to learn who we are together."

He took a shivering breath, his smile brilliant in the near-dark before his lips sought mine, soft and sweet like our first rum-soaked kiss on Luna. I allowed myself to be fully present, to prolong the glow of something that felt like joy. I could get used to the feeling again . . . and to the fire-trail sensation of Rion's hand as it skimmed down my side, lingering at the junction of my hip and thigh. His long fingers drifted over the rise of my ass and settled there.

Being me, I had to say something.

"I guess this means flirting is no longer out of the question?" I murmured against his lips.

"Be prepared for a hell of a lot more than flirting." He silenced me with another kiss and drew me in.

CHAPTER
TWENTY-NINE

MY MOUTH WAS BUSY, but my hands were not. I slipped them beneath his shirt to explore the hard planes of his stomach, reading the scars on his abdomen and chest with my fingertips. The pebbled skin of his nipples hardened against my palms and a sound of appreciation rumbled deep in his throat. Rion sat up as far as the low ceiling of the recessed bed would allow, and I tugged off his shirt, discarding it beside the bed.

The drift of his pheromones reached me in the aroma of his skin, a hint of light sweat, and a warm, earth-and-spice scent that was uniquely his. It connected with the greedy chemical receptors in my brain and triggered a wave of desire, every nerve in my sensitive changeling tissue ready to respond.

He kissed me again, slow, unhurried as his hands worked under the bottom of my shirt and peeled it over my head. His fingertips stroked down my neck, over my shoulder and collarbone to trace the knife scars on my chest. He touched the dark, ugly bruises staining my ribs and glanced up at me in question.

"I'm fine. They don't hurt," I assured him breathlessly. "I

may not be up to an all-night marathon quite yet. Just give me a little time to heal."

"Good. It gives me an excuse to draw things out." He brushed my hardening nipple with the lightest of touches. Muscles clenched deep inside my groin, wringing a groan from me as the spongy tissue over my pectorals swelled into small breasts.

"You like to tease," I accused, my voice gone ragged with need.

"Never. I plan to follow through." His fingers continued their slow, torturous circling of my areola. I fumbled with the clasp of his pants as another shiver of pleasure rocked me, then rolled out of the bed and pulled him with me so we could shed the rest of our clothes.

In the false blue twilight, he was beautiful. Wide shoulders tapered to a trim waist, his chest and abdomen scattered with light blond hair. The lightning-strike scar slashed all the way down the side of his body to twist over his powerful thigh and calf. The wicked geometry of the sharp triangle between his hip bones framed his erection, rising from a nest of tight, pale curls as he took in my naked body. My breath caught as our gazes met, his eyes dark with desire. I eliminated the space between us with one step.

"I don't know what you prefer." Arousal made my voice rough. My external erection bulged beneath the slit of skin on my mons, almost touching his cock. "Male anatomy? Female?"

"Whatever brings you the most pleasure." He dipped his head to brush his lips over my jaw and throat, his teeth grazing the flesh of my shoulder. I breathed a harsh sigh of need, and he whispered, "I'm well acquainted with both, but I want to learn yours."

He went to his knees, lips brushing the sensitive tissue on my mound, his breath a feather of flame against my skin. My erection surged out of hiding and the smooth, thick shaft leapt to full engorgement, an exquisite agony forcing a hiss between my gritted teeth. He surrounded me with the slippery-hot silk of his lips and tongue. The expert tug and glide of his mouth blurred my vision, robbing me of any coherent thought except the building pressure inside me. He brought me to crisis where I stood, more quickly than I thought possible.

"Oh, fuck, Rion . . ." I cried out against the strength of my orgasm. My knees buckled with the sensation. I slammed my palm against the bulkhead over the bed to steady myself, my other hand clenched on his shoulder as he wrapped his arms around my thighs to hold me upright.

He stood and kissed me hungrily, his lips swollen from his ministrations. My hand followed the lines of his body down to the heavy cock between his legs and caressed it until my fingers were coated in the satiny fluid leaking from the tip. I stroked it over the head of his penis, tight with his arousal. His kiss grew deeper as I continued the pressure and motion until he finally broke with a gasp.

"I won't last if you keep that up," he said with a ragged laugh. "It's been a while for me."

I tugged him into bed and did all the things I had imagined instead, exploring the track of his lightning-forked scar with my lips and tongue. My mouth strayed to his nipple, catching it softly in my teeth and drawing a low purr of pleasure from his throat. I made my way down to the tempting V of flesh between his hip and groin and moved inward.

He shivered, his cock twitching as my tongue caressed the ridge on the underside, paying special attention to the sensitive head before I took him deep into my mouth. His moan of complete surrender nearly undid me.

Rion tangled his hands in my hair and gently guided me into a rhythm, his cock riding my mouth. He soon pulled away with a stifled oath, the whisper of my name on his lips. "Dalí, take me inside you. Please."

The thick head of his penis was slick with our mingled fluids. I eased down until he buried himself to the root with a sudden upward thrust, wringing a cry from both of us. My external erection had never fully subsided; now, the twinned sensation of stroking my shaft and the pressure of him inside me sent an exquisite tremor up the nerve bundle.

Rion watched me as I rode him, his hands gripping my hips. He met each downward movement with an answering thrust until we were racing each other to the summit. He came with a wordless, guttural moan, spilling into me as my own climax detonated, every molecule in my body shattered and remade in a shower of stars behind my eyelids.

I collapsed to one side of the narrow bed. Rion rolled with me, and we remained joined from the waist down, his hand caressing the sweat-dampened skin of my back. We stayed that way for some time in the gentle aftermath.

"Well, that was more incredible than I ever imagined," I managed to say as my breathing normalized.

"Oh?" he rumbled sleepily. "You imagined?"

"Once or twice." I was more relaxed than I'd been in three years, the calm of his null against my empathic nets a treasure I hadn't realized I needed. "I'll show you, but we need a bigger bed. And some lubrication."

"That can definitely be arranged." Our lips had just met when he groaned and withdrew, tapping his implant.

"Report," he said gruffly, and listened. "Acknowledged. Let me know when the parts are aboard, and I'll pick them up in *Three*. Sumner out."

"Repair ship?" I said, disappointed.

"Right on time, damn the luck." Our bodies separated, going from warm and comfortable to cold and sticky in one move. Rion stroked my hair back. "Catch more sleep if you can."

"I don't think it will be a problem."

He kissed me before he climbed out of bed and padded

barefoot to the lavatory. I enjoyed the view of his blue-lit, very shapely ass until it disappeared behind the door.

The stupid-happy smile on my lips was something new, stretching the muscles of my face in a way I had almost forgotten. It didn't go away even when the deep heaviness born of utter contentment and great sex settled into my limbs and I let my eyes flutter closed. I was down for the count until the white lights rose to stab out my eyes at the end of the sleep cycle.

————

Repairs were rapidly accomplished with Kitryd's help, and fine-tuning of the Shontavians' new home began.

After a little discussion, we renamed the ship *Revenge*, though it was just for our use and an inside joke only our team would understand. All the identifying marks had been scoured from the hull, presumably when Alecto repurposed the freighter, and its identity transmission disabled. Ra'sho stripped the ship's old identifiers and remote piloting codes so no one could gain control from the outside. He replaced them with a quarantine beacon.

Alecto had made one careless error, if it was a mistake at all. He didn't destroy the data in the navigational computer before he set the intercept course with Sol. We had a record of everywhere the ship had been in the last five years, a potential head start tracking down Residuum's bases of operation. I couldn't imagine the bastard forgetting something like that; he was too clever. So why did he leave it? It was something we'd have to explore with great caution.

————

All too soon, it was time to say goodbye to Kitryd and its passengers.

The Shontavians waited in the bay when Sumner and I arrived. He hung back near the airlock as I walked to Naru.

The gray-skinned warriors circled me, bodies weaving in a dance-like pattern as their open mouths sifted my scent from the air. They had done this at our first meeting, their way of welcoming a creature they considered one of their own kind—and it seemed also to be their way of saying farewell.

Naru stopped in front of me. The others went still in a silent crescent behind the alpha; beings created only for war, but who had chosen to ignore their brutal conditioning in search of their own peace.

"This is more difficult than I thought it would be." My throat was tight with emotion and tears gathered in my eyes. "I will always think of you when I look at the stars."

"We will not forget." Naru's mind touched me with affection. Its enormous hand briefly rested on my shoulder before the Shontavians trooped out of the bay without a backward glance. Naru graced Sumner with a nod as it passed him. He solemnly returned the gesture and closed the airlock port behind them. I swept my palms over my leaking eyes as he joined me.

"You okay?" he asked, enfolding me in his arms, his chest warm against my back. I leaned against him for a moment, welcoming the offered comfort.

"Yeah. Let's go home."

I settled into preflight checks as Sumner did the walka-round. Once he was on board and the hatch sealed, I contacted the bridge. "We're ready to start the depressuriza-tion sequence."

"Commencing," Kitryd acknowledged. Warning lights began to flash in the bay, the heaviness of artificial gravity ebbing away as we strapped in.

"You have our contact frequency if there is ever a need to use it," I reminded the AI.

"We hope we will not." A pause. "Farewell. And thank you."

"Goodbye, Kitryd."

"The shuttle bay doors are open."

Sumner disengaged *Three*'s magnetic landing gear from the deck and eased the craft out of the bay. I got my first look at the ship from the outside: a battered and unremarkable Kadrelian freighter. It would be easily mistaken for an innocent transport headed out of the system. Once the shuttle bay doors closed, Kitryd activated the quarantine beacon. The vessel began to transmit a warning of neurotoxin contamination—something that should discourage all but the most determined scavengers from boarding to see what could be salvaged and sold.

Anyone who tried would end up a meal supplement.

I watched the freighter as it picked up speed until it was nothing more than a pinpoint of brightness against unending stars, lost against the tapestry of space.

———

Kiran Singh, it turned out, assembled a data bomb about Mother England and Batterson and primed it to explode in the event he was killed. It was transmitted to all the major networks in Sol Fed a week after his death. The press went wild. One last big story for the little prick, and one more act in the circus under way in the federal courts. Fortunately, Mother England had already turned over her data to Homeland Security as part of her plea bargain. Sumner and I secured a copy for our team before she changed her mind. The Third Front moved to dissociate itself from England's actions, with Dru taking center stage in its efforts to regroup. I was proud of her.

The Batterson case was far less satisfying. As the former President of Sol Fed, Simon Batterson was privy to so much dirt and classified information his lawyers didn't have to work hard to cut a deal with the federal government. It left a foul taste in my mouth. He would spend time in prison, but not enough.

Brian Batterson's efforts to distance the company from his father's and brother's crimes didn't have much effect on the corporation's bottom line, but he was trying to do the right thing. I hoped the board was on his side when his father got out.

The media was denied any drama in the matter of Sol Fed versus Miriam Skadi. She pled guilty to the bombing of Luna Terminal and was sentenced to life in maximum security prison. Unfortunately, it meant we had no opportunity to build a galactic case against her, obtain more testimony against England, or gain additional knowledge about Residuum. She had to know everything about the organization: who they were, where they could be found, and their ultimate plans.

Sumner and I met with her in a small private room before her transport back to Tranquility to begin serving her sentence. He wanted one last chance to convince her to do the right thing. I let him do all the talking, mostly because I didn't believe she would, and I couldn't trust myself not to tell her to have fun rotting in prison.

"Come to say goodbye?" Skadi's smirk was as ironic as ever, though she'd lost some of her arrogance. Her pale hair was drawn back in a braided queue and detention-orange coveralls gave her pallid skin a yellow tint, but her eyes still gleamed as hard and sharp as diamonds.

"I came to see if you've changed your mind." Sumner's quiet voice held no demands.

"You really don't get it, do you?" She shook her head. "I won't give you anything."

"You saved my life."

"Only because it helped get what I wanted. I'm the safest

person in the galaxy right now, with guards and bars and a kilometer of rock between me and the outside." My empathic nets picked up nothing, but fear rode her scent in the tiny room. "If I talk, that still won't be enough to keep me alive. They'll find me, and Luna will be a dust cloud sooner rather than later."

I stiffened, an echo of Alecto's words ringing in my ears. She saw my reaction and her eyes narrowed.

"Oops. I've said too much, haven't I? Let's just kiss and say fuck off, shall we?" She nodded at her guards. "I'm ready to go."

"Miriam . . ." Sumner's voice held regret, and she heard it. Her step faltered between the armed escorts for a couple of seconds. She lifted her head and kept walking.

EPILOGUE

SEVEN OF US gathered around the communications console on board *Thunder Child*. Melos joined us via subspace com, his sharp, pale features grim and determined even in grainy detail. Sumner cleared his throat.

"Is everyone certain about this?"

"Clan Sustrix is in accord," Ozzie pronounced.

Ka'pth and Ra'sho gave a synchronous nod. "As are we."

"I am ready," Melos said.

"Absolutely certain." I grinned at Sumner. He smiled back, and a flutter moved through me. Couldn't help it. This thing between us was too new and shiny to not make me slightly giddy.

"Tommi, fire at will," Sumner directed.

It should have been more dramatic. Our resignations were launched with a mild electronic blip of subspace data, nothing exciting. On the holo screen, Melos's black-gloved hand punched a button out of camera range.

"Well, it's done," Ozzie said. "As chairman of the board for our newly formed consultant agency, Sumner, what are your instructions?"

"I'm declaring a holiday." Sumner ran both hands through

his short hair and stretched. "We've been on constant missions for the last three and a half years. Nobody's seen their home worlds for a while. We have plenty of data to sort through, and it will still be here when we get back. *Thunder Child* needs some refits since she's no longer a Remoliad vessel, and when we're ready, we have our first client."

"Who?" I asked curiously.

"The new Director of Remoliad Security." He grinned at our collective surprise. "With the dissolution of the Penumbra, Director Tikker Ard announced he will be focusing on terroristic threats and organized crime, using a combination of Remoliad resources and independent contractors."

I was impressed. "That's genius." As a private entity, we could take on whatever assignments we liked, including the investigation of Residuum we'd been ordered to archive. The Director was a smart being, though painting a great big target on his own back might not be the wisest decision.

"So, we're doing the same job for more credits." Ozzie shrugged. "I like it."

"Dalí, I want you to negotiate the contract with the Remoliad." Sumner glanced hopefully at me. "We'll be treading some narrow diplomatic lines."

"I've already got some fine print in mind."

"Where to first?" asked Tommi.

"Kadrel. Our usual mechanic. From there, you can all decide where you're going to take leave and Melos can meet us when we're ready to ship out. I'll give you a date as soon as I know how long the refits will take." Sumner turned to me. "Let Brother Gor know you're going to be planetside for a while. I might tag along if that's all right."

"He'll be happy to see you." My crechemate's triumphant satisfaction he had been right about Sumner and me would be too much to bear. The smug gratification from certain lizards in the room was already fucking annoying and cluttered my empathic webs.

———

It was the first holovid marathon planned for the month-long trip to Zereid, but tonight, only Tommi and I cuddled under the thick blanket on my bunk. Ziggy and Ozzie were deep in discussion with Sumner about weapons refits, and the Andari were looking at tropical vacation destinations on their home world. That meant Tommi got to pick from the ancient films in the holo cache tonight. She had a thing for Godzilla, and a giant lizard now romped around on the screen. Definitely weird, but in the best way.

Sumner joined us while two tiny fairies sang about a moth god. "Room for one more?"

"Sure." Tommi and I made space so he could slide in behind me and get the three of us spooned into my narrow sleeping space without anybody falling out. It reminded me I needed to ask about getting my quarters refitted with a larger bed while the ship underwent modification, preferably without an upper bunk. Sumner was tall. Some of the things I wanted to do would require more headroom.

"You just got really warm," Tommy noted. "Are you thinking about sex?"

"Sorry. Can't help it."

Rion laughed and kissed my temple. I relaxed in utter comfort, his warmth behind me and Tommi's coolness in front. Her contentment and Rion's silent, restful null created a sweet stillness against my empathic nets. I shut my eyes, breathing in the moment and holding it inside me. I was grateful for this peace, something I'd been sure I would never feel again.

I fell asleep sandwiched between two beings I loved, while a giant lizard stomped the hell out of Tokyo. It was probably a metaphor for my new life, but I'd take it.

GLOSSARY OF TERMS

Third-Gender
An intersex human being, usually with a dominant set of male or female reproductive organs.

Changeling Third-Gender
A genetic mutation within the third-gender population, these individuals possess neither male nor female gonads and are incapable of reproduction. Their anatomy has specialized hormonal glands, which allow them to assume at will the secondary sexual characteristics of a male or female. They possess a vaginal-like organ without a cervix or uterus, and spongy, nerve-filled tissue in the mons, or pubic area, which can become internally or externally engorged. When externally erect, the mons can serve the sexual function of male genitalia.

The New Puritan Movement (NPM)
A human purity movement that stresses survival of the genetically pristine human race by isolation and parthenogenesis (reproduction without fertilization, which allows

unwanted genetic traits to be edited out). Quasi-religious and fanatic in that it wants to legislate mandatory genetic editing and reproduction for the citizens of Sol Fed. It views third-gender citizens, especially the increasing number of sterile changeling citizens, as a threat to humanity's survival. Discourages galactic contact with humanoid races for fear of contaminating the gene pool.

The Penumbra

A covert agency attached to the Remoliad, responsible for gathering intelligence and investigating violations of galactic law.

The Remoliad Alliance

A local galactic coalition like the United Nations which facilitates trade, diplomacy, and aid to the member planets. It also enforces galactic laws.

Shontavian Market

A black market on board a starship which remains in constant motion through the galaxy to avoid authorities. Dealing in illegal weapons for sale and trade, the Market derived its name from the sale the genetically engineered creatures called Shontavians, bred solely for fighting wars.

Sol Federation "Sol Fed"

The united colonies within the solar system that origi-nated from Earth's survivors: Luna, Mars, and Jupiter's moon, Europa. Each colony has its own militia and governor. The citizens of the solar system elect senators and a president to determine federal law.

The Third Front

A political lobbying group headed by Justina "Mother" England. Third-gender reproductive rights to unedited genetic procreation are a point of contention in Sol Fed Third Front uses financial and political influence to defeat laws encroaching upon those rights, but a fringe component headed by England also encourages sabotage and violent action against laboratories and scientists who perform genetic editing on third-gender genomes.

Zezjna

A philosophy of peace through empathy developed by the Zereid, a highly empathic/telepathic species. The term is also used to encompass a non-lethal defensive martial arts style that relies on empathic senses as well as physical skills.

Enemies and Allies

All the races depicted here are bipedal unless otherwise noted, humanoid, and oxygen breathing.

Andari

A diminutive, ichthyoid species. They live in groups led by a female alpha. Members of the Remoliad.

Cthash

A reptilian species from an arid planet system. The Cthash are born in trios. Each set of siblings is comprised of a male, a female, and an *ix*. The *ix* gender is required for mating purposes and produces an enzyme that allows the hard-shelled eggs of the female to become temporarily porous for fertilization. Members of the Remoliad.

Ferians

The collective tribes of a feline-like race, covered in short fur. They walk on two or four limbs. Remoliad members.

Kadrelians

An oxygen-breathing species with multiple tentacles used for walking and manipulation. One of the original members of the Remoliad.

Nos Conglomerate

A star-faring race that has plundered less developed civilizations for thousands of years. Opportunistic pirates and mercenaries. Genetically, they are closely related to humanity and are nearly identical in physiology. They are not allied and take advantage of any other system not affiliated with the Remoliad.

Residuum

A mysterious crime syndicate who patrons the terrorist Miriam Skadi and works to destabilize the member systems of the Remoliad Alliance.

Shontavians

A bioengineered race created by the Ursetu solely for fighting wars. Physically resistant to small arms fire, they possess four arms of equal dexterity. Though only the "alpha" line speaks, they are highly intelligent and possess strong telepathic abilities.

Pileans

An insectoid species. Family groups of the same brood share identical forehead crests and tend to engage in the same enterprises. Members of the Remoliad.

Ursetu

Another race similar to humanity in appearance and genetic traits. The Ursetu possess a strictly divided social hierarchy: the ruling caste, the warrior caste, and the casteless. Their planet created and sold genetically engineered creatures for servitude and battle for thousands of years. Newly allied with the Remoliad.

Tolkish

Lavender-skinned humanoids, one of the original members of the Remoliad Alliance. Prone to physical beauty due to the symmetry of their features and slow, graceful movements.

Zereid

A highly empathic/telepathic race. The species is bipedal and covered in short blue fur. They are skilled in diplomacy due to their ability to sense emotion. Primarily pacifist in nature, they have developed a non-lethal martial arts form for personal defense and all serve time in their military, which provides defense when necessary, but primarily offers compassionate aid to other planets. Members of the Remoliad.

Glossary of Characters

Alecto Sim

Former Minister of the Remoliad Security Council, from Tolkis. An "employee" of a mysterious crime syndicate.

Justina "Mother" England

Head of the Third Front, a third-gender rights movement. She is a third-gender human and runs Artemis Imports. Also, a smuggler.

Gor

Dalf's Zereid crechemate (blood brother). A large bipedal humanoid from Zereid.

Gresh—Andrew Gresham

Dalí's late husband. A human rights solicitor.

Sida—Rasida Gresham Tamareia
Dalí's late wife, pregnant with a child who possessed genetic material from both Dalí and Gresh when she was killed. A genetic research scientist.

Kiran Singh
A journalist prone to sensationalism who broke the story about the Batterson scandal which brought down President Simon Batterson.

Kitryd
A sentient artificial intelligence from the Sovereign Collective.

Ambassador Marina Urquhart
Dalí's mother. Former ambassador to Zereid, now Sol Fed Delegate to the Remoliad. Ambassador Urquhart is a female-dominant third-gender human.

Maritza Cortez
A Martian Drug Enforcement Agent (MDEA)

Naru
Alpha Shontavian with whom Dalí is sent to negotiate.

Dev and Michael Patil
Hostel owners. Long-term friends of Dalí and Gresh. Michael is a human rights lawyer who worked with Gresh.

Dalí Tamareia
Former ambassador turned undercover operative. A third-gender changeling.

Captain Paul Tamareia

Dalí's father. Former commanding officer of Rosetta Space Station, retired.

Agent Preeda Saetang

Lunar Homeland Security agent investigating Justina England, who aids Dalí in pursuit of Skadi.

Rion Sumner

Commander of the *Thunder Child* and its team of undercover operatives. He is a human/Nos hybrid.

President Simon Batterson

Head of Batterson Robotics, former President of Sol Fed whom Dalí had a hand in bringing down when Batterson's son, Jon, was exposed as a human trafficker. A powerful member of the NPM. There is an ongoing corporate war going on between his company and Mother England's import business.

Skadi

Miriam Skadi, the galactic terrorist Dalí believes responsible for the bombing which killed their family. Sumner's half-sister, a human/Nos hybrid.

The Crew of the *Thunder Child*

Ossixiani clan Sustrix – "Ozzie" – a Cthash pilot, second in command. Male reptilian. One of three siblings.

Tommizax clan Sustrix- "Tommi" – a Cthash medic and communications officer. Female reptilian. One of three siblings. She and Dalí have a close, platonic relationship.

Zigoxanian clan Sustrix- "Ziggy" – a Cthash weapons officer and engineer. Ziggy is *ix* — a Cthash third-gender which provides an enzyme critical to allowing a male and female to fertilize eggs for reproduction. One of three siblings.

Ka'pth and Ra'sho – a mated pair of Andari. Intelligence officers.

Melos- a Nos engineer and navigations officer.

ABOUT THE AUTHOR

E.M. Hamill writes adult science fiction and fantasy somewhere in the wilds of eastern suburban Kansas. A nurse by day, wordsmith by night, she is happy to give her geeky imagination free rein and has sworn never to grow up and get boring.

Frequently under the influence of caffeinated beverages, she also writes as Elisabeth Hamill for young adult readers in fantasy with the award-winning Songmaker series.

She lives with her family, where they fend off flying monkey attacks and prep for the zombie apocalypse.

ALSO BY E. M. HAMILL

The Dalí Tamareia Missions

Dalí

Peacemaker

Third Front

Nectar and Ambrosia: An Amaranthine Inheritance Novel

Writing as Elisabeth Hamill:

The Songmaker Series

Song Magick

Truthsong